A DOG CALLED DEMOLITION

ROBERT RANKIN

A DOG CALLED DEMOLITION

Doubleday

LONDON · NEW YORK · TORONTO · SYDNEY · AUCKLAND

TRANSWORLD PUBLISHERS LTD
61–63 Uxbridge Road, London W5 5SA

TRANSWORLD PUBLISHERS (AUSTRALIA) PTY LTD
15–25 Helles Avenue, Moorebank, NSW 2170

TRANSWORLD PUBLISHERS (NZ) LTD
3 William Pickering Drive, Albany, Auckland

DOUBLEDAY CANADA LTD
105 Bond Street, Toronto, Ontario, M5B 1Y3

Published 1996 by Doubleday
a division of Transworld Publishers Ltd

A catalogue record for this book is available from the British Library.

ISBN 0385 405162

Set in 11/14pt Monotype Bembo by Kestrel Data, Exeter

Printed in Great Britain by
Mackays of Chatham plc, Chatham, Kent

For Jim and Yvette,
The Campbells

A WORD OF WARNING

Most novels have a
beginning, a middle
and an end.

This one doesn't.

But it *does* have
a soundtrack.*

*See page 249.

A DOG CALLED DEMOLITION

1

The swine who stole my dog doesn't realize what he did to me.

ADOLF HITLER (1889–1945), 1917

The guy who said money can't buy you happiness was shopping at the wrong store.

JON BON JOVI (1962–), 1995

DOWN ON DOGS

I'm really down on dogs this week,
I've had it with the Dane.
I'm sick of all their guileless cheek,
The way the brutes complain.
It's 'give me *Pal* for which I crave,'
And 'walk me out', I'm like some slave,
And then they jog me when I shave,
I'm really down on dogs.

I'm really down on fags this week,
They make me choke and cough.
On Thursday I could hardly speak
And bits of lung dropped off.
It's 'stick him in the oxy-tent,'
And 'cut his throat to make a vent,'
And when you ask, it's 'no comment'.
I'm really down on fags.

I'm really down on beer this week,
The bugger blows me out.
It's threepence up and twice as weak
And bits that float about.
This *Fullers* stuff has done the deed,
My guts have really gone to seed,
Can nothing stop this pressing need? (Rushes to bog.)
I'm really down on beer.

I'm really down on luck this week,
But was I ever up?
If prizes were for mild and meek,
I'd win each silver cup.
My clothes hang ragged on my bones,
I'm through with love and telephones,
I'm only fit for Davy Jones,
I'm really down on luck.

I'm really down on toilet rolls, but that's another
    story . . .

And so is this —

THE REALIZATION OF
OLD SAM SPROUT

It was the kind of weather that made you feel God must be really upset about something. Cats and dogs, it was. Hammering down. It hammered down against the front-room window, filling the front room with that terrible sound television sets make when all the programmes are over. That terrible sound that wakes you up after you've fallen asleep in your armchair and gets you all confused.

White noise, it's called. Which lends dread to the thought of what *black* noise might be like.

Old Sam Sprout didn't hear the rain. The batteries in his hearing-aid had gone flat. Old Sam Sprout didn't realize that they had, he just thought the world had grown much quieter of late. Which was no bad thing, considering.

Sam sat in his armchair before his television set. No white noise came from Sam's television set. Because Sam's television set was broken. The volume control seemed to have gone on the blink, so Sam had rattled the television set about. And now the television set was broken.

So Sam couldn't watch it any more.

Not that Sam cared much about that. What Sam cared most about lay upon a Persian pouffe, equidistant between his armchair and his television set. And this was Sam's left foot. Sam, of course, had a healthy regard for his right foot also. He had no prejudice either way. A foot was a foot, be it a left one or a right. To show greater favour to one rather than to the other would be an absurd-dity, but at the present Sam really did care most about his left foot.

Because his left foot was all bandaged up.

His left foot was seriously injured.

The Fates had dealt Sam Sprout another body blow and this time one way below the belt. Sam was no stranger to accident and injury. Ill fortune had pressed upon him all the long years of his life. As a boy he had collected bad luck the way other boys collect birds' eggs. And by the time he was ten, he had broken most of his bones several times over and been struck down by such a large variety of childhood ailments, that his doctor brought medical students round to Sam's house each Friday morning to test their powers of diagnosis.

Sam was the only child in Brentford's long and dignified history to develop beriberi twice. Whenever an epidemic broke out in the borough, the emergency services never had far to look for the epicentre.

But, then, at the age of sixteen, Sam's illnesses suddenly cleared up. This came as an untimely shock to his physician, who had been making more than a comfortable income from displaying his patient and had based two bestselling novels on him.

'Are you sure you feel all right?' he asked the teenage Sprout.

'Never better,' Sam replied.

Doctor Kinn, for such was the physician's name, thumbed through his medical directory. 'Possibly he has contracted some hitherto unknown malady, which manifests itself as a facsimile of perfect health,' he said to Mrs Sprout, while wondering whether this might be the first recorded incidence of *Kinn's Syndrome*.

A vision of his name in three-point bold, atop a full-page write-up in *The Lancet*, flashed before his eyes. This was undoubtedly *The Big One*.

But it wasn't.

The weeks passed and Sprout grew stronger. His scrofula shrank and his mange became memory. His canker was conquered, his buboes were banished. His scurvy was scuttled, his trench foot transcended. And he was literally liberated from leprosy. And so on.

Even his Ghanian gut-bloat got better.

'I feel even healthier today than I did yesterday,' he kept telling his doctor.

'I fear for his life,' the great physician told Sprout's mother. 'No-one should be this healthy.'

On the morning of his seventeenth birthday, the radiant Sprout opened the front door to find three policemen on his doorstep. One of them had a dog. The dog's name was Princey.

'Are you Samuel Oliver Sprout of number four, Moby Dick Terrace?' asked one of the policemen. (The one on the left, not the one with the dog.)

'I certainly am,' said Sam. 'And I feel really well.'

'Then I must caution you that anything you say will be taken down and may be used in evidence.'

The Fates, who had spent a full year debating upon how next to mistreat Sam, had apparently reached a joint decision. Sam was now to know the sorrows attendant to *wrongful arrest*.

'But I haven't done anything,' he protested, as the officers of the law dragged him off to the Black Maria.

'What am I accused of anyway?' he continued, in a manner not unknown to Franz Kafka. 'Those who deny freedom to others, deserve it not for themselves,' he concluded. 'To quote Abraham Lincoln,' he added.

Sometime the next day, which was the day *after* Sam's birthday, which meant that Sam missed his party, Sam was released. The police informed him that there had been a clerical error, that they had, in fact, been searching for a certain Sam *O'Sprout*, the notorious baby decerebrationist and player of the Hammond organ. Samuel *Oliver* Sprout was thanked for his cooperation and returned home on the crossbar of a constable's bike. (The constable was the constable who had the dog, but he had borrowed the bike from the other constable, the one who had *not* cautioned Sprout.)

'I'm sorry about all this confusion,' said the constable,

dropping Sam off at his gate. 'Still, you've got to laugh, haven't you?'

'No,' said Sam, 'I haven't. And what about all *this*?' He gestured all about his person, drawing the constable's attention to the cuts and abrasions on his head, the severe bruising he had received during what he had been assured was 'routine interrogation'. The section of bedraggled cloth which terminated above his left knee had once been, until very recently in fact, a complete trouser leg.

'Sorry,' said the constable, shrugging like a good'n. 'Worse things happen at sea, I expect. Though I can't imagine what they'd be. Cut along now, sir, or I'll run you in for loitering.'

'Thanks a lot.' And Sam dragged himself into the house.

And 'Where's all the furniture gone?' he asked his mother.

'We've had burglars in, while you were out,' said his old mum, cheerfully. 'One of them played the Hammond organ.'

Sam said, 'I'm dead chuffed that The Fates, who have ignored me for a full year, are now once more giving me their undivided attention.'

'I shouldn't talk like that, dear,' advised his mum. 'Your father once talked like that and look what happened to him.'

Sam peered into the goldfish bowl. 'Has Dad had his ant's eggs today?' he asked.

But all that was a long time ago.

An astonishingly long time ago.

The Sam Sprout who now sat in his battered armchair caring for his bandaged left foot was eighty-seven years of age. That's *eighty-seven* years of age.

Which is old and that's a fact.

No-one who had ever witnessed the disasters which had followed Sam through his life like a faithful dog called Princey could ever possibly have imagined such longevity conceivable. Time after time The Fates had hurled down tribulations upon Sam which would surely have felled an ordinary mortal.

16

But old Sam Sprout was no ordinary mortal. No ordinary mortal was he. Oh no.

'Things haven't been too bad of late,' said Sam, reaching up for his cherrywood briar and knocking his snuff box from the mantelpiece into the roaring fire.

Such trifles as this Sam put down to pure chance.

'Quite recently I have noticed a distinct letting-up in the ill-fortune department, almost as if The Fates were beginning to relent.'

A lorry passing the front door rattled Sam's signed photograph of the Queen Mother from its honoured place on the parlour wall and shivered it to pieces on the red-tiled floor. Of course, Sam didn't hear this, as he had not heard his own voice speaking. But it *had* happened. Which possibly proves that thing about the tree falling in the forest when there's no-one around to hear it. Or possibly not.

'I think it is all down to this left foot of mine,' said Sam. 'In fact, the more I think about it, the more certain I become.'

Sam rose painfully from his armchair and limped over to the window. The rain had stopped. But as Sam hadn't heard the rain and so didn't actually know that it had been raining, he was not altogether sure just where that left him.

He could observe, however, just how much flooding there was in his basement area. And what a pity it was that he hadn't taken his washing in. Or covered up his pushbike. Or left that cake out.

Two teddyboys were unscrewing the brass numbers from Sam's front gate. A neighbour's dog, whose name was Princey, was burying a foetal pig in Sam's herbacious border.

It was just another day.

'It's just another day for some,' said Sam, 'but not for me.' He turned down his eyes to view the new damp patch that was spreading along beneath the window. 'Not for me and my bandaged foot, my bandaged foot that holds all the answers. No Siree, by golly.'

Old Sam limped off to his kitchen. As he passed through his parlour, shards of the Queen Mother's picture glass penetrated the heel of his right slipper and entered the heel of his right foot.

Old Sam ignored the pain, he had no interest at this time in his right foot. He couldn't have cared less for his right foot. His right foot did not matter. It was superfluous.

It had its uses for getting about on, obviously. But Sam wasn't dwelling on those.

'How I came by my bandaged foot would certainly put the cat amongst the Picassos if it was ever to come out before the public as a Warhol,' he said. It wasn't that his mind was wandering, it was just that he couldn't hear what he was saying.

Sam hobbled into his kitchen and fumbled about in his fridge. He was searching for a fresh pint of milk.

Somehow the fridge had become unplugged and a flood of lime-green water splashed over Sam's punctured slipper and began to soak into the bandages that swathed the foot of mystery. There was a nasty smell of rotting vegetables in that kitchen. It did not go unnoticed by Sam.

Sam sought a saucepan that still had a handle and a cup of a similar nature. Both these he tested gingerly in his hands, and satisfied that they had at least one more go left in them, he poured fresh*ish* milk into the cup and from thence to the saucepan, which he placed upon the gas stove.

'All those who dare to Dali with the supernatural will learn the importance of being Ernst, when all is revealed concerning my bandaged foot,' said Sam, as he turned on the gas.

'My bandaged foot will become an object of veneration. A bit like the Toulouse-Lautrec shroud,' Sam also said, as he searched in vain for the sugar bowl. 'I think I'll have it without sugar today.'

The coffee had run out the day before, but Sam's home-help had neglected to replenish the jar, preferring instead to abscond with his silver. 'I think I will have it without coffee as well,' Sam added, wondering why there weren't any spoons.

He did not waste time looking for the biscuit barrel. Though it was a very nice biscuit barrel, it having a photograph of the Queen Mother on it and everything, the last time Sam had opened it, a scorpion had been inside. Sam now gave biscuits a miss.

Sam took a box of matches from his waistcoat pocket and opened it. Upside down. The matches scattered about the kitchen floor, old Sam smiled a secretive smile, took out his *Ronson* and flicked back the striker.

'Ping' went the flint as it joined the matches.

Sam smiled on, took the electric lighter with the rechargeable batteries from its special socket next to the cooker, held it to the gas and touched the button.

The gas lit.

Sam's secretive smile now became one of triumph. 'I know what I know,' he said, tapping his nose with the lighter and nearly putting his eye out. 'And soon all will know what I know. And then they'll know something. Oh yes.'

Sam returned to his front room and the comfort of his armchair and pouffe. 'I must write to the Archbishop of Canterbury, to the Prime Minister, to the President of the United States, and to the Queen Mother,' said Sam. 'And also to Damien Hirst. What I have stumbled upon, in both the physical and the metaphysical senses of the word, is of such great import, that all must know of it. Whoever would have guessed,' Sam said, 'that the entire population of the world, every man, woman and child of every race, colour and creed, is slave to an invisible race of mental parasites? Whoever would have believed,' Sam asked, 'that the voices which scream in the heads of maniacs are the voices of these same evil beings? Who could ever have conceived,' Sam enquired, 'that all this would become known to me via the medium of my left foot?'

Sam shook his old head and perused the bandaged extremity. The green water from the fridge now added a certain something to its air of mystery. An aura of light shone about it.

Sam shook his old head again. 'I do believe,' he declared, 'that my whole life has been a stage, set and waiting for this bandaged foot to make its entrance. Possibly this is why The Fates have dealt so shabbily with me.'

Sam thought of the biblical Job. God had dealt pretty shabbily with him, but things had worked out just fine in the end.

'I have been tested and found not wanting,' said Sam, who hadn't slipped an artist's name into his monologue for quite some time. (Apart from Damien Hirst, of course, but Sam really *did* intend writing to him.) 'So I shall prove the world is wrong and I am Frank Lloyd Wright.'

And it was at this very moment that old Sam Sprout had the very realization which had inspired the title of his chapter.

It was the realization that *he* had been chosen.

That all *he* had suffered had been for this one reason alone.

That *he* and only *he* could alter everything. And very easily too.

'Yes!' Sam lurched from his armchair. 'Of course!' he yelled, with the light of his realization shining from his face. 'I know *exactly* what I must do and *exactly* how I must do it!'

But he didn't say more than this.

Which is hardly surprising, really.

To state what happened next, would be to state the obvious. The clues were all in place for all to view. If one thing alone is surprising, it is the fact that old Sam managed to say quite as much as he did, before the inevitable occurred.

And to state what this 'inevitable' was would once more be to state the obvious.

To state how the milk boiled over and put out the flame and how the gas built up in the kitchen, before moving on to the parlour, then along the hall, finally to reach the roaring fire in the front room at the exact moment old Sam Sprout came to his state of cosmic realization would be to state the obvious.

And none of us want that.

Do we?

And so the money ran out in the gas meter.

Old Sam Sprout opened his mouth to speak, but the voice which spoke from it was not his own. It was a dark, gruff, guttural sound. Like the baying of a monstrous hound.* A sound that was surely the dreaded *black noise* itself.

And the noise became a single word.

And that word was DEMOLITION.

*Not *that* one.

21

2

If a mule had the same proportionate power in his hind legs as a dog's flea, he could kick an ordinary-sized man 33 miles, 1004 yards, 21 inches.

G. A. HENTY (1832–1902),
Those Other Animals, 1891

SHOE HOLE

Look at the God-damn shoe hole.
Curse the *Phillips* stick-sole.
Only out for a short stroll,
When the bloody thing wore through.

Look at the state of the uppers,
Ain't no high-steppin' strutters,
Rather be home behind shutters,
Than walking these gardens of Kew.

Look at the knotted laces.
Certain they've seen a few places.
A proper pair of disgraces.
I just don't know what to do.

Wish I'd settled for cloggies.
They don't get bitten by doggies
And they stop you sinking in boggies
And cost but a penny or two.

Sod it, I think I'll go bare foot
(As long as I don't step in bear poop).
Suppose that I'd just better bear up
And stop all this hullabaloo.

Thank you.

MEGAPHONES AND CHEESECLOTH

They never found out what old Sam Sprout actually died of.
But whatever it was, it was definitely fatal.

Doctor Kinn's grandson filled in the death certificate.
'Natural causes,' he wrote, 'possibly due to complications
brought on by Kinn's Syndrome.'

And that was pretty much that.

Pretty much, but not entirely.

Only four mourners turned up for the funeral. Danny
Orion, Marmsly, Big Frank and The Kid. And they were not
there for the love of old Sam Sprout. They were there for the
money.

And they were to be disappointed.

Many others would be disappointed also, but these many
others chose to stay at home on the day of old Sam's burial,
because it was raining and they did not wish to catch a cold.
If disappointment lay in store for them, they reasoned, at least
they would suffer it in good health.

The reason for all this potential disappointment was that
old Sam had died penniless, and the reason that all these people
would take it personally was that each and every one of them

had, at some time or another, given, lent or loaned old Sam money.

Old Sam Sprout had died leaving debts of a truly staggering nature. How one man could owe so much to so many was the kind of question which might have inspired the late and legendary Winston (my silver crowns are still worth only fifty pence) Churchill to juggle about and forge into a speech. Having no good fortune of his own, old Sam had spent his life benefiting from that of others.

Never did some lucky punter come up Donald Trumps on the dogs or cop a small packet on the premium bonds, than there would be Sam Sprout hovering like the ghost of Christmas past, or something similar, ready to draw off a little of the surplus good fortune for himself.

When Danny Orion struck gold on The Shrunken Head's Christmas draw, who was it who was heard to remark, 'It would be a better Christmas for some of us if we had a pound or two to put some humble offering upon the bare table for our wife and six children'?

And when Marmsly's uncle, Uncle Marmsly, died, leaving the famous Uncle Marmsly Pewter Tankard Collection, who was it who said, 'Some of us are forced to drink from cracked enamel mugs, and then only of water'?

Or, the time Big Frank netted a cool ton on the national lottery, 'I weep that I cannot buy you a pint to offer my congratulations, could you lend me ten pounds to start the ball rolling?'

And so on and so forth. Three guesses.

The worst thing was that old Sam always made such a big deal about promising to pay the money back, that no-one ever had the face to ask him for it. Thus, when he shuffled, or jumped, or was pushed, off this mortal coil, the mourners at his funeral and many other folk besides, felt that old Sam Sprout had taken a little piece of themselves to the grave with him, and that it was more than likely that they wouldn't be getting it back.

The four mourners stood at the graveside. Two at each side. They had just lowered old Sam in. The pall bearers skulked in the shelter of the church porch, smoking cigarettes and discussing the vexed question of why it was that necrophiles were so over-represented in the undertaking trade. The rain fell heavily and they weren't going to get their top hats wet for an old ponce like Sam Sprout.

Danny Orion sighed, sniffed and blew raindrops from the end of his nose. 'Unless I am very much mistaken,' he said, 'there goes my fifty quid.'

'And my uncle's pewter,' said Marmsly, 'which, like the alchemists of old, Sprout transmuted into gold.'

'Poetic,' said Big Frank. 'And a right shame.'

'If I had a pound for every pound I've lent that old bastard,' said The Kid, 'I'd have all my pounds back and I wouldn't be here at all.'

The other three mourners nodded. You couldn't argue with that.

'How much do you reckon he left in his will?' Danny asked.

Marmsly shook his rain-sodden head. 'Not a penny,' said he. 'I bumped into his solicitor on the way here. The man is rather upset. Apparently Sprout somehow managed to borrow money from three separate building societies, putting his house up as collateral and giving the solicitor's name as the owner.'

'Is that possible?' asked Big Frank, whose mum owned her house.

'Sprout managed it. Everything's owed three times over, there's not a penny to be had. The solicitor did say one thing that I thought a bit strange. He said Sprout had died clutching a piece of paper with a few last words scribbled on it.'

'A begging letter?' Danny asked.

'No.' Marmsly gave his sodden head another little shake. 'It just said, BEWARE OF THE DOG.'

Damp shrugs were passed across the open grave.

'I suppose it must mean something,' said The Kid, 'if it was written in capital letters like that.'

'We'll never know now,' said Big Frank.

'The secret has died with him,' said Marmsly.

'Dead men tell no tales,' said The Kid.

'I wonder about that,' said Danny Orion.

In the Plume Café they sat and talked and dripped onto the lino.

'What puzzles me,' said Big Frank, sipping tea, 'is why we bothered to go to the funeral.'

'I seem to recall that it was Marmsly's idea,' said The Kid.

Marmsly offered a sickly grin. 'He *might* have left us something in his will. I thought we ought to pay our last respects, even if we didn't actually have any.'

Big Frank sipped further tea. 'If you'd mentioned bumping into his solicitor before we'd carried Sprout's coffin out of the church, we could have left you to pay your bogus respects on your own.'

'Sorry,' said Marmsly. 'But it's just that I like funerals. There's something so definitively final about a funeral. It really says The End and That's Your Lot.'

'It doesn't have to.' Danny had been thinking. Danny was always thinking, it was something he did a lot of. He had been thinking particularly about the BEWARE OF THE DOG note in its capital letters. Danny had always wanted a dog, but neither his mum, with whom he once lived (but who was now shacked up with a double-glazing salesman in Storrington), nor his Aunt May, with whom he presently lived (but who wanted him to find a place of his own), would allow him to buy one.

Danny would willingly have rented a place of his own and bought himself a dog, but he didn't have any money.

It was a great pity old Sam hadn't left him any.

'It doesn't have to *what*?' asked Marmsly, for whom no paragraphs had passed.

'Be The End,' said Danny.

'Please explain,' said Big Frank, damply.

And Danny did so.

'Old Sprout *cannot* have died penniless,' said Danny. 'He spent his entire life borrowing from other people and left debts everywhere, but what did he do with the money? It seems he never spent any, he lived in virtual poverty.'

'Is that like virtual reality?' The Kid asked.

Danny ignored him. 'If Sprout mortgaged his house three times over, there must be heaps of money hidden away somewhere.'

'We'll never know now,' said Big Frank.

'The secret has died with him,' said Marmsly.

'Dead men tell no tales,' said The Kid.

'I wonder about that,' said Danny Orion.

Madame Lorretta Rune possessed, amongst other things, the gift of post-cognition. She was able to predict the past. It was a remarkable gift, but one which had, as yet, to prove its true worth. She made a fair living from quiz shows and those terrible general knowledge competitions they hold in pubs, but it hadn't been what she asked for when she sold her soul to the Devil. Some clerical error, perhaps.

She had recently turned her hand toward contacting the dead. This had met with 'limited success', which, as we all know, is a euphemism for 'no success at all'.

Contacting the dead has always been a tricky old game. It was once called necromancy and frowned upon by the Church. Nowadays it's called spiritualism and has a church of its own. One trouble has always seemed to be that once the dear departed are contacted, they never have anything interesting to say.

Madame Lorretta, who had been boning up on the subject by attending the local Spiritualist church, felt that this particular fact was the one that proved the entire business genuine. Most people had damn all to say while living, so why should anyone expect them to have acquired some new-found eloquence when dead?

But she had, as has been said, only so far achieved 'a limited success'. So she was content to fake it for now, until she'd mastered the technique. Her gift of post-cognition was coming in quite handy for this.

An impressive woman, topping the scales at sixteen stone, Madame Lorretta held court in The Inner Sanctum of Outré Lodge, number thirty-seven Sprite Street. Here, clad usually in many yards of black crushed-velvet, she was already gaining a reputation as one who had connections on 'the other side'. She was a close friend of Danny's Aunt May, who talked a lot about her.

Madame Lorretta was snoozing upon the box ottoman when the front-door knocker knocked. She awoke and rang a small brass Burmese temple bell. This summoned her assistant, Miss Doris Chapel-Hatpeg, a small anaemic woman with nothing whatever to recommend her but for a mildly amusing name. She and Madame Lorretta had served time together in Holloway for offences of a heretical nature, which are still covered by the otherwise repealed Witchcraft Act of 1572.★

'There are four young men at the front door,' said Madame Lorretta. 'They've been there for the last ten minutes.'

'Well, nobody told *me*.'

'I'm telling you now, dear.'

'Hmmph!' It's a difficult one, is 'Hmmph!' Most people never master it. They can do 'Huh!' and even 'Phuh!', but a really convincing 'Hmmph!' is hard to come by nowadays. Miss Chapel-Hatpeg had it off to a fine art. She stomped off down the corridor and opened the front door, hmmphing as she went.

On the doorstep stood four young men, one looked very serious, one looked rather worried, the other two were stifling

★Or whenever it was.

28

smirks. The serious one was Danny, the worried one was Marmsly, the other two were Big Frank and The Kid.

'Madame Lorretta Rune?' asked Danny.

'No,' said Doris Chapel-Hatpeg.

'We've come to the wrong address,' said Marmsly. 'Let's go home.'

'Bottle job,' sniggered Big Frank, making the approved gesture.

'It's tampering with forces unknown,' Marmsly crossed himself.

'Is Madame Lorretta at home to callers?' Danny asked.

'What's it about?'

'We seek the services of a medium,' Danny said.

Big Frank, to whom the word medium meant halfway between large and small and was no good to him when it came to shirts, said, 'We've come to commune with the dead.'

'You've come to the right place then, follow me please.'

The four young men followed Doris, Danny pushing the reluctant Marmsly before him. Big Frank, as last man in, closed the front door.

The Inner Sanctum of Outré Lodge was situated in a back parlour the same size and shape as that once inhabited by the late Sam Sprout. Which didn't help much as the former had received no description.

It was carpeted in colourless Kelims, with matching wall hangings to muffle all sounds of the outer world and encourage those from the next. A sign which read 'Elvis Presley may be contacted at this address' hung humourlessly above a fireplace of neutrally toned timber. Six nondescript chairs ambushed a central table that didn't seem worth the bother. Beside the curtained window stood the big box ottoman and on this sat the large-sized medium. Potted plants were distributed hither and thus and all about the place.

All of this was 'mood lit', which is to say, 'dimly'.

Big Frank sighted Madame Lorretta and took to the tucking in of his shirt. This was his kind of woman.

Madame Lorretta rose and relocated her bulk upon the chair nearest to the fireplace (which was the one furthest away from the door). She smiled towards Danny. 'You have suffered a loss?'

'We all have,' said Danny. 'But we're hoping to make good on it.'

'You understand that I must make a small charge for my services?'

'How small?' Danny asked.

'Ten quid,' said Madame Lorretta.

'Bugger that,' said The Kid.

'It's only two and a half quid each,' Danny told him, 'You have to speculate to accumulate.'

'Count me in,' said Big Frank.

Marmsly said nothing.

'Ten quid is fine,' said Danny.

'In advance.'

Amidst much grumbling, pocket change changed hands.

'Please be seated.'

'Thank you very much.'

Miss Doris Chapel-Hatpeg left the room.

The lads sat down. Danny and Marmsly to the right of Madame Lorretta, Big Frank and The Kid to the left (looking from the door end of the room, of course. From the fireplace end it was the other way around, but it didn't affect things very much).

'We must all place our hands upon the table,' said Madame Lorretta, 'palms down, little fingers touching. When the circle is complete I shall attempt to contact the spirit world.'

'Ooooh,' went The Kid in a manner that lacked not for sarcasm.

'Sssh!' Big Frank told him.

'Thank you,' said Madame Lorretta.

'What time do you finish for the day?' Big Frank asked, but this question did not receive a reply.

Madame Lorretta said, 'I must have *silence*.'

At the word *silence*, the lights dimmed further and a haunting piece of violin music welled from behind a potted aspidistra. Big Frank, who was now in the mood to be impressed by such things, was suitably impressed.

'I must concentrate,' said she-who-would-speak-with-the-dead.

Her four damp guests squinted at one another through the mostly darkness. Marmsly moved uncomfortably in his tweed trousers. 'I want to go to the toilet,' he whispered.

'*Silence!*'

The lights went out completely and the music swelled to deafening.

'Not that bloody silent!' screamed Madame Lorretta.

The lights went up a bit and the sound down.

'Sorry!' came the muffled voice of Doris.

Madame Lorretta leaned back in her chair and did a bit of that ghastly eye-rolling which is so popular amongst those who 'have the calling'.

'My great uncle The Kid used to do that,' whispered The Kid, 'but of course he had been wounded in the head at Ypres.'

'Sssh,' went Big Frank.

'Don't keep ssshing me, I've shelled out my two and a half quid. I can take the piss if I want.'

'I will punch you,' said Big Frank.

The Kid held his counsel.

'I feel a presence!' Madame Lorretta slumped further back in her chair, putting the wind up Marmsly. 'Someone is here, someone is here.'

'Is it old Sam Sprout?' Danny asked.

'It *can* be.'

'Pardon?'

'It can be no other.'

'It could be Elvis,' The Kid whispered. 'Ouch,' he continued.

'Be warned,' said Big Frank.

31

'Oh!' went Madame Lorretta. 'Oh! Oh! Oh!'

'Good grief,' said Marmsly. 'Look at her face.'

His companions looked. It didn't look good. Madame Lorretta's face appeared to be undergoing what the chaps in the film-making fraternity refer to (correctly) as a 'lap dissolve'.

Her face was changing into another face.

'Now that *is* clever,' said Big Frank.

'It's an evil spirit,' croaked Marmsly, crossing his legs. 'And I need the toilet even more now.'

'It *is* clever though, isn't it?' Danny peered at the metamorphosing medium. The prodigious jowls were shrinking away. The bee-hive hair-do was vanishing into the top of the head. The eyes were changing colour. Actually it wasn't so much a lap dissolve, more that smart-arse computer-generated stuff that puts geniuses like Ray Harryhausen out of work.

The lips that had been Madame Lorretta's, but weren't any more, parted. A voice spoke. It wasn't hers either.

'Hello, lads,' said the voice of old Sam Sprout from the face that was now his also.

'Well, I'll be dipped in dog shit,' said Big Frank.

'Do dogs *please*.' Sam Sprout's face contorted.

'Sorry,' said Big Frank.

'Sam,' said Danny. 'Is that really you?'

'It is,' said the face.

'Then where did you hide the money, you old bastard?' asked The Kid.

'Money? What money?' The face looked genuinely puzzled.

'Our money for a start. The rest would be nice also.'

'Dead men pay no debts,' said old Sam Sprout.

'It's *tell no tales*,' said The Kid, wondering just how this was done. 'Definitely *tell no tales*, I've been saying it all afternoon.'

'Well, this dead man can pay no debts. Damn me, I haven't even got a pair of strides here to call my own.'

The lads looked on in silence. That seemed a bit of a bummer, not even having a pair of strides.

Danny scratched his chin. 'We were hoping that you might direct us to your hidden hoard of booty.'

'I've no boots either,' said old Sam.

'Any socks?' The Kid asked.

'Nope.'

'Shirt?' asked Big Frank.

'No shirt, no.'

'No shirt!' Big Frank whistled.

Marmsly let out a strangulated cry. 'I've just wet my damn trews,' said he.

Danny shook his head. 'Good grief,' said he. 'Here's old Sam with no trews at all and Marmsly wets his. There must be a moral in that somewhere.'

'Aren't you cold wherever you are, without any clothes?' asked Big Frank.

'Nah,' said old Sam. 'The sex keeps me warm.'

'The *sex*?' Four voices said this. In unison they said it.

'Of course the sex.'

'You have *sex* where you are?' Danny said this.

'Certainly do. All the time. Get up in the morning, have sex, breakfast, more sex, lunch, then sex, dinner, then sex. Then bed-time. Then sex, of course.'

'Bloody Hell!' said Big Frank. 'And that's what Heaven's like?'

'Heaven be buggered,' said old Sam Sprout. 'I'm not in Heaven, I've been reincarnated as a rabbit in Hyde Park.'

3

Save the planet, kill yourself.

THE CHURCH OF EUTHANASIA, 1995

PELTED WITH STONES
ON THE COMMON

Pelted with stones on the common,
Because of my new-style hair-do.
A fine affair,
I do declare.
A riotous and rare do.

Pelted with stones by foreign students,
Yelling the words of Marx.
A kettle of fish.
An unsavoury dish.
I'd rather be eaten by sharks.

Pelted with stones by Jehovah's Witnesses,
'Cos I wouldn't purchase *The Watchtower*.
A bleeding cheek.
I bought one last week.
And anyway, I'm a Catholic!

SHADES OF RUDYARD KIPLING

(Or why Danny's Aunt May won't allow animals in the house)

During that rough old period we had after the Boom Years finished,* Danny's Aunt May thought it might be a good idea to supplement the modest income she made from the Tupperware parties and take in a lodger.

Danny's Aunt May was living in Dacre Gardens at this time, opposite the abandoned cement works, so she put aside her first thought of an advert in *Country Life* and settled for a postcard in the window of Peg's Corner Shop.

Aunt May cleared all her late husband's tweed suits from the wardrobe, gave the tiny back bedroom a good flicking over with a feather duster and awaited the rush.

Now Danny's Aunt May was not a silly woman and being a regular patron of the Walpole Cinema (this being the time when they showed proper British films), she was well acquainted with tales of aged lodgers who died and left their fortunes unexpectedly to kindly landladies.

Aunt May's postcard read: FURNISHED ROOM TO LET. WOULD SUIT RETIRED GENTLEMAN OF MILITARY BACKGROUND. (In capital letters.)

'Someone around the eighty-year mark,' Aunt May told her friend Mrs The Kid, who lived around the corner in Purple Haze Terrace. 'And looking as much like Wilfred Hyde-White as possible.'

Her first applicant was a beturbaned bus conductor whose credentials were quite unsuitable.

Her second was a young man named Stewart, who wore a quiff and a most unusual brand of aftershave. He was similarly rejected.

Colonel Bertie C. Bickerstaff, late of the Khyber Rifles,

*The one we're still having (satire).

arrived on a bright summer's morning, crocodile-skin travelling case and polo sticks clutched in wrinkled sunburned hands.

He was eighty if he was a day, a gentleman if ever there was one and his resemblance to Wilfred Hyde-White was quite uncanny.

'Your servant, ma'am,' said he and was received into Aunt May's little terraced house with a degree of accord that Aunt May would normally have reserved for a visiting member of the royal household (should one have ever chosen to make a visit) or the Dalai Lama (Aunt May having a go at Buddhism at the time).

Colonel Bertie C. Bickerstaff was not a hard man to please and although his conversation seemed somewhat limited – 'Your servant, ma'am,' to Aunt May and 'Man's a damn fool' to the milkman – he fitted into the house of Danny's aunt the way the toad of yore fitted into its hole.

He had been ensconced therein for some three months before he chose to make, what seemed at the time, an innocent request.

'Mind if I bring one or two small house plants up to me quarters, ma'am?' he enquired. 'To make meself feel more at home, as it were.'

'Certainly you may,' said Danny's aunt. 'Feel free to treat this house as your own.' It was a poorly chosen remark, but at the time it seemed appropriate. After all, the old fellow didn't look short of a few bob and none of us are getting any younger.

'Your servant, ma'am,' said the colonel.

The first consignment of plants arrived the next Tuesday. A swarthy individual, smelling strongly of the Punjab, knocked upon Aunt May's gaily painted front door and announced, 'Plants for Colonel-Sahib, missy.'

'Colonel,' called Aunt May, up the flight of twenty-three stairs, 'your plants are here.'

'Jolly good show,' bluffed the old boy, blustering down. 'Jolly good show.'

The box was not a large one, but it seemed unduly weighty. Aunt May had to join in the struggle to hump it up the stairs.

'Mostly packaging,' said the colonel, apologetically. 'My eternal thanks, ma'am, my eternal thanks.'

Well satisfied to have earned the eternal thanks of a rich old lodger, Aunt May started down the stairs.

'Drop the driver-johnny a couple of rupees, would you, my dear?' the colonel called after her.

Aunt May parted with a two-bob bit.

The driver-johnny thanked Aunt May and departed, leaving the air heavily scented with vindaloo.

Over the next few weeks there was a lot of coming and going in Dacre Gardens, and all of it at Aunt May's house. A great many discarded packing cases, bearing inscriptions in Urdu, found their way into Aunt May's back garden. The same number of two-bob bits left her purse.

Aunt May began to grow a tad uneasy.

'I don't like to mention it to the old gentleman,' she told her friend, Mrs The Kid. 'After all, he does pay his rent on time and his resemblance to Wilfred Hyde-White is quite uncanny.'

'It's probably just a hobby,' her neighbour replied. 'My hubby, Mr The Kid, collects encephaloids. I don't mind, it's quiet enough.'

'He's been bringing home some very strange things lately.'

'He needs *them* for his work.' Mrs The Kid reddened about the cheek areas.

'No, not your hubby, I mean the colonel.'

'Oh.' Mrs The Kid enquired as to what sort of things these might be.

'Mosquito nets, a lot of old leather suitcases. He stays up until all hours. I can hear him muttering away and banging about. I think he must be making something.'

Mrs The Kid's face took on the look of grave concern which she always kept in reserve for moments such as this.

She aroused her husband who was sleeping peacefully in the front parlour, his feet in the tub of fuller's earth and his head in a brown paper bag★.

'Mosquito nets and old leather suitcases,' mused Mr The Kid, once he had been given a synopsis of the story so far. 'Anything else you can think of?'

'He collects bones from the butcher.'

Mr The Kid smiled mysteriously. 'That elephant's foot umbrella stand you have in your hall, has he asked to borrow that, by any chance?'

Danny's aunt nodded.

'*Eureka!*' went Mr The Kid, which made everybody jump. 'I know what he's up to then.'

'You do?' asked his wife and her friend, Danny's aunt.

'It is obvious.' Mr The Kid preened at his braces. 'Consider the facts: a retired colonel of the Khyber Rifles takes up lodgings in your house. He begins filling his room with plants, then with hide suitcases and bones and seemingly unconnected oddments. To my mind there can be only one logical explanation.'

'And what, pray tell us, is *that*, Mr Sherlock Holmes?' asked his wife.

'The nostalgic colonel is building himself a jungle.'

Aunt May gasped.

'And an elephant!'

Aunt May fainted.

'I suppose you think that's very funny,' said Mrs The Kid, as she applied the smelling bottle to Aunt May's nose.

'Simply applying Occam's razor, my sweet,' said Mr The Kid, returning to his tub and paper bag.

★A popular homoeopathic remedy for curing gout.

'I'll take you home, dear,' said Mrs The Kid, once Aunt May had been adequately revived. 'And we'll go and have a word with this colonel of yours.'

As the two ladies approached the tiny terraced house at the end of Dacre Gardens, they were both equally surprised to see the large foreign-looking lorry that was parked outside.

The word 'surprise' however was hardly adequate to describe their feelings as they watched an enormous packing case being manhandled with the utmost care through the front door. On the side of this packing case were printed the words BENGAL TIGER. HANDLE WITH CARE (in capital letters).

'Now there is a thing,' said Mrs The Kid.

'And there is another,' said Danny's aunt, as she spied a crowd of little brown-skinned men approaching from the direction of the abandoned cement works. They were banging gongs and blowing whistles. 'Surely those would be native beaters, wouldn't they?'

'What, people who beat up natives?'

'No, natives who beat.'

'Oh, I see.'

The porters who had been manhandling the packing case into Aunt May's house, emerged from the front doorway in considerable haste, bundled into the foreign-looking lorry and departed at speed.

Danny's aunt looked at Mrs The Kid.

And Mrs The Kid looked at Danny's aunt.

They both looked towards the approaching native beaters, the half-open front door, and then back at each other once more.

'I think we had better get all this sorted out right now,' said Mrs The Kid, in a most determined tone. 'Come on, let's do it.'

'After you, my dear,' said Danny's aunt.

As she pushed the front door fully open, Mrs The Kid

became immediately aware of the unusually pungent odour which filled the little house.

'Smells a bit like the hot house at Kew,' whispered Mrs The Kid, 'only more so.'

Aunt May, who had her eyes tightly shut, opened them a crack.

'Oh my goodness,' she said, closing them again. 'Gracious me,' she continued, as she opened them a second time and became fully aware of the bizarre transformation which had taken place in her house during the few short hours that she'd been out. Palms and ferns and vines and grasses rose from rows of aspidistra pots and choked up the hall. From the reproduction coachlamps above the Queen Mother's portrait, spotted lemurs skipped and chattered. The distinctive diamond-shaped leaves of that tree which is sacred to the Bodhisattva shone richly from the direction of the kitchenette. All in all the effect was one that would have had the likes of Gunga Din, or indeed Saboo, feeling well at home.

Overhead, indeed coming from the direction of the back bedroom, a curious trumpeting arose.

Mrs The Kid clapped a hand to her cheek. 'Tsetse fly,' she said, knowledgeably. Aunt May was feeling faint once again. 'Shall we come back later?' she asked.

Mrs The Kid was now adamant. 'We will see this thing through *now*,' she said, with the kind of spirit that made folk like Scott of the Antarctic, Lawrence of Arabia and Jones of Indiana exactly whatever it was they were.

Mrs The Kid advanced along the hall, beating at the vegetation with her parrot's-head umbrella. 'Follow me,' she cried, making an assault upon the stairs. The lemurs chattered with glee and curious reptiles stuck their scaly heads out from the greenery and blew raspberries.

Upon gaining the upper floor, the two ladies espied what was surely the tail-end of a King Cobra protruding from the bathroom. Over this they stepped, most nimbly.

The back-bedroom door stood ajar. Clumps of exotic foliation showed about the hinges and the smell of Kew's-hothouse-but-more-so was more-so than ever. The landing window had steamed up and the light which fell upon the newly mossed linoleum lacked not for arboreal ambience.

The two ladies looked at each other once more.

Then a terrible shout was heard.

'Where's me damned mahoot?' went this shout. 'Mahoot, be damned, where are ya?'

The shout was the shout of Colonel Bertie C. Bickerstaff, late of the Khyber Rifles.

Mrs The Kid put her hand to the back-bedroom door and gave it an almighty push. As the door swung in and the two ladies stared, a singular sight was seen.

The lower jaws of Mrs The Kid and Danny's aunt fell slack when they saw what they saw. Because it can truly be said that they had never seen anything like it before, nor ever have they wished to see it since.

There it stood, in the middle of the floor.

The colonel's mad creation.

It was as Mr The Kid had foretold.

An elephant.

But no ordinary elephant, this. Here was a grotesque parody of an elephant. A mockery. A monstrosity.

Styled out of ancient suitcases, plaster of Paris and chicken wire, a length of garden hose serving for a trunk, two bicycle lamps for eyeballs and a pair of brass *Peerage* hunting horns serving as the mighty tusker's ivory glory, this travesty stood some four feet high and atop it, in a makeshift houdah, formed from Aunt May's favourite wicker commode, sat the colonel, all in shorts and tropical kit, a .577 Cordite Express double-barrelled sporting piece across his lap.

'Wot ho, me dears,' called the old loon as he spied the boggle-eyed twosome. 'Climb aboard and join the shikar. Damn me!' he continued, pulling out his pocket watch and rattling it at his ear. 'Those bally native beaters are late.'

'They're outside in the street,' said Mrs The Kid. 'Now see here, Colonel—'

'Bring'm in,' cried the colonel. 'Bring'm in. Don't stand on ceremony. The hunt is on.'

'There'll be no the-hunt-is-oning here, if you don't mind.' Mrs The Kid folded her arms, which those who knew her knew to be a bad sign.

'Would you care for a cup of tea, Colonel?' asked Danny's aunt, she being one of those individuals who believed that no matter how dire the circumstance – leg blown off by terrorist bomb, cobblers held fast between the teeth of a Dobermann – a cup of hot sweet tea is a universal panacea. These individuals have names like Elsie of Hartlepool or Doreen of Huddersfield, but they never receive the acclaim of the Scotts, Lawrences or Joneses.

There's no justice in this world.

'No time for tea, me dear,' chuffed the colonel. 'Have to hunt down old Shere Khan. Damn treacherous man-eater that one. Been bothering the cattle, doncha know.'

'Cattle?' Aunt May shook her well-baffled bonce.

Mrs The Kid pointed to the left front leg of the colonel's mount. 'There's your umbrella stand, dear,' she said.

An Indian in white livery came puffing to the bedroom door. 'We track down tiger to lair beneath box ottoman in front parlour, sahib,' he said.

Aunt May fainted.

'Forward, my mahoot!' bawled the colonel, cocking his shotgun.

Now, at this time things really got moving. The native beaters sighted the tiger through the front window and broke into the house, Mrs The Kid became suddenly entangled in the coils of a boa constrictor and the colonel let fly with his .577.

A neighbour, taking this report to be a gas mains explosion, called for the fire brigade, who arrived in record time and began training hoses on the house and winching up the big ladders.

The native beaters, who had not been able to squeeze themselves into Aunt May's house, were somewhat incensed by the drenching and replied with a hail of stones and flower pots.

The tiger, sensing that perhaps the time was right to make a break for it, escaped through the scullery window.

Aunt May slept on, oblivious to it all.

Order was finally restored at about three fifteen, when a heavily armed rapid-response team abseiled in from helicopters.

Though many were wounded in the rioting and mayhem, there was only one fatality.

And that was Colonel Bertie C. Bickerstaff, late of the Khyber Rifles and now late of Dacre Gardens also.

His body was carried reverentially down the twenty-three verdant stairs of 23 Dacre Gardens by four native beaters and laid to rest upon a makeshift bier of milk crates.

There was some talk of the natives wishing to cremate him there and then, but the rapid-response team soon put a stop to that.

The coroner's report stated that the old man had died from multiple injuries, impacted fractures and burst whatnots, almost consistent with 'being trampled to death by a rogue elephant'.

Aunt May doesn't live in Dacre Gardens any more, what with all the publicity and everything, she decided to open her house up as a safari park. The novelty certainly seems to have caught on, because there are now three more such parks in Dacre Gardens alone and the word is out that the council may be converting some of its maisonettes in Moby Dick Terrace into wildlife sanctuaries.

It is sad to record that Colonel Bertie C. Bickerstaff died

penniless, so Aunt May did not come into an inheritance. Apparently, a single week before the old warrior took his final salute, he entered into some kind of financial agreement which involved him making over all his not-inconsiderable personal wealth to another party.

This party was a certain Samuel Sprout.

4

People can only talk about you if you exist.

ERIC CANTONA, 1995

PET HATREDS

He took his pet hatreds out for a walk,
On a very strong piece of chain,
For they seemed to dislike the populace,
And would bite people time and again.

He left them outside the hardware shop,
While he purchased a packet of nails,
And when he came out, his pet hatreds had gone.
He was happy and moved to Wales.

THE MARK-TWO DANNY ORION
(Or a change is not always as good as a rest)

Danny Orion sat upon a bench in Walpole Park. He was well
peeved. The day, as they say, had not been his.

Soaked to the skin at old Sam's funeral, then striped up for two and a half quid by Madame Lorretta.

Danny shook his head. And for the entire episode to come screaming to a halt with a duff old gag about rabbits in Hyde Park . . . It was all too much.

Danny sniffed. He was sure he was catching a cold. Marmsly had gone home for a hot bath and a change of trews. Big Frank had taken Madame Lorretta to the pictures and The Kid had shot off to visit his aunt, who had a sealife centre in her kitchen sink.

Danny sniffed again. In the far distance a man walked a dog, which made Danny sad as he was greatly desirous of such a beast. In the middle distance some children played hopscotch and bowling the penny. And in the near distance, on the bench next to Danny, a poet sat composing links to go between the background music.

> 'The rain is gone,
> And my name's John,
> And I've a bench,
> To sit upon,'
>
> composed the poet.

'Good grief,' said Danny. It was definitely time for a change. What he needed for certain was *a change*. If there was one thing capable of lifting himself out of himself, then that one thing would be *a change*.

I'll go home, thought Danny, but there was no change there.

The pictures then. Still no change.

Danny sniffed a third time. What was it his old dad used to say about *a change*? Before his old dad buggered off with the waitress from the Plume Café? 'Out with the old and in with the new,' was that it? Danny recalled vaguely that this had some connection with drink and vomit.

46

I could change my job, thought Danny. But this was not possible, as Danny didn't have a job.

I could go round and see Mickey Merlin, thought Danny, and this seemed far more practical. Danny had not seen Mickey Merlin in a very long time.

Danny rose from the bench, found his trouser pockets and stuck his hands into them.

> 'Then he got up,
> And I stayed here,
> Soon he'll be far,
> But I'll be near,'
>
> > composed the poet.

'Aw, shut up!' said Danny.

Mickey Merlin lived in a converted lock-keeper's hut on the Grand Union Canal near to where Leo Felix sold used motor cars.

'With a single turn of the screw, I could flood twenty square miles of the home counties, should I so wish . . .' he used to say. But it was a damnable lie, because his stretch of canal had dried up years ago. Hence the lock-keeper's hut becoming available. And everything.

It being now four of the afternoon clock and Tuesday of the early week, Mickey Merlin was tending to his live-stock. A long-handled spade in one hand and a bucket in the other.

He was mucking out his rabbits.

Danny appeared, slouching up the tow-path, lighted Woodbine stuck in his mouth. 'Good-afternoon, Mickey,' he said.

'I know you just lit that up,' replied the other, 'so I'll trouble you to come across with one for me.'

Danny shrugged. 'My last,' he said, unconvincingly.

'You're a pain in the neck, Danny. And mean with it.'

'I've had a most depressing day. I've come round here to ask for some advice.'

'Then I advise you to give me one of your Woodbine.'

'Those rabbits really smell,' Danny observed.

'It's not the rabbits that smell, it's all the . . . Look, are you going to give me one of your Woodbine or not?'

'Not,' said Danny.

'Then clear off,' said Mickey.

Danny got out his fags. 'Have one then,' he said to the man with the spade and the bucket.

'You must understand that any advice I give you, may not necessarily be the correct advice. I am subject to making the occasional slip up.'

'Like when you advised Big Frank to roll about naked in the nettle bed as a cure for his piles?'

'Well, he didn't complain about them for a couple of weeks, did he?'

'Not about the piles, no.'

'I don't do medical advice any more,' said Mickey, as he led Danny into his converted hut.

'In exactly what way is this hut converted?' Danny asked.

'Thoroughly,' said Mickey and that was the end of that conversation.

The next conversation lasted a little longer. Not much, but a little. It was one of those intimate conversations which old friends (who go back a *long* way) have.

'Would you like some tea, Danny?'

'Yes please.'

'I have only coffee, I'm afraid.'

'Coffee would be fine.'

'Black or white?'

'White please.'

'Sorry, I don't have any milk.'

'As it comes then.'

'Sugar?'

'No thank you.'

'I've already put it in.'

Spot on, thought Danny, who hated tea, didn't take milk in coffee and always had sugar.

'What I want is a bit of a change,' said Danny, accepting his coffee and seating himself on Mickey's camp-bed.

'*Don't sit there!*' cried Mickey.

Danny jumped up and shifted himself to the ancient wicker commode which stood by the door.

'There,' said Mickey. 'Now you've had a bit of a change. Finish your coffee and go away.'

Danny sighed and sipped his coffee. 'It's not as simple as that. I want to completely change my life, my entire outlook. I'm tired of being what I am.'

'And what are you?'

'Dull and dogless.'

'You're both of those, true. Have you thought about changing your job?'

'I don't have one.'

'Well, I can't employ you. You can't actually do anything, can you?'

'I can think about things,' said Danny. 'I think a lot about things.'

'It's a poser.' Mickey Merlin scratched his head.

'You've dandruff there,' said Danny.

Mickey ignored him. 'There's one thing we might try, but, well, no, perhaps not.'

'What? What?'

'Well, it's just possible. Hand me down my book of spells.'

'Book of spells?' Danny showed a degree of surprise.

'Oh yes.' Mickey drew back his shoulders. 'Seventh son of a seventh son.'

'Son of a gun.' Danny lifted down an ancient leather-bound volume from the shelf and blew away the dust of ages.

Mickey took the book upon his knees and idly turned the pages. 'Rooty-toot,' said he. 'This takes me back a few years.'

'Do they work?'

'Do *what* work?'

'The spells?'

'Of course they work. They wouldn't be spells if they didn't work, would they?'

'Like the boomerang, you mean?'

'Like the *what*?'

'You know. What do you call a boomerang that won't come back?'

'A stick,' said Mickey. 'But I know what you mean. They work all right. My many-times great grand-daddy wrote these spells. Surely you've wondered about my name.'

'No,' said Danny.

'You can't, perhaps, think of a famous magician who had the same name as me?'

Danny thought. 'Oh yes, of course.'

'There, told you.'

'*Mickey* Mouse,' said Danny. 'In *Fantasia*.'

'Not Mickey bloody Mouse.' Mickey Merlin slammed shut the book. Little animated coloured stars burst all around it.

'Only joking,' said Danny. 'Merlin, of course.'

'Of course.'

'Paul Merlin and Debbie Magee.'

'Get out of my hut.'

'I'm sorry, but come on, Mickey. I've already had a run-in with a medium today. A magician I really don't need.'

'Well, sod yourself then.' Mickey rose to put back the book.

Danny gave his lip a chew. 'They *really* do work?' he asked.

'You *really* are a stupid prat, Danny.'

'Another reason I need a change.'

Mickey reopened his book and turned pages once more. 'Hm,' said he. 'The spell of Temporary Temporal Transference, what do you think of that?'

'I think it's somewhat alliterative. But no offence, I told you I think a lot. What does this spell do?'

'It affects a temporary temporal transference.'

'Oh I see.'

'No you don't.'

'No I don't, please explain.'

'Your consciousness, your thinking processes in fact, are temporarily transferred into someone else's head. And theirs into yours. You swop bodies. It's only temporary, of course. Lasts until you go to sleep. Then you wake up back as yourself.'

'You have got to be joking.'

'Do you remember the day Big Frank's Morris Minor found its way into the top of the vicar's oak tree?'

'Wasn't that the day after he punched you for having him roll about in the nettle bed?'

'Or when The Kid was bitten by a cheese sandwich?'

'Shortly after he sold you those socks with no leg-holes in them?'

'Correct.'

Danny scratched his head.

'You're going grey at the temples,' said Mickey Merlin.

'Well, you can't take the credit for that. I was going grey before I came in here. I've been growing grey since . . .'

'Since you ran over my foot at school with your bike.'

'Well, I'll be dipped in dog sh—'

'Careful what you say when I've got the book out.'

'Quite so. Temporary Temporal Transference, eh? And I could be anyone I wanted to be, for just a while, until I fell asleep?'

'That's the kiddie.'

'But what about the person who suddenly finds themself in my body? They might go mad and throw *me* off a bridge, or something.'

'I'll be here to look after *your* body. I'll tell whoever it is that they're having a bad dream. I'll take care of it, you can trust me. Magician's Code of Conduct and all that sort of thing. Rhinocratic oath.'

'I miss Viv Stanshell,' sighed Danny.

'We all miss Viv Stanshell,' said Mickey. 'So what do you think? Care to give it a try? If that isn't a change, then I'm banjoed if I know what is. You can't be Viv Stanshell, by the way. No dead people.'

'I wonder which brat-pack Hollywood star has the biggest—'

'Number of Oscar nominations?' Mickey asked.

'Dick,' said Danny.

'*Danny?*' said Mickey.

'*Dick* Whitby,' said Danny. '*He* has the biggest number of Oscar nominations.'

'So you want to be him? You want to be a famous brat-pack Hollywood star with the biggest—'

'Number of Oscar nominations. Yes.'

'You wouldn't fancy being, say, Mother Teresa?'

'No!' said Danny. 'Would you?'

'Not a second time, no.'

'A second time?'

'Certainly, don't you recall reading in *The Sunday Spurt*★ about Mother Teresa once dancing the night away topless at a disco in Calcutta?'

'No, I don't!'

'They hush these things up,' said Mickey. 'It's a conspiracy, you know. There's magicians all around the world doing this sort of thing all the time. I was Hugh Grant once for an evening.'

Danny did not dignify this remark with a reply.

'Isn't Dick Whitby gay?' Mickey asked.

'Good grief,' said Danny.

'Well listen, it will take me about half an hour to get things set up. You sit outside and decide who you want to be. Give the matter some *really* serious consideration. OK?'

'I will,' said Danny, taking his leave.

★　　★　　★

★Yes, that is SPURT, to avoid the court action.

The sun was heading down behind the Godolphin Chemical Works by the time Mickey Merlin appeared at the door of the converted hut to beckon Danny within.

Danny had been pacing up and down outside, shaking his head and going, 'Yes him', followed shortly by '*no not* him', again and again and again. In fact, Danny had all but reached the conclusion that although he was fed up with being himself, he really wasn't all *that* keen on being someone else.

'Enter,' said Mickey. 'All is in preparation.'

Danny followed him into the hut.

The converted hut had undergone further conversion. But this of a religious nature. The interior was now candlelit, a pentagram had been chalked on to the wooden floor, inscribed within a double circle containing the names of power. Mickey Merlin wore a black silk gown, which stretched from neck to ankle and was embroidered in silver thread with many an enigmatic logo. He certainly looked the part.

'Who enters?' he intoned, in a deep dark voice. 'Say, a seeker after truth,' he continued, in his own.

Danny raised a doubtful eyebrow. 'A seeker after truth,' said he.

'What is your desire, oh humble one?'

'Well, you see I . . .' Danny sighed.

Mickey frowned and tut-tut-tutted.

Danny sighed again and shrugged. After all, this wasn't *really* going to work, was it? But the least he could do was to play along. Mickey was going to an awful lot of trouble just to cheer him up.

'What is your desire, oh humble one?'

'I wish to be Temporally Transformated, please.'

'And with whom do you wish to exchange bodies?'

Danny sighed and he sniffed also. He *had* caught a cold. He knew he would. It was all old Sam Sprout's fault. 'I can't make up my mind,' said Danny. 'I've narrowed it down to about half a dozen, but you see, I don't know what they're doing today. They might be lying in bed with a cold or something.'

'They don't have colds in Hollywood,' said Mickey.

'All right,' said Danny. 'I know who I want to be.'

'OK, we'll run it from the top then. Go out and come in again.'

'Must I?'

'Just do it.'

'Okey-doke.' Danny went out and came in again.

'Who enters?' asked Mickey, in his deep dark voice.

'A seeker after truth,' said Danny.

'And what is your desire, oh humble one?'

'I desire the spell of Temporary Temporal Transference.'

'Then you've come to the right place, moosh. Step into the circle.' The seventh son of a seventh son positioned Danny at the pentagram's centre.

'I will begin the recitation,' said Mickey. 'When I reach the line SCARABUS NOSTROS ONAN (in capital letters), speak the name and all will be done. Do you understand?'

Danny nodded. Mickey really did look ever so serious. 'I understand,' said Danny.

Mickey removed himself to a little rostrum he had set up next to the primus stove. On this stood his book of spells. Mickey flung wide his arms. 'We begin,' said he, 'with the banishing ritual of the pentagram, in order to cleanse the air of any undesirable presences, then we open and consecrate the temple.'

'And will all this take long?' Danny asked.

'No, I did it while you were waiting outside.'

'Fair enough.'

'So, we'll get straight on to the really tasty stuff.'

'Jolly good.'

'Oh, and by the way, while the ceremony is in progress it would be fatal to take a step outside the pentagram.'

'*What?*'

'Well, it's no big deal, is it? You *can* stand still, can't you?'

'Mickey, I'm beginning to have my doubts about all this.'

'A change is as good as a rest,' said the magician. 'And I've started now, so I'm jolly well going to finish. Can't leave a job half done.'

'Mickey, I . . .'

Mickey Merlin raised his arms. '*Globalis et isipadis et medmanis, et mehanis.*'

'Mickey, this isn't a good idea.'

'*Daedulas, Daedulas, consumat consumat.*'

'I think perhaps I'll just look for a job.' Danny suddenly shivered, it seemed to have grown a bit nippy.

'*Testiculos habet et bene pendentes.*'

'Mickey . . .' Danny rubbed at his arms, it was growing *extremely* cold *extremely* fast. He lifted a foot and prepared to do a runner. A little blue crackle of light twinkled about the pentagram's edges. Danny lowered his foot and stood very still.

'Mickey stop this,' he said.

But Mickey looked in no mood to stop. One of the reasons that witches and magicians often practise their fearful arts in the middle of forests or on wild lonely moors, is because magic is a very noisy business. It involves a great deal of shouting. Neighbours banging on the walls do not help the aspiring practitioner of The Left Hand Path.

'*Tantalus, Salamandus, Acraphantus.*' Mickey was really working up a lather now. Sounds of thunder rolled from without and the floorboards trembled within.

Danny looked down at the pentagram. Perhaps if he rubbed it out. He put forth a tentative foot. Blue flame crackled. Perhaps not.

'*Et pharna, copacantus, lefsphatus,*' shouted the magician. The camp-bed was bouncing, things tumbled from shelves, window panes rattled. Lightning now flashed.

'Mickey, stop this.'

'*SCARABUS NOSTROS ONAN*' (in capital letters).

'Mickey Merlin! Listen to me!'

There was a bang and there was a whoosh and then there was a whoosh *and* a bang. Things turned this way, then turned that and then went rather quiet.

Danny Orion sat upon a bench in Walpole Park. He was well peeved. The day, as they say, had not been his. Soaked to the skin at old Sam's funeral, striped up for two and a half quid by Madame Lorretta and now . . .

Danny Orion looked down at himself.

But it wasn't himself.

It was Mickey bloody Merlin.

Danny sighed, but he didn't sniff. Mickey Merlin hadn't caught a cold.

In the far distance another man walked his dog, in the middle distance some other children played at hopscotch and bowling the penny, and in the near distance the same poet sat composing links to go between the background music.

> 'Where are we now,
> And who shall we be,
> When our measure runs out,
> To eternity?'

composed the poet.

'Aw, shut your face,' said Danny Orion.

5

It came outta nowhere, just to say 'I'm back again'.

THE SCREAMING BLUE MESSIAHS, 1982

THE KID

The Kid put on his mackintosh,
And fiddled with the belt.
'It's not the way it used to be,'
He said, and if you'll pardon me,
I do believe he told the truth,
Because that macky smelt.

The Kid put on his Homburg (black),
And worried at the brim.
'This isn't mine, it's poorly made,'
He said, and in the Homburg's shade,
The grass grew up between his toes
And one day covered him.

The Kid went back to Birmingham
To see his family.
But they had gone without a trace.
They'd vanished into outer space.
Which goes to show you what can happen,
Dum-de-dum-de-de.

When The Kid was a kid there'd been a chap living in his street who'd met a magician. His name was Boscombe Walters and this is his story.

THE BOSCOMBE WALTERS STORY

'The cruel fact of the matter,' sighed the sympathetic dermatologist, 'is that some people are simply born – how shall I put this? – ugly. While some have complexions like peaches and cream, others resemble glasspaper, or places of acute volcanic activity. Sadly you are one of the latter.'

And there was no doubt about it, Boscombe Walters was one ugly bastard. And it wasn't just the pustules. It was the entire physiognomic caboodle. The heavy jowls. The flaccid mouth. The bulbous nose. The terrible toad-like eyes.

These now glared balefully at the handsome dermatologist.

'But it needn't be a handicap,' this fellow was saying. 'Many a man born without the advantage of conventional good looks has gone on to find fame and celebrity. Has won the respect of his peers and the love of a good woman. Think of, well . . .' He paused for thought. 'Think of Sidney James, or Rondo Hatton*.'

Boscombe thought of them. Both were dead, he thought.

'It's not what a man looks like. It's what he has inside him.'

Boscombe raised a grubby mit to squeeze a prominent boil on his neck and release a little of what *he* had inside *him*.

'Oh, please *don't*,' implored the doctor. 'The surgery has just been redecorated.'

Boscombe returned his mit to his lap and scratched his groin with it. 'So what you're saying,' he growled, 'is that you can do sweet sod all to help me.'

Doctor Kinn, for such was the physician's name, coughed

---

*Now legendary star of *The Creeper* and *The Brute Man*.

politely. He had come to dread the weekly sessions with this unsavoury little man. An aura of evil surrounded him, which made him about as welcome as King Herod at a baby show. 'Go out and live your life,' the doctor advised. 'Rejoice that you are alive. Revel in your existence. Think positively.'

Boscombe rose negatively from his chair. 'Bloody quack,' said he.

'Excuse me?'

'I said, bloody quack. As in doctor, rather than duck.'

'You can collect your usual prescription at the reception area,' said Dr Kinn, moving papers around on his desk. 'And, er, come back and see me in, what shall we say, six months?'

Boscombe hawked up a green gobbet of phlegm the size of a glass eye and spat it onto the carpet. 'That to you,' said he.

'Make that *one year*,' said the doctor. 'And see yourself out.'

Boscombe had recently taken to wearing tropical kit, as it made the mosquito net he had stitched onto his solar toupee in order to conceal his face, seem a little more in keeping. The khaki shorts, however, flattered neither his beer belly nor his bow legs.

From the surgery in Abaddon Street to the chemist's on the main road is a fairly short shuffle, and as it was term time there were no children about for Boscombe to cuff as he passed upon his dismal way.

A cat or two to kick at though.

Beneath his breath the ugly man cursed darkly. He would do for that bloody quack. Pop around at lunch-time and loosen his bicycle brakes, watch him sail down the hill towards the traffic lights, then—

Boscombe Walters sniggered. 'Then *splat* and physician heal thyself.'

There was no spark of goodness in Boscombe. He was ugly through and through. From the outside to the in and out

59

again. Boscombe cared for no-one and no-one cared for him. And that was just the way he liked it. Ugliness suited him fine. He'd made a career out of it (although not one that was likely to bring him fame and celebrity and the love of a good woman). Boscombe's problem was the spots. The boils! The buboes! If only he could rid himself of these, then everything would be as fine as it was ever likely to be. Which, though far from perfect, was perfect enough for him.

Boscombe took a short cut down an alleyway, on the off-chance that there might be dustbins to ignite, or ladies' items upon a line that he might add to his collection.

Sadly there was neither, but as he slunk along, muttering sourly, he did chance to notice a bright little card that was pinned to a back entrance gate.

It had the look of those printed postcard jobbies which always add that essential touch of colour to the otherwise drab interiors of telephone boxes.

This one, however, did not promote the skills of some lady 'trained in those arts which amuse men'. This one bore a mysterious logo and the words:

DR POO PAH DOO. OBEAH MAN.
HERBALIST. SKIN SPECIALIST.
BMX CYCLE REPAIRS.
(in capital letters)

Out of habit, born from badness, Boscombe plucked the little card from the gate and crumpled it between the fingers of his rarely washed hands. He was about to cast it groundward when a little voice inside his head said, 'Hang about there, pal.'

Boscombe sniffed deeply, brought up another ball of phlegm and sent it skimming back along the alleyway. And then he uncrumpled the card. DR POO PAH DOO. *SKIN SPECIALIST!*

'Luck,' said the ugly man. 'Luck indeed.'

But was this luck? What was an Obeah Man? Something to do with voodoo, wasn't it? And that was all crap, that kind of thing. 'Nah,' said Boscombe, recrumpling the card. 'Waste of time.'

But then, DOCTOR. SKIN SPECIALIST. HERBALIST? It had to be worth a try. It couldn't hurt. And a spotty man *is* a desperate man.

Boscombe thrust the card into a pocket of his safari jacket and pressed open the gate. It moved upon groaning hinges to reveal a squalid backyard. There was a mound of mouldy papers and a black cat.

Boscombe skirted the mound and kicked the cat.

'Meoooow!' it went.

The back door was open. Boscombe didn't knock.

It was dim and dank within. A dour hallway led to a flight of uncarpeted stairs. A sign on the wall read, 'Dr Poo Pah Doo. First Floor.' Somewhere in the distance a dripping tap spelt messages in morse.

Boscombe trudged up the stairs. This house smelled none too good. This house smelled of dampness and old bed linen.

This house smelled like Boscombe's house.

On the first floor was a single door and upon this a brass plate which bore the name of Dr Poo Pah Doo.

Boscombe knocked.

'Come on in then,' called a deep, brown voice. 'And bring yo' bike.'

Boscombe entered.

The room was souped in ganja smoke. A single bulb, yellow-hued and naked, cast a wan crepuscular glow.

Bits and bobs of bicycles brought an occasional glitter. But there was nothing here that really offered welcome.

'Welcome,' said something.

Boscombe strained his toad-likes. Close by in the fug something sat. It was a beefy-looking something and it wore a top hat decorated with chicken feathers. Two large dark hands tinkered with an alloy chainset.

'What de trouble?' asked Dr Poo Pah Doo, for such was this something. 'Bin doin' de bunny-hops and done twisted yo' frame?'

'I don't have a bike,' said Boscombe.

'Well, I don't do skateboards. Trucks too damn expensive.'

'Don't have a skateboard either.' Boscombe turned to take his leave. This obviously *was* a waste of time.

'Where yo' damn well goin'?' asked the Obeah Man. 'What yo' problem anyhow?'

'Skin.' Boscombe had one hand on the door. 'I saw your sign. Skin specialist, it said.'

'And in capital letters.' The tall top hat rose to expose the face beneath. It was an African face. A noble warrior's face. Fierce, with piercing almond eyes, but smiling a mouthload of golden teeth. 'Come here. Let's have a look at you.'

Boscombe did a two-step shuffle, raised his mosquito net and inclined his head towards the sitter.

'Whoa!' went this body. 'Not so God-damn close. Yo' got a real rake of trouble and grief there, boy. Yo' should get someone fix that for you.'

'Someone?'

Dr Poo Pah Doo sniffed at Boscombe. 'I can smell yo' aura boy and it don't smell good. It smell wicked. Yo' wicked 'cos yo' ugly, or ugly 'cos yo' wicked? Which it be?'

'You spades know bugger all!' said Boscombe, who numbered racism amongst his more appealing qualities. 'I'm off.'

'Yeah. Yo' do that. Come in here, uglying up my workshop. I not make yo' pretty.'

'As if you could.'

'Oh, I could do it, wicked man. I could do it. But I won't. Go on now. Scoot.'

Boscombe stood his ground. 'What *could* you do?' he asked.

'I could fix up that face of yours. Make that face as smooth as a baby's bum bum.'

'How?'

'There's ways.'

'What ways?'

'Old ways.'

'Mumbo Jumbo.'

'If yo' think it's that, then that's what it is. It don't work unless yo' believe. Why do yo' think I sit here fixin' bikes all the damn day?'

'Probably because your old ways ain't worth shite,' Boscombe suggested.

'Then reckon yo' know best, wicked man. Go on now, scoot. Believe in nothing. Be wicked ugly man all yo' God-damn life. See if I care.'

'How much?' Boscombe asked.

'How much I care? Not much. Not damn all.'

'How much to make my face as smooth as a baby's bum bum?'

'Hundred pounds.'

'How bloody much?'

'Hundred pounds. How much it worth to yo'? I charge you two hundred pounds and that's my final offer.'

'Done!' said Boscombe, who didn't intend to be.

An hour passed and during this time various prayers were offered up to less-than-Christian deities. Some salt was thrown. A frozen chicken was symbolically sacrificed.

A cheque for two hundred pounds changed hands and a bottle of yellow pills came into Boscombe's possession.

'Trust it must be,' said the Obeah Man. 'Now go, wicked man. Take one pill each day at dawn and look not into a mirror until the seventh day. Then all be done.'

'As smooth as a baby's bum bum?' Boscombe asked.

'As smooth as a baby's bum bum.'

Boscombe went off whistling, he had omitted to sign the cheque.

★　　★　　★

The days dragged into a week. Boscombe took one pill each dawn and on the seventh he rushed to his mirror.

And there a great wonder was to be revealed.

Boscombe blinked and blinked again. The hideous pustules had vanished without a trace. The skin, so long pitted and ghastly was now pure and unsullied, sensuous and soft.

The horrible pimples were gone.

So too were Boscombe's nose, ears and eyebrows.

And as he stared, his left eye smoothed over, closely followed by his right.

Boscombe was about to remark upon the somewhat Gothic turn that events had suddenly taken, when his mouth vanished, leaving his entire visage as smooth as a baby's bum bum.

And he suffocated.

LITTLE EPILOGUE BIT

Dr Kinn, who viewed the spot-encrusted face of the deceased said that he 'appeared to have died from natural causes', but declined further examination of the body on the grounds that he was 'far too ugly to look at closely'.

'Quack indeed,' said he, as he rode off on his BMX to his chess evening with Dr Poo Pah Doo.

6

The past is a foreign country: they do things differently there.

L. P. HARTLEY (1895–1972)

Death to false metal!

MANOWAR (1980–)

WHAT'S IN THE LEDGER
FOR ME, FRANK?

What's in the ledger for me, Frank?
Anything down in the book?
Any great winnings,
From humble beginnings?
Tell us, Frank, have a quick look.

See if the bonds are up smiling,
Or the pools have come through with the goods.
Run through my sweepstakes,
And old bingo backdates,
See if I've won any puds.★

★Christmas puds, in a raffle, possibly.

65

Check on my lottery numbers,
And crosswords I did as a boy.
Horse racing winners,
Records by Guinness,
Ring if you have any joy.

(I really am pleased I've got my own accountant.)

Hello, yes, Frank, it's me speaking.
Tell me what luck has transpired.
Not one brass nickel,
Or fish and chip pickle?
Frank, you dull bastard, YOU'RE FIRED!

HEADS AND HANDBAGS
(Or how Danny finally made a decision)

Discovering just what your friends *really* think of you is, of course, one thing you can do, if you happen to find yourself in someone else's body for an evening.

It's one of the things Danny did. He went along to The Shrunken Head and did it.

He wasn't too surprised by the responses. The general opinion seemed to be that Danny Orion was all right, not a bad bloke, a bit idle, always whinging that he couldn't have a dog of his own, mean with his fags.

As Mickey Merlin, Danny bought drinks all round, ran up an enormous bar tab and got commode-hugging drunk.

Well, he wouldn't have a hangover in the morning, would he? Because when he became Mickey, he'd no longer had the cold he'd caught at old Sam's funeral, had he? No and no. So.

'More drinks all round,' he called out once again, and (hopefully), 'Has anyone seen my girlfriend tonight?'

When Danny woke up in the morning, Danny was no longer
Mickey. He yawned, sniffed, concentrated his thoughts.
Concluded that he *didn't* have a hangover. Then he tried to
remember how the evening had finished.

It had finished, he so recalled, with Mickey Merlin's
girlfriend giving him a—

Danny chuckled. At least Mickey will be pleased to wake
up in his own bed, he thought. I trust he stuck to his
Magician's Code of Conduct and got me home in one piece.

Danny opened his eyes and blinked up at his ceiling.

No, it was *not* his ceiling.

It was the ceiling of Mickey Merlin's converted hut.

No. It was *not* that ceiling either.

It was the ceiling of a police station cell.

Oh no! Danny tried to rise, but could not. He craned his
neck and peered at himself. He was strapped down. There
was a kind of leather belt arrangement over his chest, two
more secured his wrists. *Oh no!* Danny's eyes did startings
from their sockets. What was he wearing?

He was wearing a skin-tight mini-dress of red PVC. Fishnet
stockings. On his right foot a black patent leather shoe, with
a winklepicker toe and a high stiletto heel.

On his left foot, a large white bandage.

And. *Oh shit!* His left foot was hurting like the very Devil.

'Mickey, you *bastard!*' Danny's scream rang about the little
cell. Ring, ring, ring, it went. And then Danny's tongue went
taste, taste, taste, about his upper lip area. That *was* lipstick
he was wearing, wasn't it?

It was.

Danny's brain turned a number of cartwheels. Mickey
Merlin had done this to him. Dressed his body up in drag
and then got him into trouble with the police. The dirty
trickster. What a way to treat a friend.

'Mickey . . . you . . .' Danny cleared his throat. 'Mickey
. . . you . . .' Danny coughed several times. 'Mickey . . . ?'

There was something very strange about Danny's voice.

It did not sound right at all. Rather high-pitched, it was. And with a regional accent. But not any region of the British Isles.

'*Mickey?*' Danny tried the name again. He tried to make his voice go deeper. But it wouldn't. Danny ran the tip of his tongue around the inside of his mouth. His teeth were rather straight, weren't they? They'd been all over the place yesterday.

'Mickey,' said Danny, once more. Just to hear the sound. Then.

Danny craned his neck once more.

Looked down along himself once more.

Down along the tight red PVC mini-dress.

The tight red PVC mini-dress with the high breast definition under the leather strap arrangement.

'*Tits!*' Danny screamed this word with considerable vigour, and that voice went ring, ring, ring, all around the cell once more. That voice that wasn't his.

That *woman's* voice.

'Aaaagh!' it went. 'I've got tits! I've got tits! I'm in the wrong body. Help!'

'Shut the Hell up in there.' Something, possibly (probably) a truncheon, went bang upon the cell door. The nasty little sliding hatch thing slid aside. A policeman's face leered in. 'Keep it down, Audrey, or I'll have the guys give you another strip search.'

Audrey! Danny rolled his head (or Audrey's head) from side to side, wrestled to free himself (herself) of the straps. Kicked his (her) legs. 'Let me out of here. Help! Help!'

'Wrap it,' said the policeman with what was definitely an American accent. Just like the one Danny/Audrey had. 'The priest will be here in a minute to give you the last rites. Not that it's gonna help you, Audrey. You know you shouldn't have put the last head in your purse. Careless that was.'

'*Head* in my *purse*?' The eyes that weren't Danny's crossed. 'What are you saying?'

'You've lost your appeal, honey. Guilty as charged on all sixteen counts. You got just half an hour left before you fry in Old Sparky, the electric chair.'

'*No!*' screamed the voice of Audrey. 'No! No! No!'

'Yes, yes, yes. God-damn serial-killing bitch. We're gonna fry you slowly, tease that current up and down, up and down. Melt ya a bit at a time. Make it last real long.'

'No!' Danny jerked the head of Audrey back and forwards, up and down. And he screamed and he screamed and he screamed.

And then he passed out.

He awoke, a quivering wreck, to find Mickey Merlin grinning down at him. 'And let that be a lesson to you,' said the magician. 'Getting my girlfriend to—'

His words were cut short as Danny leapt at his throat.

'Get off me! Ooh! Ah!' Mickey punched Danny in the ear, knocking him backwards across the converted hut. Danny snatched up a frying-pan and swung it at Mickey's head.

Mickey ducked and punched Danny in the stomach.

Danny doubled up, but he did manage to get one good welt in with the frying-pan, as he went down.

Right on Mickey's left foot.

Mickey took to hopping about. 'You sod you. You've broken my bloody toes.'

Danny croaked and gagged and spat out words such as tits, head and handbag.★

'Served you right.' Mickey slumped down onto his bed and worried at his foot. 'You can pay off that bar tab at The Shrunken Head also.'

★Which is the English for 'purse'. Or rather 'purse' is the American for handbag. They call a purse, a 'pocket-book'. Quite mad, the Americans. Quite mad.

'I damn well won't.'

'You damn well will, or it's back to the States with you, and *The Electric Chair*.'

'You *wouldn't*.'

'Call an ambulance,' moaned Mickey Merlin. 'And call it right now. Or you're in big trouble, Orion.'

Danny rose groaning to his feet. 'Do you have any change for the telephone?' he asked.

Of course the ambulance wouldn't come. They won't for a couple of broken toes. Danny had to call a mini cab.

Big Frank arrived in his mum's Morris Minor.

He didn't charge Mickey. Well, after all, Mickey *had* stood Big Frank drinks all the previous evening, hadn't he?

Danny waved Mickey off and then returned to the converted hut, where he had been ordered to finish mucking out the rabbits, do the washing-up and make the bed. And *not* to touch anything, especially the book of spells, which Mickey had kissed goodbye and told to be good. Danny touched that first and received for his disobedience an electrical charge that sent him reeling.

Danny sat down upon the bed, pulled out his packet of Woodbine and found it empty.

'I had three left yesterday,' Danny complained. 'That bugger Merlin must have smoked them.'

Danny rootled about amongst Mickey's private items, unearthed a packet of Rothman and smoked one of those instead.

He was still as well peeved as ever.

He *had* had a change. This was true.

Two changes, in fact.

But they hadn't got him anywhere.

And the second one had been positively terrifying.

'I wonder why that Audrey's left foot was all bandaged up,' Danny wondered. (Because, as yet, he did not know about the particular significance bandaged left feet were to play.)

And he didn't actually care much, either.

He puffed upon Mickey's cigarette and thought about things.

He was going to have to earn some money to pay off Mickey's bar tab. And in order to do that, he would have to take a job. But taking a job is the last thing a young man of resourcefulness and talent should ever have to do. A young man of resourcefulness and talent should live off his wits, play the field, wheel and deal and things of that nature. But was Danny a young man of resourcefulness and talent?

On the evidence so far?

Well . . .

'It looks like I'll have to take a job,' said Danny.

Obviously not.

'No,' said Danny. 'Stuff that. I know exactly what I'm going to do.'

And he did.

Gathering himself to his feet, Danny took his leave of Mickey Merlin's converted hut. He left a note. It said, HAVE GONE TO GET MONEY TO PAY OFF YOUR BAR TAB AND COMPENSATE YOU FOR YOUR LEFT FOOT. GET WELL SOON. DANNY.

The note was written in capital letters and it *was* full of good intentions.

In the light of what would later happen to Danny, it might be argued that it was not a 'good' note. A 'good' note would have been one which read, HAVE GONE TO *SEEK EMPLOYMENT* AND – etc, etc. The difference is subtle, but significant.

If Danny *had* gone to seek employment, then he would never have become embroiled (which is a 'good' word, *embroiled*) in the series of matters and incidents and intrigues and conspiracies and adventures and dangers and hair-raising how's-your-fathers that he did, in fact, become *embroiled* in.

And so there would have been no story to tell.

71

Not even one which did not have a beginning, a middle or an end.

But Danny did *not* go to seek employment.

So *embroiled* did he become.

Oh yes!

7

He that dies pays all debts.

WILLIAM SHAKESPEARE, *The Tempest*

TEACHING BEETLES TO SWIM

Taught the old cockroach to dance.
Folk said I hadn't a chance.
But hours with a stick,
For once did the trick,
And soon I will open a ranch.

Taught the old bed bugs to sing.
Folk said it's not the real thing.
But experts agree,
That it's them sing (not me),
And it's done without aid of a string.

Taught the old deathwatch to jive.
Folk said, that can't be alive.
It's all an illusion.
Please stop this confusion.
Wait still for the van to arrive.

At last I taught beetles to swim,
Through methods perplexing and grim.
I sat up all night,
Till they all got it right,
And some grew quite handsome and slim.
Beautiful things, beetles.

THE SPROUT FILES

Now, they do things differently in America.

Like calling a handbag a purse.

In America, if you were invited to attend a top-secret meeting, a chap who looked like Gary Busey would beat upon your door at about five o'clock in the morning.

He would be wearing a dark suit and mirrored sunglasses and when you opened your door, he would clap a gun to your head, frisk your pyjamas for hidden weapons, then bundle you into a black Lincoln Continental.

You would then be driven out to an airfield, endure further frisking at the hands of a chap who looked just like the first chap's twin brother and then be bundled into an unmarked light aircraft.

This aircraft would fly you to a desert, where yet a third Gary Busey lookalike would be waiting. There would be a bit more frisking, followed by another bundling and then a long ride in an old bus with blacked-out windows.

Eventually you would arrive, still in your pyjamas, somewhat hungry (although well frisked and bundled), at a high-security air base in the very middle of nowhere.

Here the frisking would be of an electronic nature and a guard, who looked for all the world to be none other than the ever-popular Gary Busey himself, would scan you all over with a sort of wire coathanger device.

If he pronounced you 'clear', you would be allowed to

proceed further. If not, all your fillings would probably have to come out. But if you *were* allowed to proceed further, then it would be along numerous metal-clad corridors, through countless security checks and steel doors which only opened to the application of Gary's special plastic card. Then down in a lift to what seemed the very bowels of the earth.

At last you would receive your final bit of bundling and find yourself in a narrow, windowless room, where men with hooded eyes would be sitting at a long black table.

Whatever happened then, of course, would be anyone's guess because it would be *top secret*. But it is reasonable to suppose that some frisking might well be involved.

In England, however, we do *not* do things differently.

In England we do them the same as we always have.

In England, if you were asked to attend a top-secret meeting, you would probably receive a letter in the post. You'd take the Underground (or a taxi, if you weren't short of a few bob), to one of those big official-looking buildings in the heart of London. Most likely the one with the brass plaque outside which reads MINISTRY FOR SECRET AFFAIRS (in capital letters, but very smart ones).

You'd walk up the steps, past a chap in a commisionaire's uniform, who was the dead-spit of Lionel Jeffreys. This chap would salute you and give the revolving doors a little push to help you on your way.

A rather attractive lady of middle years would peruse your letter of invitation, smile enticingly and direct you to the lift. Here the lift attendant (surely the commissionaire's *doppelgänger*) would whisk you up at a sedate three miles per hour to the third or fourth floor.

He would then escort you to the appropriate door and knock on your behalf, tipping his cap and politely refusing the small gratuity you offered him.

The top-secret meeting room would have a very familiar air to it. It would be broad and high and panelled in oak.

There would be a framed portrait of Her Majesty the Queen, a few busts of noble Victorians and a couple of overstuffed leather Chesterfields. A grand-looking desk with a blotter and brass trough lamp would stand before Gothic mullioned windows which looked out onto a view of Big Ben and The Houses of Parliament.

The chap who sat behind this desk would not look like Lionel Jeffreys. He would look like Gary Busey and he would demand to know why you were still wearing your pyjamas.

You would smile and attempt to explain that you weren't really there at all. That, in fact, all the foregoing had merely been a literary device to demonstrate a difference between the English and the American way of doing things.

Gary would laugh and turn into a lobster. You would be frisked, injected with strange, mind-altering drugs and wake up hours later in Portmerion, wearing a blazer and a badge with a penny-farthing on it, all set to star in a thirteen-part television series that no-one could understand.

So, absolutely no change there then!

America may have the edge on us when it comes to secret air bases in the middle of deserts, but if *weird shit* is your Trust House Forté, then it's England every time.

'Good-morning, Mr Vrane.' The gentleman behind the grand-looking desk rose to greet the young man who had entered the top-secret room. 'I trust your journey here was without incident.'

'I took the Underground.' The young man's voice was the merest whisper, he put out a hand and the gentleman behind the desk shook it. It was one of those special handshakes, but then they always are, aren't they?

The gentleman reseated himself and indicated a choice of Chesterfields. The young man sat down upon the nearest.

The gentleman behind the desk was a squat and girthsome body.

Those areas of his clothing which were neither black nor

white were both, being pin-striped. His face had the colour of Budgens' economy ham. A hue which is found nowhere else, except possibly in a certain region of Tasmania where white men fear to tread. The gentleman wore moustachios beneath his nose and a toupee on his head. A monocle served as an optical aid and a *Salmon-Odie* ball-and-socket truss offered him all the support he needed. Even on the hottest of days.

The young man was a different kettle of carp altogether. He was tall and sleek and high of cheek-bone. Sharp white suit, sharp white shirt, sharp white shoes. His nose was sharp and it was white. His eyes were black. All of them, including the white bits. *And* his teeth. They were utterly black. But he had arranged to have them done later in the day. So no-one was going to notice.

'Parton Vrane.' The gentleman leafed through a buff-coloured folder which contained many sheets of buff-coloured paper. 'Very impressive credentials. And completely remodi-fied, I see.'

'Fully armoured.' The young man tapped at his chest with a bony knuckle, raising sounds such as might be raised from the striking of a cracked bell (though not a particularly large one. Say one about ten inches across and made of brass). 'I can pass for human any day of the week, except possibly Tuesday.'

'And your genus?'

'*Blattodea*,' said Parton Vrane.

The gentleman consulted his buff-coloureds. 'That's *cock-roach*, isn't it?'

The young man made agitated rattling sounds with his fingers but his voice remained soft and without the vaguest hint of emotion. '*Blatta Orientalis*, oriental cockroach, or black beetle,' he said.

'Quite so. Well, you're a splendid specimen, Mr Vrane. You're booked in to have your teeth bleached at two, I understand.'

'And the eye modifications done.' Parton Vrane blinked. His eyelids rose from beneath, covering the all-black eyes. It was a rather alarming sight.

'Yes, I think that's most essential.' The gentleman coughed politely and moved papers about on his desk. 'Now, you are aware of exactly what your mission entails?'

The young man, if such he was (which now seems rather doubtful), nodded. 'Seek and destroy,' he said.

'Ah, no. It has been so up until now, but on this particular occasion we wish you to seek and *contain*.'

'I do not understand,' whispered Parton Vrane. 'My kind are bred by your kind, specifically to destroy *their* kind. Such is the way it has always been.'

'Yes, well, we've been having a bit of a rethink about all that. You have read the files I sent you?'

'The Sprout Files?'

'Samuel Oliver Sprout, yes. We don't know how he discovered the existence of the creatures we call the riders. *They* got to him before *we* could. We know his left foot was involved and we know *they* sent the dog.'

'The same dog?'

'It's always the same dog.'

'And you want me to contain *that*?' Parton Vrane's voice was soft and cool as ever.

'My chaps will issue you with the wherewithal.'

'If your chaps have the wherewithal, why not send them?'

'Because, my dear Vrane, my chaps can't see the damn creatures, can they? We cannot see into that range of the spectrum, unlike your good self. If we human beings could see the damn things, then we wouldn't be in all this trouble now.' The gentleman's face suddenly took on a worried expression and he flapped his hands above his head. 'I *am* still clear, aren't I?' he asked in an anguished tone. 'There isn't one of those things on *me*?'

Parton Vrane studied the air above the gentleman's head. 'You are still clear,' he said. 'If one of them was riding on you it would be controlling your thoughts, you would never have called me to this meeting.'

The gentleman regained his composure. 'My apologies,' said he. 'It's just, that, well, when you know they're there, waiting to pounce on you . . .'

'I'm sure it must be very distressing. I would offer you sympathy, but, as you know, I do not possess any.'

'Quite so.' The gentleman shuffled further papers, made a stiff upper lip and an even stiffer lower one to join it. 'Containment,' said he. 'The department is assigning you the roll of the dog-catcher. We want this particular beastie caught alive.'

'To what possible end? These creatures are parasites, vermin; they feed off human emotions. I have been bred and trained to seek out the worst of them, those which pose a positive threat, and, where possible, destroy them. That is what I do, and rather well too, even if I do say so myself.'

The gentleman raised an eyebrow and his monocle fell out. Had there been a flicker of human emotion present in Vrane's remark? A smidgenette of pride, perhaps? 'Look,' he said. 'My chaps have been working on a containment strategy. We want to put an end to this dismal business once and for all, wipe out *all* these beasties at a single stroke.'

'A sort of inter-dimensional ethnic cleansing?'

The gentleman, who had been refitting his monocle, raised his eyebrow once more and lost it once again. Was that sarcasm? 'Was that sarcasm?' he asked.

'I have no concept of sarcasm. But surely the riders have existed upon this planet for as long as mankind. They share the same space, although they are not composed of the same matter. You can only hope to keep the worst of them at bay.'

'Just bring me the dog,' said the gentleman, 'and leave the rest to us. We will provide you with the wherewithal.'

'Ah yes.' Parton Vrane composed his fingers on his lap. Their joints bent curiously back upon themselves. Aware that this was unacceptable he thrust his hands into his jacket pockets. 'Speak to me of this wherewithal,' he said.

The gentleman opened a desk drawer, brought out an item and pushed it across his blotter.

'And that is it?' asked Parton Vrane.

'That is it.'

'But it is—'

'A hammer, Mr Vrane. Find out whoever the dog has entered, bop him on the head and bring him here. What could possibly be simpler?'

'To smash him repeatedly upon the head until his skull has caved in and his brains are reduced to jelly, killing him and therefore the parasite that feeds upon him. That could be simpler. Far simpler.'

'Quite so.' The gentleman idly turned the hammer back and forth upon his blotter. Then without any warning he snatched it up and flung it at the head of Parton Vrane.

Vrane did not move a muscle. He possessed no muscles to move. But within his head neurofibril webs cross-matted, registered the speed of the approaching object, gauged its mass and damage potential. As if in slow motion he withdrew his left hand from its pocket, raised it and plucked the hammer out of the air. He returned both hand and hammer to pocket in the twinkling of an all-black eye with a retractable lower lid.

'Impressive.' The gentleman smiled. 'Where did it go?'

'Left jacket pocket.' Parton Vrane displayed the hammer.

'I never saw you catch it.'

'We see things at a different speed, as you know full well.'

'I do. So, Mr Vrane, time you were on your way. Teeth to bleach, eyes to dye and lids to rearrange.'

'Seek and contain?'

'That's the spirit.'

'I think,' said Parton Vrane, 'that you are making a very grave mistake.'

'I do not recall you being asked to *think*,' said the gentleman in a most ungentlemanly manner. 'I only recall you being *ordered to serve.*'

'I will do my duty.'

'See that you do.'

'I will.'

'Goodbye.'

'Goodbye.'

And that was the end of the secret meeting.

Outré? Bizarre? Outlandish? Totally incomprehensible and downright stupid? Call it what you will. But it goes to show, if it goes to show anything, that Brittania still rules the waves when it comes down to good old-fashioned weird shit.

And it's early days yet.

8

Dog days: The period between 3 July and 11 August, when Sirius the dog-star rises and sets with our sun. These are the hottest days, when dogs and men become a little mad.

Anybody who hates children and dogs can't be all bad.

W. C. FIELDS (1880–1946)

BRAND-NEW BLUE BOOK JACKET

It's the brand-new blue book jacket,
That makes a fellow sing.
That makes a fellow sing and shout,
And splash his savings all about.
Others speak of Jan and Dean,
But I of the blue book jacket.

It's the cut-down cardboard carton,
That's worn upon the head.
That's worn upon the heads of men,
Who strut about in packs of ten.
Others speak of Don and Phil,
But I of the cardboard carton.

It's the deaf and dumb-dumb waiter,
That gives me some relief.
That gives me some relief from those,
Who say it's down to looks and clothes.
Others speak of Pearl and Ted,
But I of the dumb-dumb waiter.

It's the fabled fowl of feathered folk,
That help to turn the tide.
That help to turn the worms and stuff.
'He's mad!' they cry. 'Enough! Enough!'
Others speak of Bud and Lou.
And I run out without paying.

SO WAS THE TITANIC★

As Danny entered The Shrunken Head a great roar of applause
went up.

Danny stared about the deserted bar. It was, well, deserted.
Danny looked to left and right. A ripple of chucklings reached
his ear. He took a step back, went out of the pub and then
came back in again.

This time gales of laughter filled the air.

Danny spun around in circles, fists raised. 'Who's doing
that? Who's there?'

Further laughter.

'Come on out, where are you hiding?'

More laughter still.

Then silence.

★Those who have ever entered the gents' toilet in a public house will
recognize this phrase, which is inevitably scratched onto the con-
traceptive dispensing machine just below the British Standard's Kite
Mark. (It always gets a big laugh.)

Sandy, the sandy-haired landlord stuck his head up from beneath the counter. His head wore a merry smile upon its face. 'What do you reckon, eh?' he asked. 'Is it good, or is it good?'

Danny said, 'What?' and, 'Eh, what?' also.

'Canned laughter.' The barman displayed a remote controller in his hand. He gave it a flip.

'Canned laughter?' Danny asked. And canned laughter echoed all around.

'Brilliant, eh?' The landlord gave the controller another flip and laid it on the bar counter. 'I got the idea while watching TV. There was this series about a bar in America and they must have had one of these things fitted, because every time anybody said anything, whether it was funny or not, and it was mostly *not*, I can tell you, great guffaws of laughter went up. And I thought, Sod it, if the Yanks have it in their bars, why shouldn't we have it in ours?'

'Yes,' said Danny, 'but—'

'Voice activated, you see. Must be how theirs works.'

'No,' said Danny. 'It's—'

'I'm going to put a sign up outside. You know the kind of thing, FORGET KARAOKE, FORGET QUIZ NIGHTS (that bloody fat medium woman wins all those anyway), THE SHRUNKEN HEAD'S LAUGHTER BAR WELCOMES YOU. In capital letters like that, except for the bit in brackets, which is what they call an "aside". Pretty smart, eh?'

'Yes,' said Danny. 'I mean, no—'

'Well, make up your mind. Is it *yes*?' The barman flipped the controller and laughter rolled about the place. 'Or *no*?' Hootings of mirth went every-which-way.

'Please yourself,' said Danny. 'I may not be drinking in here much longer, I am expecting to come into a great deal of money.'

The laughter was deafening.

'Switch the bloody thing off,' shouted Danny.

'It *is* off.'

'Oh.'

'By the way,' said Sandy, 'Mickey Merlin was in here last night and he said that if you came in today, you could drink as much as you liked at his expense, on his tab.'

'That was very thoughtful of him,' said Danny, stifling some laughter of his own. 'I'll have a large Scotch then. And a steak and chips belly-buster.'

'I'll bet there's a catch in it,' said Sandy. 'He's a vindictive bastard, that Merlin.'

'Ahem.' Danny took to patting his pockets. 'On second thoughts I think I'll stick with a half of light ale and a cheese roll. I'll pay for them myself.'

Sandy did the business. 'So tell me all about this great deal of money you're expecting to come into,' he said.

'It's top secret.' Danny gave his nose that tap you do when something *is* top secret.

'Oh yeah?' The landlord gave Danny that 'old-fashioned look' you do when someone is pulling your plonker.

'I'm not kidding. I'm on to something big and I'm not going to tell anybody what it is.'

'Some kind of investment deal, is it?'

'No, it's not.'

'An insider on a horse race, then?'

'Not that either.'

The landlord scratched at his sandy head.

'You've dandruff there,' said Danny, but the landlord ignored him.

'I know,' said Sandy. 'I'll bet you're thinking of breaking into old Sam Sprout's house and searching for his hoard of money.'

'That's right,' said Danny. 'I mean . . . *what*? How did you know *that*?'

'Call it an inspired guess. It's just that I passed his place this morning and they were boarding the windows and they'd put up this big sign which said, KEEP OUT. NO SEARCHING FOR HIDDEN HOARDS OF MONEY. THIS MEANS

YOU. And I knew it didn't mean *me*, so I naturally assumed it must mean *you*.'

'That's ludicrous, why should it mean *me*?'

The landlord scratched his head once more. 'No, you're right. So it's not that then?'

'No,' said Danny. 'It's definitely not that.'

'But I thought you just said—'

'I was joking.'

'I'll switch the machine on again then. No point in wasting a joke like that.'

'No point at all.'

Sandy switched the machine back on. 'Ha, ha, ha,' it went.

'Ha, ha, ha,' said Danny, tucking in to his cheese roll.

He went home, Danny did, after the meagre lunch that was also a late breakfast. Home to his Aunt May, who really wished he'd get a place of his own.

Danny sat upon the sofa and thought about things.

He thought about things all through the afternoon, and into the evening and awoke to the sound of white noise issuing from the television set and the realization that he had been thinking about things in his sleep.

'Damn,' said Danny. 'I've missed that American TV series about the bar with the laughter machine in it.' And indeed he had. 'Time to go to work then.'

Ah, work.

Danny switched off the television set, crept upstairs to look in on his Aunt May, who was sleeping peacefully, a gherkin beneath her chin and lettuce leaves strewn all round her bed.★

'Sleep on, Aunty,' whispered Danny.

'I'll try,' said the old one. 'Lock the back door on your way out.'

Danny crept downstairs, went out the back way and locked the door behind him. From Abaddon Street, where Aunt May

★An allopathic remedy for gout.

kept an orderly house, to Moby Dick Terrace, where Sam Sprout had once tried to, was a couple of back alleyways.

Danny had a torch about his person and some tools in a bag, of the type which counsels for the prosecution always refer to as 'house-breaking implements'. And, indeed, Danny was certainly going off on his way with 'intent'.

During his extended period of thinking, he had been reasoning the whole thing out. Old Sam *must* have stashed his loot away somewhere in his house. Unless he had a Swiss bank account, of course. But ordinary folk like Sam didn't have Swiss bank accounts. How did you get a Swiss bank account anyway? Phone up Switzerland? Perhaps there was a Swiss bank in London.

'Look,' said Danny to himself, as he crept along the alleyway. 'If he *did* have a Swiss bank account, then he must have had a chequebook. And if he had a chequebook, then he must have hidden *that* somewhere in his house. Of course, he might have hidden his chequebook in one of those safety deposit box things they have in banks. In which case he must have had a key to fit it. And he *must* have hidden the key in his house. Of course, he might have hidden the key in another— Aaaagh!'

Danny fell over a dustbin and landed in a smelly heap.

'It's in the house,' he told himself. 'Whatever it is, it's in the house. All I have to do is find whatever it is. How difficult can that be?'

Danny found his way to the alleyway which ran along the rear of Moby Dick Terrace (the even-numbered side), he counted along the back gates. Number two, number four. The back gate of number four was all grown over with weeds and showed no sign of forced entry. Which was promising. Danny took out a tool suitable for the job and forced an entry.

He put his shoulder to the gate and eased it open. Then he shone his torch about. The small backyard was filled by a jumble of broken furniture. It was severely broken, ripped apart, reduced to its component parts, then veritably shredded.

That someone had done a very thorough job of searching the furniture was eminently clear.

'Personally I wouldn't have done that,' whispered Danny. 'Personally I would have searched it carefully and then sold it.'

He scrambled as quietly as he could over the mound of splintered wood and shone his torch upon the back door. It was nailed shut, with very large nails. Danny shone his torch around the downstairs windows. These were securely barred.

'Hmmph!' went Danny, in a manner of which few, bar Miss Doris Chapel-Hatpeg, were actually capable. 'This doesn't bode too well.' He shone his torch up the wall. The windows on the first floor weren't barred. In fact, the one over the scullery was open a crack. It was an up-the-drainpipe job.

'Piece of cake.'

Now, let's be honest here. Have *you* ever tried to climb a drainpipe? It's possible to do when you're a child. But as an adult, forget it. The fastenings come out of the wall and you plunge to your death through a greenhouse roof.

Danny once had a friend called McGebber. McGebber was nineteen when he chose to climb a drainpipe. He had come home after a lock-in at The Shrunken Head and, not having his keys and not wanting to wake up his mum and being drunk and everything, he decided that shinning up the drainpipe was a 'piece of cake'. He got almost to the bedroom window before the fastenings came out of the wall.

McGebber would certainly have been killed, as he and the drainpipe swept down towards the greenhouse, but, as chance would have it, he fell instead through a crack in the time-space continuum and found himself at Normandy in the year 1188. As this was the year in which Henry II was gathering together an army to begin the third crusade, McGebber, who had always wanted to see a bit of the world, joined up. Sadly he was shot in the neck by one of Saladin's archers during the siege of Damascus. Which goes to show that drainpipe climbing inevitably leads to a fatal consequence.

Another chap, called Bryant, came to an even more bizarre, but no less destructive end when he climbed a drainpipe at the rear of the Walpole Cinema. It appears that unknown to him, the vanguard of an inter-stellar strike force was—

'*Piece of cake!*' Danny lifted the sash and slipped in through the bedroom window. He had taken the opportunity to avail himself of a ladder from a neighbouring garden. Which showed not only a certain degree of enterprise on his part, but that even though the plot was prepared at any moment to slip off on another tangent, he, at least, was keeping his mind on the job in hand.

Dull bugger that he was.

Danny now shone his torch all around the bedroom. It was empty and it was gutted. The floorboards had been ripped up and the plaster broken from the walls. Some very 'brutal' searching had been carried out in here.

'I find this somewhat disheartening,' said Danny, as he stepped nimbly from one floor joist to the next, in order not to fall through the ceiling of the room below.

Beyond the bedroom lay further scenes of devastation. The landing floorboards had been upped and bore-holes drilled into the walls. Stair treads had been knocked out. Danny slid carefully down the banister. Whoever had done all this, and Danny reasoned that it was probably old Sprout's solicitor, had done it 'with a will'.★

Danny's torchlight explored the ground-floor carnage. The fireplace in the front room had been prised from the wall. The kitchen sink was a thousand icy fragments. In the back parlour on the red-tiled floor lay a framed photograph of the Queen Mother. The glass was broken. Danny picked it up and shone his torch onto the face of Britain's favourite grandmother.

★Possibly some kind of pun?

'Well,' said Danny, in a very gloomy voice. 'Whoever gave this place a going over certainly did a number on it. If there was anything to find, I reckon they must have found it.'

'I wouldn't be too sure of that.' This voice was a harsh grating whisper. A real nappy-filler it was.

Danny jerked about and shone his torch into the face of a young man who stood passively by, his hands in his white trouser pockets.

'Who . . . ?' Danny's torchlight went flick-flick up and down the young man, highlighting the neat tailor's-work, the sharp white cheek-bones and the sharp white nose. The flashing white of the teeth. 'Who are *you*?' Danny managed.

'Never mind who. Would you mind turning away your torch? My eyes are most sensitive to direct light.'

Danny swung the beam down. And then he swung it back up. There was something not altogether right about this young man in white, something uncomfortable. Danny moved the beam to a point some inches above the young man's head. He was not altogether certain why. Something inside seemed to be saying, 'Do it.' There was nothing there.

Nothing.

Nothing.

Danny shook his head. Blinked his eyes. Of course there was nothing there. But why did that make him feel bad inside? Threatened?

A voice in his head was saying, '*Clear. He's a clear. Kill the clear.*' Danny pinched at his eyes.

'Turn down your torch,' whispered the young man. 'Go on your way. There is nothing for you here.'

Danny curled his lip. He didn't like that whispery voice. Not one bit. It was sarcastic. Cynical. Sneering. It was taking the piss out of him.

'Please go,' whispered the young man. 'You are in great danger here. The beast has not left the house. You will become contaminated.'

'What beast? What are you saying?' Danny's knuckles grew

white in the darkness as his fingers tightened on his torch. He would smash this evil young man. Yes, *evil.* That's what he was. *Evil. Smash the clear. Kill the clear.*

'Turn away your torch.' The young man put up his hands. On the attack? It looked like he was on the attack. 'I know what you are thinking. How you are feeling. Irrational hatred. But those are not *your* thoughts. Try to remain calm. Just turn around and leave by the way you came. Do it quickly. Trust me.'

'Trust *you?*' Danny raised the torch. The beam swept up to the ceiling as he plunged towards the hateful young man. '*Kill the clear.*'

A hand grasped his wrist. Another caught him by the ankle. He was lifted from his feet, flung backwards. His torch went spinning from his grip, smashed down somewhere.

Went out.

'Go quickly,' whispered the voice. Somehow *less* evil, now that its owner could not be seen.

Danny was floundering about on the cold tile floor. He didn't seem to be able to figure out which way up was.

'Go,' went the whisper. 'Be just another person. That's the safest thing to be. There is still time. Hurry. Just go.'

'Who are *you?*' Danny managed.

'My name is Vrane. I am here to contain the beast. I would prefer to do that before it enters you.'

'Strangely, I have no idea what you're talking about.'

'The beast,' said Parton Vrane. 'The dog.'

'Dog?' Danny said. 'Is there a dog here? Old Sprout's dog?' Danny's fingers were feeling all around in the darkness. A lump of wood. A half-brick. Something. Though the voice seemed less evil, he had seen the face. Seen the *space.* This one had to be killed. This *clear.*

Clear? Danny shook his night-bound head. What's a *clear?* And as he thought it he forgot it.

Instantly.

'Oooh,' groaned Danny. 'What happened? Ouch. I must

91

have fallen down the damn stairs. Where's my torch? Hold on.' Danny's eyes went blink, blink, blink. It didn't seem to be all that dark any more. He could make out shapes. It was a bit like looking through a red filter. No, it wasn't like *looking* at all. It was more as if he was *feeling* with his eyes. Sensing things rather than seeing them. Radar, was it? No, of course not. You didn't have radar in your head. But this was something new. Perhaps he had concussion. What was he doing here anyway? And where was *here*?

Danny tried to rise. He put his hands to the cold tiles and tried to push himself upright. But his hands slipped away. His hands were covered in something sticky. Danny gaped at his hands, sensing their image, sensing the cloying substance. It was blood! His hands were drenched with blood!

'I'm bleeding!' Danny staggered to his feet. He stumbled into the corridor, clawed his way up the banister. Danced across the floor joists of the back bedroom. Through the window. Down the ladder. Away and away. Running. Running.

But Danny wasn't bleeding. The blood that caked his fingers wasn't his. Time had passed for Danny. Time that he would not recall. Something evil had occurred.

For there was blood.

Much blood.

The walls of the back parlour were streaked with it. From the middle of the floor, where a dark puddle lay deep, the trail of something that had been dragged was quite apparent. It had clearly been dragged into the kitchen.

Although the door was now closed.

One day soon that door would be opened to men in blue uniforms and others in white protective suits. And these men would gaze into that kitchen, horror-struck by what they saw. A room quite red, its each wall coloured. The work of a painter from Hell.

With blood. All over. Thickly. Two coats' deep.

The ceiling though was still white.

But for the word.

Writ big the word was. Six-inch letters.

DEMOLITION was the word.

In capital letters.

And written by a left hand. They would know that it was written by a left hand because there upon the shattered sink was the very left hand that had been used to write it.

It was the left hand of Mr Parton Vrane.

They would never find the rest of his body.

9

On 16 April 1943 Dr Albert Hofmann fell off his bicycle and changed the world for an awful lot of people.

> Facts you really *should* know No. 1.

Practise random kindness and senseless acts of beauty.

> DISCORDIAN DOCTRINATE NO. 23.

NAYLOR'S HANDBAG

All the wonders of the world
(which number seven),
Or the glories of the Lord
(who lives in heaven),
Can scarce at all compare,
Nor can even Samson's hair,
To that Tommy Naylor's inter-stellar handbag.

All the colours of the rainbow
(or the *spangles*),
Or the theories of Pythag'
(who knew the angles),
Just don't come up to scratch,
Jackie Trent and Tony Hatch
Are as nought before that Tommy Naylor's handbag.

All the thirty shades of green
(the Micks speak well of),
Or the gasworks by the Thames
(I love the smell of),
Just haven't got a chance,
Nor has fair Salome's dance,
To hold a candle to that Tommy Naylor's handbag.

(Chorus)
Naylor's handbag – the peasants stand and cheer.
Naylor's handbag – all your troubles disappear.
Naylor's handbag – I think that Naylor's somewhat queer.

And as far as I'm concerned, he can stick his handbag!
I ask you!

ATAXIOPHOBIA

It is the way of man to seek order from chaos.

To impose order upon chaos.

To search for pattern and meaning and if none can be found, then to invent it.

Like time, for instance.

Man conceived time and sliced it into hours and minutes and seconds. And then man said, 'Here is time, I have it upon my wrist, it is now under my control.'

Which, of course, it is not.

At one of his famous lectures delivered in the nineteen sixties, that greatest genius of our age, Sir Hugo Rune, was interrupted, while in full and magnificent flow, by his arch detractor, Rudolph Koeslar.

Rune had been expounding upon his theory of APATHY★,

★A-PATH-TO THE REASON WHY – see *The Book of Ultimate Truths*.

when Koeslar had the temerity to declare that Rune was 'a lazy scoundrel, who had never done an honest day's work in his life'.

'*Work?*' asked Rune. 'And what is *work?*'

'Work,' answered Koeslar, 'is what honest folk do for eight hours a day, five days a week.'

'Impossible,' said Hugo Rune. And then went on to prove it.

WHY IT IS IMPOSSIBLE TO WORK EIGHT HOURS A DAY, FIVE DAYS A WEEK

(From the calculations of Hugo Rune.)

There are 365 days in a year. In a leap year 366. Let us be generous and begin with 366.

Days in the year:	366 days
Eight hours of sleep each day equals a total of:	122 days
Leaving—	244 days
Eight hours of rest each day equals a total of:	122 days
Leaving—	122 days
You *don't* work Saturdays and Sundays, so subtract:	104 days
Leaving—	18 days
You *do* have an hour for lunch each working day:	10 days
Leaving—	8 days

Out of these eight working days, you must surely have at least one week's holiday a year.

Which leaves you with a single day to work on.
   And that's Christmas Day.
   And nobody works on Christmas Day.

Suitably chastened, Koeslar slunk from the hall as the mangy dog he was. The audience set to counting upon its fingers, but none could disprove Rune's calculations, because they were so demonstrably correct.

There will always be those who will quibble over details and seek to claw back a day here and there.

But to those we must say then, What about days off sick? Or time off being late, or leaving early?

No. It is proved.

No more can be said.

Order from chaos? Forget it.

And there are those who would seek order from the chaos of a story which lacked a beginning, a middle and an end. Those would see a definite pattern emerging. A pattern composed of short stories (seemingly unrelated) juxtaposed with a rambling plot about a chap called Danny, around whom events appeared to revolve.

And those astute enough to reason this out would conclude that before returning to Danny, another 'seemingly unrelated' short story was probably on the cards.

And they would be correct.

THE DOG-FACED BOY

Having been told to 'expect a letter in the post', Alan left his fourteenth interview in two weeks in something of a huff. He now had little faith in the promises of youth employment officers and began to realize that he should make the best of a bad job (which was no job at all) and start to get used to a lot of spare time.

He didn't bother to go back to the agency, instead he caught a 65 at the Broadway and rode back on it to Brentford and The Plume Café.

A pleasant cuppa, he thought, and somewhere to sit that is out of the rain.

The waitress, with the come-to-bed eyes and the do-it-and-die husband, brought a cup to Alan's table.

'Do you have any money today?' she asked.

Alan fumbled in his trouser pockets. 'I have some string, a penknife, a couple of cigarette cards and my front door key. And a threepenny bit and that's it.'

The waitress had just read her horoscope – 'a kind gesture will be returned'. 'Keep your threepence,' she said, 'it's on the house.'

'Why thank you,' said Alan, who managed a smile.

The waitress smiled back and returned to the counter.

Alan sat a-sipping of the thin grey liquid and a-peering through the fly-specked window at the rain-danced street beyond. A figure was hurrying towards the café, *Sporting Life* held over his head, tweed collar turned against the inclemency of the weather.

This figure was Naylor and Alan knew Naylor well enough.

Thomas Henry Naylor, owner of a handbag which he claimed had been given him by a Venusian. Also owner of two pairs of winklepickers and a snooker cue, a snooker cue which he had won from Lenny Hall for staying an entire night alone in St Mary's churchyard. A snooker cue which he had snatched from the grasp of Lenny Hall when Lenny Hall had refused to hand it over. A snooker cue with which he had laid Lenny Hall low. Thomas Henry Naylor. Dodgy, dishonest, violent.

Alan hoped he would hurry by.

He did not.

Thomas Henry Naylor pushed open the shattered glass door of the Plume Café and sighted its only customer.

'Al baby,' said he.

I hate that, thought Alan. 'Hello, Tommy,' he said.

'Al baby, are you in luck.'

Alan considered this to be a statement, rather than a question, so he said nothing.

'Oh yes you are,' said Naylor. 'You're in lots of luck.'

'I am?' asked Alan, who could not imagine just how he might be.

'You are,' said Naylor. 'And I will tell you why.'

Tommy Naylor sat down at Alan's table. He hailed the waitress with the come-to-bed eyes and ordered two cups of coffee. When these arrived he pushed one across the table to Alan. 'Drink up,' he said. 'We have to get moving.'

'We do?' Alan said, as he pushed his now-cold tea aside.

'We do, my boy, we do.'

Alan hated the 'my boy' almost as much as he hated the 'Al baby'. In fact, Alan cared little or nothing for Tommy Naylor and really, really wished that he would go away and leave him in peace.

Tommy Naylor grinned at Alan, indifferent to thoughts he could neither hear nor read upon his face. 'I have shares in a sideshow,' he said. And then he paused, hoping for a reaction. He didn't get one though.

'A sideshow,' he said once more. 'I am going to become the proprietor of a fairground attraction.'

Alan was mildly intrigued and managed to sniff out a brief, 'What kind?'

'A FREAK SHOW,' said Naylor, in a voice so loud as to make the come-to-bed eyes of the waitress grow wide.

A freak show?

It is strange how a short phrase, or even a fragment of a

99

phrase, is capable of conjuring up memories, sometimes memories of something you had hoped forever to forget.

No sooner had the words 'A FREAK SHOW' left Naylor's mouth, than terrible memories returned to Alan. Memories of a small, hairy face with eyes so sad, which peeped at him from a tiny roped-off enclosure.

As a child, Alan's father had taken him to see THE DOG-FACED BOY. The old chap had paid the sixpences for admission, and the proprietor, a tall gaunt man with a black handlebar moustache, had led the two of them through the gaily painted canvas hoarding, along a dingy corridor and into a tiny back room which had been painted a garish yellow.

A crowd of people was pushing and shoving and the air was rank with the stench of cheap cigar smoke and perspiring flesh.

Alan's father had edged the boy to the front and as the gaunt proprietor yanked back a length of ragged cloth which served as a curtain, Alan found himself almost face to face with the main attraction.

Seated upon an ancient highchair in the corner of that yellow room was a little boy. He wore a strangely old-fashioned knickerbocker suit of blue velvet, with white lace collar and cuffs. He could have been no older than Alan was himself. But he had the face of a dog.

Beneath matted eyebrows two clear brown eyes, two oh-so-sad brown eyes, peeped out at Alan, and a small silly mouth chewed upon nothing, again and again and again.

Alan drew back in horror, but the crowd was thick behind him, and the crowd was laughing. Mocking barks and howls. Alan pressed his face against his father's hand and wept frightened tears.

'How would you like a job?' asked Naylor.

'Job?' The images retreated, a dull ache remained. 'What job?'

'Huckster,' said Naylor. 'You know, roll up, roll up. That kind of thing.'

'No, I wouldn't.' Alan rose to take his leave.

Naylor rose with him. 'Of course you would. You're unemployed, aren't you? A bit of easy money wouldn't go amiss, would it?'

'I'll have to think about it.' Alan edged towards the door.

'No, you won't. Come on, I'll show it to you. It's a bit ancient and knackered and needs a lick of paint.'

Alan had a sick premonition. 'I don't want to see it,' he said.

'Of course you do.' Naylor took him by the arm.

The rain hadn't let up. If anything it fell more heavily. It rattled upon the corrugated iron roof of the old warehouse. Naylor fumbled a key into an enormous padlock. 'It must have been here for years. Stored away. A friend put me on to it. He used to be in the business. You just wait until you see it.'

Alan didn't want to.

The padlock swung away and Naylor pressed open the door.

The hinges groaned dramatically and the damp light fell across an expanse of concrete, exposing green canvas dust-sheets which sheltered something large. Alan felt cold and ill.

'I'll wait here,' he said.

'Of course you won't.' Naylor steered him inside, closed the door, switched on a light. Neon flickered, flared and glared.

'Now,' said Naylor. 'Just wait until you see this.' He stalked towards the mysterious something that lurked beneath the canvas dustsheets. 'Just you wait.'

Alan watched as Naylor took up a canvas corner. He shrank back against the door, dreading what he knew he must surely see. He shut his eyes, that he should not. But there was no safety there. There was only the image. That hairy face, those tragic eyes. The mouth that chewed and chewed.

'Behold!' cried Naylor, flinging back the dustsheet.

Alan peeped.

JOHNNY GULL, read the Victorian script (in capital letters), THE FATTEST MAN IN THE WORLD.

Below was a lurid representation of a huge swollen giant munching upon a cream cake and smiling the way a dead animal does.

Alan began to laugh. Tears ran down his face. He staggered to and fro, pointing at the image, rocking with laughter. He clutched at his stomach.

He laughed and he laughed and he laughed.

And then he blacked out.

When Alan awoke, he found himself in bed.

He tried to lift his head, but he could not.

To move his hands. No, they were strapped at his sides.

He blinked. The light was too bright. It shone into his eyes. He tried to speak. But he could not.

A face loomed at him. It was the face of Naylor.

'He's coming round,' said this face.

'Give him some air then.'

Naylor's face drew back. The light rose.

'How are you feeling?' asked Naylor. 'You've been out of it for quite a long time.' He leaned forward and twisted something at Alan's head.

Alan moved his head stiffly and glanced all around.

He was in a tiny room. Paint flaked from its walls. Yellow paint.

There was a dull, medical smell in this room. And other smells also. Naylor stood with a smile on his face, he puffed upon a cheap cigar. Another man stood by him. A tall, gaunt man with a grey handlebar moustache. He wore a surgeon's gown and rubber gloves.

'About that huckster's job,' said Naylor. 'There's been a slight change of plan. My pal Mr Henderson here,' Naylor gestured to the gaunt fellow who was now peeling off his gloves, 'says that fat men won't really pull a crowd any more. But that, as we had the booth and everything, all we needed to do was make a few alterations.'

Naylor displayed a small hand mirror and what appeared to be an old-fashioned blue velvet suit with a white lace collar and cuffs. 'Of course, we needed a really good freak.'

He held the mirror towards Alan's face.

Alan did not want to look.

10

Antipericatametaparhengedamphicribationes.

TITLE OF A BOOK BY RABELAIS.

I have nothing. I owe much. The rest I leave to the poor.

THE LAST WILL OF RABELAIS.

SHOUTING AT DOGS

I love it, I do,
I shout till I'm blue,*
I yell at the spaniel and peke.
I howl at the dachs
And the ill-tempered collie,
And baffle the bulldog with Greek.

I swear at Alsatians,
And dreadful Dalmatians.
I say 'up your pipe' to the Dane.
And 'get on your bike,'
To the old English sheppy.
Which drives the poor blighter insane.

*In the face.

I holler 'you noodle'
At each passing poodle.
And terriers get their come-uppance.
(But as for the *Corgi*,
I treat them like royalty,
Or else I would live on a pittance.)

Yes, I love it you see.
It's pure bliss to me.
Abusing the canine élite.
Of all life's wee pleasures,
There's none to compare,
With shouting at dogs in the street.
Woof woof – SHUT UP!

A DOG IN SHEEP'S CLOTHING

Certainly some of the blame for what happened to Danny must lie with his mother. But not all.

Ever since the days of Edward Gein, 'The Butcher of Plainfield',★ criminal psychologists have been flogging us the notion that the deviant behaviour of the son is all down to the influence of a dominating mother.

But are we really buying that?

During the summer of '57, when old Eddie was prancing about on his moonlit lawn, dressed to the nines in a suit of tanned human skin, there must have been a million dominating mothers in America.

There was just, however, the one Edward Gein.

At his trial in 1886 for the violation of graves, Henri Blot was asked by the magistrate whether he could explain just what had driven him to commit his abominable crimes. Blot

★The original inspiration for Norman Bates in Robert Bloch's *Psycho* (as if you didn't know).

shrugged and then replied with an off-hand remark which sent shivers racing around the courtroom.

'Everyone to his taste,' said Henri Blot. 'Mine is for corpses.'

And there perhaps you have a piece of it. A matter of personal taste?

Agreed the personal tastes of Blot and Gein★ were somewhat extreme, but tastes they were none the less. Where the unholy two slipped up was in not finding careers for themselves where they could have indulged their personal tastes without upsetting people.

As do so many many others.

It has long been recognized that necrophiles are somewhat over- represented in the undertaking trade. That foot fetishists work in shoe shops. Masochists become traffic wardens, and rampant heterosexuals, Tory politicians. And while we admire the man (or woman) who chooses medicine for a profession, do we ever think to question the motives of the dentist or the haemorrhoid specialist?

Why should a man (or woman) wish to spend his (or her) working life with his (or her) hands inside the mouths of almost total strangers, or worse still up their . . . ?

Which brings us to country vets. We've all seen those James Herriot programmes. We all know what those lads get off on!

'Everyone to his taste.'

It makes you think.

But, of course, it would be ludicrous to suggest that this applies to every profession. Naturally there are many where public service and a selfless dedication to duty are uppermost in the hearts and minds of the workers. Where the unsavoury taint of ulterior motive could never be applied.

★Not to be confused with the other *Blot and Gein*, popular music hall stars, Barrington 'Inky' Blot and Charlie 'Madam it's a whippet' Gein, best remembered now for their evergreen Cockney singalong *Underneath the Armpits*.

Like the police force, for instance.

To even hint that the police force is a natural haven for bullies who like dressing up in uniform and hitting people with sticks would be to overstep all bounds of reason.

Something you'd never catch *me* doing!

And anyway, I personally know several librarians who spend much of their leisure time dressing up in uniforms and hitting each other with sticks. And what's wrong with that, eh?

Nothing!

But where does this leave us?

Good question. Firstly it leaves us *not* blaming our dear little white-haired old mothers every time we're caught in an open grave adding to our nipple collections. And secondly, it teaches us to think very carefully before committing ourselves to a career in computer programming, if our abiding passion is for the decerebration of chickens, or teaching beagles to smoke.

But then . . .

But then there just might be another factor involved, an outside factor. One which no criminal psychologist or self-styled expert has touched upon. An outside factor which involves neither nature nor nurture. An invasive force, capable of entering an individual and driving him to the very extremes of human behaviour. Possibly one which the church has already come up against.

'*In my name shall they cast out devils.*'

     Mark 16:17   Oh yes.

And so with all that said (and most eloquently too), let us turn our attention once more to Danny. Three months have passed since his nocturnal visit to the house of the late Sam Sprout. Three months, during which he has been going through changes.

★ ★ ★

You would hardly have recognized him. His friends sometimes didn't. His *ex*-friends, for as often as not he would pass them right by in the street without even acknowledging their existence. It was almost as if they just weren't there.

He didn't socialize. But he was very polite. In the off-licence, where he now worked, he was renowned for his politeness. Especially to the older ladies. The ones who would phone up for that extra bottle of gin to be delivered. He would pop round during his lunch hour or half-day closing and drop it off.

Mr Doveston, the off-licence manager, had nothing but praise for him. Danny was charming and eager to please. He was punctual, he was proper, he was neat and he was nice. Mr Doveston could find no fault in this young man.

'I hesitate to say this,' he told his chums at a Rotary Club get-together, 'but I truly believe the lad to be a living saint.'

'Does he still live with his Aunt May?' asked a chum in an inflated rubber suit with neck harness and crotch spurs★.

'No,' said Mr Doveston. 'He moved out. He now has his own place. It's only a rented room, but I understand he's done it up very nicely, although I've never seen it myself. It's in Moby Dick Terrace.'

'Ah *there*.' The chum adjusted the torque on his latex insertion piece. 'That's where the, *you-know* occurred.'

'What *you-know*?'

'You know what *you-know*. The murder. The bloodbath, walls daubed, human body parts.'

Mr Doveston said, 'Hmph!' And well did he say it. 'That was nothing more than an elaborate hoax. Inspector Westlake, who I might add is a very close friend of mine, told me that the blood was not human and neither was the hand. That's why there has been no murder enquiry.'

'It's probably a cover up,' said Mr Doveston's waterproof chum. 'A conspiracy.'

★This was a Rotary Club 'Specialist Evening' (allegedly).

Mr Doveston shook his hood and adjusted his nipple clamps. 'Ask the inspector yourself, if you don't believe me. He's over in the corner chatting with Long Jean Silver.'

'Not Long Jean Silver, the amputee porno queen?'

'She's this month's guest speaker.'

'But that woman's a living leg-end.'

'She certainly is.'

And she certainly *is*.

As it was Mr Doveston's evening off, Danny stood all alone behind the off-licence counter. And for the first time ever it was actually possible to get a close look at him.

He was tall, but scholar-stooped. And the hair upon his head, which had been greying at the temples, was quite white. For a man of twenty-three this was unusual, but it suited him and added some distinction, something special. It gave him a certain dignity. His face was lean and spare, the eyes, grey, had a sparkle to them. Almost as if always bathed in a film of water. The nose was long and finely drawn. The wide mouth crayoned in with red. Precise cheek-bones cleanly shaven. A pervading air of soap-scrubbed. The hands were delicate, the fingernails polished. Grey suit. White shirt. Company tie. Shoes shined black, Biro in the top pocket.

A personable young man. And one who, if your daughter were to bring him home, would not have you reaching for your knobkerrie. Very nice.

The off-licence door swung open to the push of a customer who stepped onto the farting doormat*.

'Good evening, sir,' said Danny. 'And how may I help you?'

The customer, an aimless youth in a holey sweater and greasy black jeans, said, 'I'm just looking around.'

*This distant relative of the whoopie cushion is greatly favoured by off-licence managers, who prefer it to a doorbell. Why? Who can say?

'*Keep an eye on that bogtrotter,*' said the voice in Danny's head.

'I will,' said Danny.

'What was that?' asked the youth.

'I said, *I will* . . . be glad to help you, if you need any help.'

'Yeah, right.'

Another push. Another fart.

'Good-evening, Danny,' said Mrs Roeg, widowed in her forty-fifth year and now in her forty-seventh. A fine-looker with a taste for *Jim Beam* and menthol cigarettes.

'Good-evening, Mrs Roeg,' said Danny. 'And how may I help you?'

Mrs Roeg ran a long pointy tongue back and forth beneath her painted upper lip. 'Now what will I have?' she asked.

The question was, of course, rhetorical. Mrs Roeg knew exactly what she was going to have. And Danny knew exactly what she was going to have. And Mrs Roeg knew that Danny knew exactly what she was going to have. And Danny knew that she knew. And so forth.

But in an off-licence you pretend that you don't.

'Was it wine?' Danny asked.

'No.' Mrs Roeg's pale blue eyes danced along the 'heavy duty' shelf. Well, her vision did anyway. Her eyes stayed inside her head (for now).

'Well, la-de-da,' said Mrs Roeg.

'*That old tart hates your guts, Danny boy.*'

'She does not,' whispered Danny behind his hand.

'*Put the machine on her, you'll find out.*'

'It will be a pleasure to prove you wrong.'

'Did you say something?' Mrs Roeg asked.

'No, sorry, only clearing my throat.' Danny cleared the throat that didn't need clearing.

'I think I'll take a bottle of *Jim Beam* and twenty *Consulate*.'

'*Don't forget the machine.*'

Danny took down the bottle and the pack of cigarettes. He placed them on the counter just beyond the woman's reach and picked up the bar-code-reading light-pen thingy that was attached by a cable to the cash register.

'This brand?' Danny asked, turning the pack of cigarettes onto its side. Mrs Roeg reached out her hand and, as she did so, Danny ran the light-pen over her wrist. She didn't notice. Folk never did.

'They're fine,' said Mrs Roeg.

Danny applied the light-pen to the bar codes on the bottle and the cigarettes. On Mrs Roeg's side of the cash register the liquid crystal display showed the prices. On Danny's side it read out something quite different. The words SMARMY YOUNG UPSTART glowed in capital letters. Danny looked up from them and smiled. 'Will there be anything else?' he asked, as he accepted the credit card.

'No, that's all.'

The business was done, a signature signed, a bottle wrapped, a carrier bag shaken, a wrapped bottle placed therein and a packet of cigarettes. Mrs Roeg smiled once more and went on her way.

Danny watched her depart. Danny wasn't smiling.

'*The bogtrotter's slipped a can of Carlsberg up his jumper,*' said the voice in Danny's head.

'I saw him, we share the same eyes, you know.'

'*But not the same instincts. A summary caution, do you think?*'

'I do.'

Danny came around the counter and approached the young man. 'Might I be of assistance?' he asked.

'No. I don't think I want anything, actually.'

'I see.'

It was fast. It was *very* fast. Danny shot out his left hand, caught the young man by his left wrist, twisted it viciously up his back. The first two fingers of Danny's right hand were suddenly up the young man's nostrils.

A can of *Carlsberg Special Brew* bounced onto the linoleum and rolled slowly across to the counter.

Danny's mouth was close to the right ear of the now

squirming youth. 'Come into my shop again,' whispered Danny, 'and I'll break both your legs. Do you understand?'

'Yes, yes,' went the lad in a high-pitched nasally tone.

'Bite his ear off as a lesson.'

'I will not!'

'You won't what?' The young man struggled.

Danny flung him towards the door. 'Get out. Go on, and don't come back.'

'I won't.' And with a step so light and quick that the doormat hardly raised a growl, the young man left the off-licence never to return.

'Bite off his ear?' said Danny. 'What kind of talk is that?'

'Just my little joke. Ha ha.'

'I shouldn't have brought you out with me tonight. You stay in the shed tomorrow.'

'Oh no, please, sir, don't lock me in the shed.'

Danny laughed. 'Then behave yourself. Bite his ear off indeed. Whatever goes on in your head?'

'I don't have a head, Danny, that's why I'm inside yours.'

Danny grinned. 'And for the most part I enjoy the experience.' He turned towards the cash register. 'And showing me how to rewire that thing so it reads out what people think. That *was* clever. How do you know such stuff?'

'Danny boy, I know all kinds of stuff.'

'Yep. I reckon that you do.' Danny did a little skipping kind of a dance back to the counter. 'And do you know what?'

'Probably, but go on just the same.'

'I'm chuffed,' said Danny. 'Dead chuffed.'

'And why, as if I don't know?'

'Because I have you, my own holy guardian angel, to protect and advise me. Am I one lucky guy, or am I not?'

'You certainly are, Danny. You certainly are.'

But he certainly wasn't.

Most certainly he was *not*.

11

If all the Chinese in the world were to march four-abreast past a given point, they would never finish passing it, though they marched forever and ever.

BASED ON US MARCHING REGULATIONS, 1936

PLUME GÂTEAU

Dear Sir,
    With reference to that Plume Gâteau,
    I bought from you a week ago,
    The bugger's furry and the icing's grey.
    I do not wish to be a boor.
    It's not the money (I'm not poor),
    It's just I wanted it for Tom's birth-day.

    And when I come to cut this cake,
    My knives they bend and then they break.
    It seems a wicked take-on trick to me,
    I've always found your standards high,
    So pardon that I raise this cry,
    But this is more than a cal-am-it-y.
              It's a bloody rip off!
                    Yours sincerely.

Dear Sir (a reply came by return of post),
    We much regret this incident,
    We find it without precedent,
    And all the staff concerned have now been fired.
    We've had the baker shot at dawn,
    And burned his house and all the corn,
    That is used for making bread and cakes for the
        entire population of Northern Canada as
        a punishment.
                                    Yours truly.

I didn't get my money back though!

AS HARD TO SAY AS SNPHZJT

'So, what have you to report?' asked the gentleman, glancing up from his desk to the man in the whitest of suits.

The man who was not altogether a man, but mostly a cockroach.

'Everything is going exactly according to plan,' said Mr Parton Vrane.

'This would be the *Above-Top-Secret* plan, rather than the *Just-Plain-Secret* plan?'

'Correct. I proceeded to the house of the late Mr Sprout and waited. Sure enough, a likely subject appeared on the scene. A Mr Danny Orion. I temporarily disabled Mr Orion and then summoned the beast, which was hiding in the picture of the Queen Mother. It entered Mr Orion, who engaged me in combat. I allowed him to rip off my hand and thrust my body down a drainhole.'

'And how is the hand?' the gentleman asked.

'Oh fine.' Parton Vrane displayed his left hand. 'I grew another. No problems there.'

'Splendid. Go on with your report.'

'Convinced that I was dead and no threat remained to it, the beast then went on his way within the subject. I have been keeping him under close surveillance. He is showing no signs of psychotic behaviour as yet. I suspect the beast has spun him the usual yarn.'

'That he is a holy guardian angel, come to protect and advise?'

'That's the form. The subject keeps smiling and talking to himself. He's taken a job at the local off-licence.'

'Ah,' said the gentleman. 'That is significant.'

'Agreed. Normally the subject withdraws totally into the world the beast creates for him. This is a new development. Do you want me to bring them in yet?'

'Oh no, not yet.'

'I don't think we should wait too long.'

'There you go, thinking again.'

'People will die,' said Parton Vrane.

'I'm not altogether sure. Something different is occurring. Any – how shall I put this? – *creative activity*, on the part of the subject?'

'Indeed,' Mr Parton Vrane nodded. 'He has rented an allotment patch. He spends most of his spare time there.'

'Horticulture?' The gentleman shrugged. 'Surely not.'

'There is an allotment *shed*. He spends much of his spare time in it.'

'Have you seen inside?'

'No, he's painted over the windows and he keeps it well padlocked.'

'They're building another one. I knew it.'

'Another shed?'

'Not a *shed*.'

'Another *what*, then?' asked Parton Vrane.

'Vehicle. Animated robot, ersatz zombie, Frankenstein's monster, call it what you will.'

'I don't understand.'

115

'Then allow me to explain. You know how the beasts first came to be discovered?'

'Of course. But if you're in the mood to re-tell the whole story, I'd really like to hear it again.'

'You would?'

'Absolutely.'

The gentleman raised an eyebrow, was Parton Vrane taking the piss or what? The gentleman composed himself. 'Right then,' he said. 'Are you sitting comfortably?'

'No, I'm still standing up.'

'Well, let's assume you're sitting comfortably.'

'Fair enough.'

'Then I'll begin. The story proper begins in the year 1905, when that great philosopher, scientist and mathematician, Sir Hugo Rune, first postulated his theory of relativity.'

'But I thought it was Einstein's theory of relativity.'

'Different theory. Rune's theory was in regard to the Earth's exact position in the universe, that it is at the very centre, with everything else relatively far away.'

'It sounds a rather foolish proposition.'

'Nevertheless, he proved it conclusively.'

'How?'

'I'm coming to that. Will you stop butting in?'

'Sorry.'

'Right. Now, Rune's theory works in this fashion. If you could draw a straight line of infinite length, a never-ending line which stretched on and on for ever and ever in either direction, then any point you chose upon that line must, by definition, be at its very centre. There could not be more infinity on one side of the point than the other, could there?'

Parton Vrane shook his head. Of course there could not.

'So,' continued the gentleman, 'if you stand at any point on the planet Earth and look straight up, what are you looking into?'

'Infinity?'

'Infinity. From wherever you choose to stand. In every direction. No more infinity if you stand at the South Pole and look straight up, than if you stand at the North. Equal amounts of infinity in every direction. Ergo, the planet Earth is right at the very centre of the universe.'

'What about if I stood on another planet somewhere else? Wouldn't that make the planet I was standing on the centre of the universe?'

'An interesting theory,' said the gentleman. 'How would you go about demonstrating this then?'

'Well, I wouldn't, would I?'

'No, you would not. Because you cannot stand upon another planet, only this one.'

'Someone else might be standing on another planet.'

'The point is, Mr Vrane, that they are *not*. No life exists upon other planets. Because *all* life exists here, right here at the very hub of the universe. On planet Earth.'

'*All* life?'

'*All*. Life, as we define it, is a localized phenomenon, occurring only at the central point. You are aware that infinity only works in one direction, aren't you? That although you can go on doubling the size of something for ever, in all directions, you cannot divide something in half an infinite number of times?'

'Why not?'

'Because eventually you will have something so small that it weighs less than the light which falls upon it and at that point it simply ceases to exist in this universe.'

'Well I never knew *that*.'

The gentleman raised another eyebrow. That *was* sarcasm. It *was*. 'So,' said he, 'Earth at the very centre and *all* life on Earth. Where does that take us to?'

'Does it take us to the experiments of Dr James Bacon in the 1920s?'

'It does. Dr Bacon's work was with spectroscopy, the

117

science of analyzing the spectrum, which is the distribution of colours produced when white light is dispersed by a prism or some such means. Dr Bacon's research took a radical departure. He wanted to know what would happen if you projected darkness through a prism. Would there be a negative spectrum?'

'Again a rather foolish proposition, on the face of it.'

'On the face of it. However, the redoubtable Dr Bacon persevered. In his opinion darkness was, in fact, black light. He constructed test apparatus to project a shadow through an opaque prism cut from obsidian. Few of his notes remain extant, but we know that he succeeded and that he perfected his dark-light goggles, or nightshades, as he called them. And that he was the first man ever to see into the negative spectrum and view the creatures that dwell within.'

'The riders.'

'The riders. Invisible to normal vision. Another order of being, sharing our planet. And sharing *us*.'

'Makes your flesh crawl, don't it?' whispered Parton Vrane.

'You *are* taking the piss, aren't you?'

'Unthinkable. Pray continue with your most interesting narrative.'

'I will. Dr Bacon saw them. At first he thought it must be some trick of the light. The black light. And so he put on his nightshades and went out for a stroll in the park.'

'Didn't he keep bumping into things?'

The gentleman raised both eyebrows. Very high. And lost his monocle once more. 'I don't know. But he sat in the park and he watched people passing by. Except he couldn't see *people*. Because he was looking into the negative spectrum. But he *could* see what was riding upon the people. The other beings. He described them as pale and flimsy, humanoid, with oversized hairless heads and large black slanting eyes.'

'That's what they look like,' said Parton Vrane. 'Apart from the really bad ones. The real *beasties*.'

'Dr Bacon returned to his laboratory,' the gentleman

continued. 'And there, with the kind of courage which made Clive of India, Gordon of Khartoum and Tom of Finland whatever they are today, he looked through his nightshades into a mirror.'

'And got a somewhat unpleasant surprise. But tell me this. We know that these creatures are capable of controlling the thoughts of the individuals they ride upon. How come the creature on Dr Bacon did not control *his* thoughts? Stop him being able to see the creatures, in fact?'

'Theories abound.' The gentleman shrugged. 'Some say that the creature slept, others that it was aloof to the thoughts of Dr Bacon and did not see that he could pose a threat. Whatever the case the creature did nothing. Dr Bacon stared into the mirror and the creature on his shoulders stared back at him. And Dr Bacon determined that at all costs he would remove this creature from his person.'

'Which he did.'

'Which he did, although we do not know how. After he had removed it he went once more for a walk in the park. This time without his nightshades. And now he could see them clearly. With the creature removed from him, his eyes were well and truly open. Dr Bacon had become the world's first *clear*.'

'And then his troubles began.'

'They did. He could see the creatures, but the creatures could see that he was clear. That one of their number was no longer *riding* upon him. They pressed hard upon the thoughts of their unwitting human hosts. Dr Bacon was pelted with stones by small boys. Attacked in the street. An angry mob surrounded his laboratory.'

'And they killed him.'

'The Coroner's report said "suicide". But then it would say that, wouldn't it? We don't know how he died, he was working on a means to rid humanity of the creatures. His left foot was injured in some way. Heavily bandaged. Gangrene, blood-poisoning, murder, who can say?'

'Which takes us almost up to the present day. Thankfully.'

'Thankfully?' As the gentleman had already raised both his eyebrows, he now raised his moustache.

'Go on,' whispered Parton Vrane. 'Finish the story.'

'The nineteen fifties. The Cold War. Suspicion, intrigue, espionage. Experiments with electronic camouflage. Radar invisibility. Genetic engineering.'

'The creation of my kind,' said Parton Vrane, 'designed to withstand atomic radiation, regenerate lost limbs, see in the dark.'

The gentleman nodded. 'Into the black light. Although we did not understand it then. It came as a shock when your kind described what they were able to see.'

'My kind being naturally *clear*.'

'Exactly. The scientists working on the genetic experiments were urged by the creatures that possessed them to close down the project and destroy all of your kind.'

'But they did not.'

'They tried. And they would have succeeded. But for your father. He had observed that when a man dies, the creature riding upon him dissolves. He contrived to kill each scientist in turn by drowning. Once the creature had dissolved, he resuscitated his victims. I was one of his successes. There were a few failures. But a core of *clears* was established. We exist within this building as virtual prisoners.'

'Is that like virtual reality?' Parton Vrane asked.

The gentleman ignored him. 'We are *clear* and cannot be reinfected, but it is not safe for us to walk the streets.'

'It's not safe for *me* to walk the streets. I have to burrow underground most of the time.'

'Quite so. Which brings us up to the present day. We know the creatures exist. We suspect that for the most part they are benign, although parasitic. But there are those amongst them who are destructive. A breed within a breed, capable of transferring from one person to another.'

'The mad-dog element.'

'Correct, which brings us around once more to the matter of vehicles, animated robots, ersatz zombies and Frankenstein's monsters.'

'Which was the matter I asked you about.'

'The creative activities. It goes back to Edward Gein and beyond. The collection of body parts. I believe the creatures are aware that their days are numbered. They know we're on to them and that it is only a matter of time. So they are trying to engineer vehicles for themselves other than man. Do you recall that case a few years back? A Colonel Bickerstaff tried to build himself an elephant? There have been many other such cases. Do you know, I'd really like you to take a look inside this Orion's allotment shed. See what he and his "holy guardian angel" are cooking up.'

'You think Orion is building another elephant?'

'We have a file on Orion,' said the gentleman, 'as we have a file on everybody. This Orion doesn't want an elephant. What he wants is a dog.'

'A dog called Demolition?'

'I think he'd prefer one called Princey, but it's not what he's going to get.'

'I'll see what I can do.'

'You do that.'

And that was the end of that secret meeting. There hadn't been much in the way of action, but there rarely is at secret meetings. There had been plenty of exposition though, which may have helped to tie up a few loose ends, or possibly confuse things further. It's hard to say really. As hard to say as SNPHZJT.

12

I loathe people who keep dogs. They are cowards who haven't the guts to bite people themselves.

AUGUST STRINDBERG (1849–1912)

You will find that the woman who is really kind to dogs is always one who has failed to inspire sympathy in men.

MAX BEERBOHM (1872–1956)

PARDON MY LINES

Pardon my lines, Ben Andrews.
Pardon my way of speech.
My range of old suitcases,
My love of colourful braces,
My fear of foreign places,
And my hatred of the beach.

Pardon my lines, Ben Andrews.
Pardon my book of rules.
My legs that scarcely bear my weight,
Which well account for my ambling gait,
My accent and my empty plate,
My stolen transport tools.

Pardon my lines, Ben Andrews.
Pardon my lack of class.
The scales that in my kitchen rust,
The layers of unhampered dust,
My crass Napoleonic bust,
Which really is a farce.

Pardon my lines, Ben Andrews.
Pardon my way of speech.

'All right,' said Ben, 'you're pardoned. Now
   whose round is it?'
'Yours, I think.'

VINCENT TRILLBY

After locking up the shop and depositing the evening's takings in the night safe of the high street bank*, Danny took a stroll over to the allotments†. It was a fine, moony evening and a few last birds were chirruping away amongst the old oaks along the riverside. Danny whistled as he strode up the path between the picturesque huts and the well-tended plots.

A wonderful thing, an allotment.

Adam was the first allotment holder, you know. Or perhaps he was just God's gardener. He didn't get paid, that was for sure and he came in for a lot of rough handling all because he'd taken a bite or two of a Granny Smith, which hardly seemed fair.

It wasn't his fault anyway. It was all Eve's fault. Did Adam and Eve have a dog?

And *who exactly* did their sons marry?

---

*The one run by Big Brother, who's always *listening*.
†This is one week later, by the way.

Danny had never had much to do with religion. But now he had his own personal holy guardian angel, he thought he might be prepared to give it a bit of a go.

Mind you, he wasn't actually certain which denomination his particular guardian angel was. The being who had taken up residence in his head was somewhat cagey about supplying any details. Danny couldn't even persuade it to tell him its name. And as the voice was inside his head, and not heard through his ears, he actually couldn't tell whether it was male or female.

It was all a bit bewildering.

When the voice had first spoken, Danny had gone all to pieces. Thought he was cracking up. *Had* cracked up.

But the voice had been gentle, soothing, it had offered him advice. Calmed him. Promised him things.

Things like a *dog*.

A *magic* dog.

The dog he was now constructing in his allotment shed.

The *top-secret* dog.

Danny reached the heavily padlocked door of his hut. He felt good inside, did Danny. Warm. At peace. He was certainly getting the change he so wanted, and marvellous times lay ahead. The future was full of hope.

Oh yes.

Danny sat down upon the clapped-out bench before his hut and kicked his heels idly in the dust. It was good here, on the allotment. He'd got the hut and plot really cheap. His guardian angel had known the very chap to phone at the council offices.

The chap had been more than keen to offer Danny the plot.

Mind you, it was a funny old plot.

Circular it was, about thirty feet in diameter. And the land was quite black. Hard and black, as if burned. Nothing grew upon this plot. Not a blade of grass. Danny had thought this somewhat odd, but as he only wanted the use of the hut, he didn't care too much.

The other allotment holders gave his plot a wide berth. This suited Danny also, as privacy was the name of the game in which he was the star player.

Indeed Danny's plot, had it been able to speak, would have had a strange tale to tell. But, as with other allotment patches (barring that owned by a certain Mr Cox in Orton Goldhay), it was mute.

So its tale must be told here, on its behalf.

(With the promise that this will be the last separate tale told for a while. But it *is* a really good one.)

It concerns Vincent Trillby.

Exactly who Vincent Trillby was, why he came and where he eventually went to will never be known for certain. But his brief appearance upon Brentford's regal acres caused a great sensation at the time. A time all of thirty years ago now. But one still spoken of.

If only in low whispers.

Trillby appeared one Wednesday morning, late April, in the year of '66, marching in a determined manner along the almost-crescent of Mafeking Avenue.

He was not a tall man. In fact, the appellation 'short-arsed little bastard' fitted him as snugly as a knitted bed sock. He wore a grubby black frock-coat, battered brogues and a hat of his own design. Those who viewed his passing felt that here was a man who could take just a tad more care over his appearance, without fearing to incur the accusation of Dandyism. They also felt that here was a man to whom this was better left unsaid.

And given that in later casual conversation, Trillby would claim that he could turn milk sour and deflower virgins with a single glance, they were probably wise to keep their counsel.

Vincent Trillby walked alone. Short and dark and determined. Such men as he make poor companions. But excellent Nazi Reich führers.

But let us not stone the man yet, for he has done us no harm. That in the months to come he would be directly responsible for the mysterious disappearance of Barrington Barber for sixteen days, and the fact that *nothing* would ever grow again on the thirty-foot diameter circle in the middle of The St Mary's allotments, was not to be known at this moment of his coming. So, let's just behave ourselves, shall we?

Of Barrington Barber, what might be said? Well, Barrington was one of those tragic bodies who go through life with the permanent conviction that The Fates have personally singled them out for bad treatment. In the case of old Sam Sprout, this was correct. But not in the case of Barrington Barber.

He was fine. Folk liked him, he liked folk. But it was not enough. Something in his psyche was all in a dither. He was certain that he was always being picked on and that dire plots were forever being hatched with the implicit purpose of doing *him* down. And the more his friends assured him this was *not* the case, the more assured did he become, that it *was*.

Barrington saw spies behind every lamppost and heard his name whispered in every half-overheard conversation. 'Those two blokes over there talking about me think I'm paranoid,' he was often heard to remark. (Though it rarely got a laugh.)

The day Vincent Trillby arrived was the day on which Barrington had become convinced that he was about to become the next victim in a particularly malicious series of dustbin burnings which was at that time plaguing the area.

He was taking no chances and was dowsing down his bin with the contents of his teapot, when there came a knocking upon his gaily painted front door.

'Oh mercy me, by Crimmins,' gasped Barrington, making the sign of the cross. 'It will be the gutter press. I've been *outed*, I just know it★.'

Barrington Barber walked through his kitchen, through his back parlour and up the short hall to the front door, as a man bound for execution. He was doomed, and he just knew it. With the resignation of the well and truly damned he swung the front door open.

On the doorstep stood Vincent Trillby.

Barrington looked over his head and then up and down the street. Then he looked under his head and observed the raggy clothes. And then he looked directly at his head and became all pale and bewildered.

'What do you want?' he managed.

'Could I have an aspirin to go with this glass of water?' asked Trillby, producing a full glass from his pocket.

Barrington looked at the glass and once more at the man and decided he didn't like either.

'Aspirins give me a headache,' said Barrington. 'Milk of Magnesia upsets my stomach and I have a proprietary brand of shampoo in my bathroom that gives me dandruff.'

'I've come to the right place then.' Vincent Trillby presented Barrington with a well-thumbed calling-card. It read, VINCENT TRILLBY. RECONVENER.

'Is that in capital letters?' Barrington asked.

'No,' said Vincent Trillby. 'It only looks that way. Might I just come in for a moment? I think it's about to rain.'

Barrington Barber peered up at the bright blue sky. 'You have to be joking,' said he. 'You've as much chance of getting in here as, well, as there is of there being a storm.'

The sky began to darken and the rain began to fall.

★   ★   ★

★The fact that this was 1966, that Barrington was *not* a homosexual, and that the term *outed* did not, as yet, exist were as nothing to this man.

'More tea?' asked Barrington Barber.

'And another biscuit, if you have one.'

Vincent Trillby now sat in Barrington's favourite armchair. He had his feet up on the Persian pouffe. Barrington took the little stranger's cup and plodded off to the kitchen.

'Why did I let him come in?' he asked himself, as he topped up the teacup. 'What am I doing leaving him alone in my front room?' he also asked and, 'Short-arsed little bastard!' he added, although beneath his breath.

When Barrington Barber returned to his front room his manner was, to say the least, a little brusque. 'Drink your tea and then piss off,' he said. 'And there's no more biscuits.'

Vincent Trillby accepted his tea with a show of great gratitude. 'I am forever in your debt, sir,' he said.

Barrington scowled purposefully upon his unwelcome guest. Vincent Trillby, for his part, appeared immune to all hostility.

Around and about the walls of Barrington's front room were the trophies which spoke fluently of his particular hobby.

'I see that you are a terrantologist,' said Vincent Trillby.

Somewhat startled by his visitor's unusual perceptiveness, Barrington said, 'Yes, I am.'

'I collect myself,' said Vincent.

Barrington scratched at his head, releasing flakes of dandruff. 'How can you collect *yourself*?' he asked.

'No. I collect – comma – myself.'

'Oh I see. A matter of punctuation. Your accent has me slightly addled. Where exactly are you from?'

'I'm from down under,' said Vincent, and the matter was allowed to drop.

About an hour later Barrington was to be seen trudging through the rain *en route* to Brentford Station, where he would collect Vincent Trillby's heavy suitcase from the left-luggage office. Trillby, at this time, lazed upon Barrington's bed, his sinister footwear soiling the eiderdown and his stumpy little hands behind his head.

He was smoking Barrington's pipe.

Vincent Trillby had come to stay.

That night, Barrington Barber took Vincent up to The Flying Swan to meet the lads and get acquainted. Vincent got in a generous round (which was never repeated and which proved later to have been purchased with pennies from Barrington's darts club money), raised his glass and said, 'Skol,' and, 'Good health.'

'Where are you from?' asked Archroy*. 'I can't place your accent.'

'I'm from down under,' said Vincent Trillby. 'Do you know where I might rent an allotment patch?'

Now, whether this question was merely conversational, as had been the terrantology remark, or whether Vincent Trillby really wanted to rent an allotment patch, was not immediately knowable, but the effect that it had on The Swan's patrons was – how shall we say? – *marked*.

All conversation ceased and twenty-three pairs of suspicious eyes turned upon Vincent Trillby.

Neville, the part-time barman, was the first to speak. 'What do you want with allotments, mister?' he asked. 'Are you from the Customs and Excise?'

Vincent shook his head. And apparently unfazed by the electricity in the air, he said, 'I need a plot of land.'

Barrington took the small man to one side and put him wise. 'You do not just walk into someone's local and start asking for an allotment patch,' said he, making furtive side glances towards those he *knew* to be talking about him. 'People are apt to become apprehensive and possibly hostile. An allotment is a place of sanctuary. A sacred place. Visiting

*Who had yet to take up Dimac or find the Ark of Noah.

one's allotment is a bit like being a Moslem and making the pilgrimage to Mecca.'

'How much like?' asked Vincent Trillby.

'Not much really. But listen, certain things take place on allotments. Certain things which are not, in the eyes of the law, strictly above the bread board. Certain plants are grown, certain spirits distilled. I don't wish to go into this too deeply, but I'm afraid you have as much chance of getting an allotment patch around here as there is of . . .' He sought something suitably absurd with which to make his point. 'As there is of Sam Sprout over there getting a round in.'

'So, what are you all having?' asked Sam suddenly.

'About this plot of land,' said Vincent.

How it came to pass that a week later old Arthur Card became fatally entangled in the coils of his garden hose and died leaving his allotment patch to Vincent Trillby was anyone's guess. But those who had their suspicions kept them to themselves. Vincent Trillby was already acquiring a reputation as a man it was better not to cross.

Those who came into proximity with his diminutive person generally went upon their way with lighter pockets and heavier hearts. Catholics crossed themselves as he marched by.

Babies filled their nappies.

Archroy called round at Barrington's one morning to bid him the best of the day and assure him that whatever the dreaded eventuality currently filling his mind might be, it was nothing he should worry himself about (and possibly to scrounge a cup of coffee). Vincent Trillby appeared in the doorway, drinking a cup of coffee and wearing Barrington's dressing-gown.

'He's gone away for a couple of weeks,' said Vincent. 'Now clear off or I'll set my dog on you.'

Archroy took his leave.

It soon became noticeable, to those who notice such things, that although Trillby was still about, he was for the most part only observed during night-time hours, and with furtive expression and scurrying feet.

And it was Archroy who was the first to notice that something was strangely amiss with the late Arthur Card's allotment patch.

Archroy, John Omally* and Father Moity stood upon the brim of the once-plot and stared down into what looked for all this wonderful world like a very deep crater indeed.

'It wasn't here last night,' Archroy assured the other two lookers-down. 'I noticed it this morning as I was on my milk round.'

John Omally lifted the flat cap he wore at the time and scratched at a curly forelock. 'Is it *dug*?' he asked. 'It has more the look of being *caused* rather than *dug*.'

'It's that Vincent Trillby,' said Archroy. 'I've seen him skulking around here at night. I tell you, that man is up to no good. We should go round and confront him. Strike him, if needs be.'

Father Moity sucked upon the briar he smoked at the time and fingered his clerical collar. 'I am not so certain that there is anything to confront Trillby with. After all, this is his plot now and he will no doubt tell us that he has been turning the sod. Adding that we should bugger off and mind our own business.'

'I think he's in league with the Devil,' said Archroy, suddenly.

'And I must be off about business of my own,' said Father Moity, hoisting up his cassock and having it away on his toes. His appearance in the story had been brief, and, even for a man of the cloth, quite without any lasting merit. 'Farewell.'

John Omally peered down into the darkness beneath. 'It is a very deep pit,' said he, 'and I cannot see its bottom.'

*Who had yet to become a legendary hero, in the mould of Wolfe of Quebec, Robin of Sherwood, or Eve of Destruction.

Archroy chewed this observation over for a moment or two, coupled it with his own last remark and came to a sudden, though not altogether welcome, conclusion. '*The Bottomless Pit*,' said he.

'The *what*?' asked John, who had been idly kicking stones into the hole and listening in vain for a sound.

'The bottomless pit. John, what is the date?'

Omally, who owned neither watch nor calendar, but had a good memory, said, 'The sixth of June.'

'And the year?'

'1966, of course.'

'Hoopla!' said Archroy. 'The 6-6-66, now there's a thing.'

'So what?' asked John.

'What's the time?'

Omally shrugged. 'I was pretty impressive knowing the date, please don't push things.'

And ding-dong (merrily on high) went the church clock of St Mary's.

'It's five-thirty,' said John. 'And opening time.'

'Not tonight.' Archroy put on a desperate expression. 'Five-thirty p.m. and, if I'm not mistaken, the trouble will start at six minutes past six.'

'You've lost me,' said John Omally. But Archroy hadn't.

'We'd best go round to Barrington's house *now*,' said the lad. 'See if the villain is there. Time, as they say, is running out.' And the two men ran out of the allotments.

As they rushed towards Mafeking Avenue, Archroy breathlessly explained the theory that was blooming in his head. 'It's that Vincent Trillby,' he spluttered. 'He gets the allotment and he builds The Bottomless Pit, or he digs it, or causes it to appear, or something. And if I'm not mistaken he's waiting for that very moment that only occurs once every century, to release all the horrid nasties onto unsuspecting mankind.

'According to the Book of Revelation, the great beast's number is 666. So that exact time would be six minutes past six on the sixth of the sixth, sixty-six. Double whammy. This Vincent Trillby is old Nick himself.'

Omally huffed and he puffed. He wasn't any too keen to hear this kind of talk. But it somehow made all kinds of sense. 'Didn't he say that he'd come from *down under*?' asked John, as he huffed and he puffed.

And the two rushed on. Archroy quoting all he knew of The Book of Revelation and Omally shaking his head and rolling up his sleeves. Presently they reached Mafeking Avenue.

'Number twelve,' said Archroy.

Omally counted the houses as they ran. 'Number six, number eight, number ten, number . . .'

'Number fourteen,' said Archroy. 'Now there's a thing.'

'And there's another,' said Omally, as the sky suddenly darkened. 'Is that a great big storm coming or what?'

'*Or what*, would be my guess. Back to the pit. Back to the pit.'

And back towards the pit ran they.

It was all quite exciting really. Although there certainly was an element of danger involved. The Devil incarnate about to unleash all the horrors of The Bottomless Pit upon the plain God-fearing people of Brentford.

And everything.

By the time they reached the allotment gates, they were pretty much out of breath. Omally had sworn that he would never smoke another Woodbine, and Archroy that if he should survive, he would become a monk.

The storm was getting up a treat. Black clouds tumbled in the heavens. Lightning pitched and struck. Wind whistled, thunder biffed and banged. Rain showers seemed imminent.

'There! There!' cried Omally. And there, there, he stood. Although still small, he was awesome, his old frock-coat whipped about him in the wind and his self-styled hat showed two distinct peaks.

Somewhat horn-like.

133

And he stood, mouthing something on the very rim of The Pit.

'Lord save us,' gasped Archroy. 'What do you reckon the time is?'

Omally gagged for breath. 'I heard the clock chime. Maybe five past six.'

'We've got to stop him.' Archroy snatched up half a brick from a pile quite conveniently placed and advanced upon the terrible figure. Omally did likewise. An icy wind was rising and it was getting darker by the moment.

'You go that way, I'll go this,' shouted Archroy.

Lightning exploded from every side and the wind grew stronger and stronger.

Trillby stood with his hands raised as high as his short arm's length would allow. He ranted and raved with his eyes glowing red. The ground rocked and shivered and screams could be heard welling up from the darkness below.

It was horrible!

Archroy flung his half-a-brick—

And missed.

Trillby turned upon him. 'Too late, too late,' he crowed. 'Now is *my* time. You all die. All. All. All.'

'You first!' Omally threw his missile.

Vincent Trillby caught it in the left ear. He swivelled around on the rim of the pit, spitting fire and brimstone, laughing like a loon.

John Omally kicked him in the cobblers.

Vincent Trillby staggered back and tumbled, down into the pit of his own making. Down and down. For ever and for ever.

The sound that followed might well have been described as indescribable. The earth heaved and the pit closed like a great hungry mouth snapping over a fish finger.

And all went very quiet. And the sun came out again.

★   ★   ★

Barrington Barber appeared at the allotment gates. 'Hello, lads,' said he. 'How's tricks?'

Archroy scratched at his head. 'Where have *you* been?' he asked.

Barrington Barber scratched at *his* head. 'Well. The last thing I remember is, I was dowsing down my dustbin when there was a knock at the door . . . then it all sort of goes blank. What are you blokes doing here anyway?'

John Omally now scratched at *his* head. 'Hey, Archroy,' said he, 'what *are* we doing here?'

13

A hen is only an egg's way of making other eggs.

Popular Aphorism.

POTS IN THE SHED

Nigel found those pots in the shed.
Held one high above his head.
His sister in her rubber mac,
Called to him to put it back.

But Nigel was completely captivated and
    could not hear her at all.

Nigel's sister skipped in the lane,
When suddenly a cry of pain,
Shook the calm and village air,
And shortly after, in despair,

Came Nigel with his head all cut and
    a bloody big bump on his forehead.

Nigel's sister laughed with glee.
'That serves you right, believe you me,
You never heard a word I said,
You should have left those pots in the shed.'

But Nigel didn't hear that either
because he had concussion.

THE DOG FORMERLY KNOWN
AS PRINCE

There were pots in Danny's shed. Fine big pots they were. Terracotta pots. And there was a broken hoe, an old-fashioned rat trap, some bails of wire and a bit of a bench with half a bag of solid cement tucked away beneath it*.

On the bench were many curious items: odd roots and dried vegetable matter, pickled things in jars, the remains of Aunt May's favourite fox-fur stole, marbles and magnets, medical textbooks and motor cycle manuals. But, taking up the greater part of the bit of a bench, was an overlarge something covered by a pink nylon bed sheet.

Danny went, 'Tarraaah!' and flung the sheet aside.

And by the light of a single hurricane lamp his wonder was revealed. And lo his wonder was a dog.

It was Princey the Wonder Woofer.

Danny viewed the magnificent construction, so realistic as to be awesome. It was a dog all right. And *some* dog. A great big, lovable, floppy-eared, cold-nosed, waggy-tailed, golden-haired Labrador of a dog. Good boy, Princey. Good boy there.

---

*Many theories abound concerning why there is always half a bag of solid cement in every garden shed. The best being that it is a tradition, or an old charter. Or something.

Danny whistled. 'Beaut,' said he. 'It's coming on a treat.'
He ran a loving hand over the canine head, tickled it beneath
an ear, stroked his knuckle under the chin. It looked perfect.

You couldn't see the joins or stitches. And it didn't look
like a stuffed dog either. It looked like the real McCruft's,
just standing still, waiting for the command to fetch a stick
or beg a biscuit. Danny gave it a pat upon the back. 'Good
boy,' said he. 'Good boy there.'

'*You like it then, Danny boy?*'

'I love it. But will it really work? I mean how *does* it work?
Is it radio-controlled, or what?'

'*Voice-activated, of course.*'

Danny clapped his hands together. 'It's brilliant. But what
makes it go? Is it clockwork or does it have batteries?'

'*Secret, Danny. I can't tell you everything.*'

'But what I don't understand is, how do you work on it?
I mean, you're a discorporate being. You don't have a body.
But each time I come here, a bit more's been done. And I
can never figure out *when* you did it, because you're always
with me.'

'*I have my methods, Danny.*'

'Yes but how . . . ?'

'*Leave it, will you?*'

'Yes, but, all I want to know is—'

'*Leave it!*' This time Danny felt the voice. It echoed about
in his head. It actually hurt.

'Oh.' Danny put his hands to his temples. 'Not so loud.
Stop.'

'*Time to go home, Danny. Time to go home.*'

'Yes. OK. Right, I'll do that.'

'*Good boy, Danny. Good boy there.*'

Inspector Westlake paced up and down the hall. The hall was
in a house and the house was in Moby Dick Terrace. Number
eight. Inspector Westlake's hands were in his pockets and his
chin was on his chest. He had a bit of a sweat on also.

The inspector was a *professional* policeman. No mucking about. Things done by the rulebook, because that's what the rulebook's for. Tall the inspector was. Imposing. Long neck.

They have long necks, policemen, don't they? Or perhaps it's just the haircuts. A bit like soldiers, or any of the armed services really. Simple rule of thumb there: if the job demands that you have your hair cut off, tell them to stick the job. Inspector Westlake hadn't told them to stick it. He was a career policeman. In the force until pension.

Tall, imposing, long neck, professional. Hard bastard. Gaunt, chisel-featured, bitter mouth.

He paced.

At intervals he ceased pacing and turned towards a wall, where he gently kicked at the skirting board. Then he shook his head, returned his chin to his chest and resumed pacing.

Mid-morning sunlight fell upon him through the stained-glass panels of the front door. A colourful erotic confection styled in the manner of Peter Fendi. Each time the inspector paced in the direction of the front door his chin rose a little and his head cocked upon one side. And thoughts of the Long Jean Silver came to him.

But each time he paced back again, towards the rear parlour, his face became grave and his chin pressed firmly down.

The front door swung open and banged against the wall. A young constable, of the type so useful in supplying comic relief when things get really heavy, tripped over the doormat and fell into the hall.

'That's a bit premature, lad,' said Inspector Westlake.

'Excuse me, sir?'

'We haven't set the scene yet. All I've done is pace.'

'Sorry, sir. Should I go out and come in again?'

'I think that would be for the best. Yes.'

The young constable went out and came in again. This time the door didn't bang and he didn't fall over the mat.

'That's much better,' said Inspector Westlake. 'Now go on, tell me what you want.'

'Pardon me, sir, but the Soco's here.'

'Socko the magic clown?'

'No, sir. Soco. *Scene of Crime Officer*. And the forensic people and the press.'

'Is the street cordoned off?'

'Yes, sir.'

'Bunting?'

'No, I'm Constable Dreadlock, sir.'

'*Bunting*, lad! Those little flags on a long string that you hang out for coronations and royal weddings.'

'Don't think I quite follow you, sir.'

'Well, you cordon off the streets for a royal wedding and you hang up bunting. I would have thought that was patently obvious. Never mind, Constable *Dreadlock*, did you say?'

'It's a Polish name, sir. It means "he who comes in the middle of the night bearing a box of chocolates".'

'How very interesting. Well, don't just stand there like a candle in the wind, Dreadlock. Send in the clowns.'

'Er, yes, sir, I'll do that.' Constable Dreadlock offered a formal salute and departed. He knew, as all his fellow officers knew, that Inspector Westlake was a certifiable loon. But *he* wasn't going to be the one to speak up about it and lose his pension. He was a professional.

A very short, fat, round, bald-headed fellow, wearing a yellow tweed suit, wire-framed specs and a goatee beard, and evidently designed to contrast with the inspector, now entered the hall. 'Inspector Westlake,' said he.

'That's a coincidence,' said the inspector.

'No, no, no.' The fat man shook his baldy head. 'I'm Gould. But don't be formal. Call me Fridge-Magnet.'

'Fridge-Magnet, did you say?'

'It's a Cherokee Indian name. Father was a Cherokee Indian serving on an airbase here. Secret one, very hush-hush. And you know how they name red Indian children—'

'It's native American, isn't it?'

'Is it? Well, they name them by holding them up by the

river and calling them after the first thing they see. But it was raining, so I got baptized in the kitchen.'

'Would you like to see the body?' asked Inspector Westlake.

'Oh, there's a body, is there?'

'Parts of one, yes.'

'Parts of one.' Fridge-Magnet Gould smiled broadly and rubbed his hands together. 'Let's have a look then.'

Inspector Westlake pushed open the rear parlour door. Mr Gould peeped in. And whistled. 'Well,' said he. 'Well . . . er . . . yes . . . well . . . that's definitely . . . parts of a body . . . yes indeed.'

'And along the mantelpiece.' Inspector Westlake pointed.

'Mm, yes.'

'And threaded onto that drying-line before the window.'

'Mm, there too. Rather festive, a bit like—'

'Bunting.'

'No, *Gould*,' said Mr Gould. 'I think I'd better get one of my chaps to take some photos.'

'I'll comb my hair then.'

'Yes, you do that.' Fridge-Magnet Gould shook his bald head and waddled away up the hall. 'Oh, Inspector,' he called back, 'do you have any idea of the identity of the body?'

Inspector Westlake took out his regulation police notebook and flipped through the pages. 'A Mrs Roeg,' said he. 'Glenda Roeg.'

'Done to death,' said The Kid, to roars of applause. 'Ripped up and spread all about.'

'You're winding me up,' said Sandy, and laughter filled the air.

'Turn off that bloody machine,' said Big Frank. 'It's not funny and nobody likes it.'

Sandy looked around the pub. The lunch-time crowd that normally packed the place was a bit lacking. In fact, other than for Big Frank and The Kid, there was only Marmsly to be seen. And he was going off to the toilet.

'Typical,' said Sandy. 'You bend over backwards to please people and they spit in your eye.'

Big Frank tried to picture that, but the effort was too great for him.

Sandy switched off the canned-laughter machine.

'Ripped up?' he said. 'What, like sawn up, or hacked, or torn limb from limb?'

'I think limb from limb would have it,' said The Kid. 'I shinned over the back fence and had a squint in through the parlour window. I couldn't see too much, there was a policeman in there having his picture taken. But the limb-from-limbing appeared to be quite comprehensive.'

'Urgh,' said Sandy. 'Weren't you sick?'

'Oh yes,' said The Kid. 'All over the place. Give us another Bloody Mary please.'

Sandy did the business. 'I'm glad I don't live in Moby Dick Terrace, that's the second murder in a few months.'

'Could happen anywhere,' said Big Frank. 'It's just a coincidence. Two murders in the same street, blood every-where, bits of body strewn all around.'

'You don't see some kind of pattern emerging then?' asked The Kid, with a smirk on his face.

'Nah.' Big Frank shook his big head. 'I used to work in a morgue, remember. One year we had eight young women, all raped, strangled and mutilated in identical ways, just coincidence. And before that it was tobacconists, heads cut off and bottles of Tizer stuck in the neckholes. Coincidence again. You get a run on a certain type of crime. It happens all the time.'

The Kid hid his face and stifled his mirth. 'You prat,' said he.

'You what?'

'Nothing. So it's just a coincidence, that's your opinion?'

'Bound to be.' Big Frank took a big swill of beer.

'But Mrs Roeg.' Sandy shook his head sadly. 'Good-looking woman, what a waste.'

The Kid looked up at the barman. 'So it wouldn't have been a waste if it had been an ugly-looking woman?'

'Certainly not,' said Sandy. 'We've a surplus of ugly-looking women in this country. And ugly-looking men, come to think of it. Look at Big Frank here, for instance.'

'True enough,' said The Kid.

'Bollocks,' said Big Frank.

Marmsly returned from the toilet. 'Your bog's been vandalized,' said he.

'I know,' Sandy said. 'I did it myself. Gives the Gents a bit of character, I thought. I'm trying to attract a rougher clientele to the pub. What do you think?'

'Very nice,' said Marmsly. 'Does this mean that all the yobbos you previously barred will be invited back?'

'Certainly does. You see, with the laughter machine driving away all the respectable customers, I didn't have any choice.'

Marmsly shook his head. You couldn't argue with that kind of logic. 'Smart move,' said Marmsly. 'We'll drink elsewhere in future then.'

'I should,' said Sandy. 'It'll be Hell in here. I'm thinking of selling up before the trouble starts.'

And as if on cue (for such is the only way to do things) the saloon-bar door opened and in walked Danny Orion.

'Hello each,' said Danny.

'Blimey,' said Big Frank. 'It has returned. It speaks to us once more.'

'What *do you* mean?' Danny asked.

'He means,' said The Kid, 'that you haven't been in here for months. Not since you got the job in the offy.'

'Of course I have. Haven't I? No, maybe I haven't. I can't quite seem to remember.'

'You *haven't*,' said Marmsly. 'So did you get the sack, is that it? Good thing too. It's bad luck to work in an off-licence.

Uncle of mine worked in an off-licence and he came to a very sticky end. It's a strange story, but I'll tell it if I may.'

THE TALE OF MARMSLY'S UNCLE

'No thanks,' said Danny.

'Oh,' said Marmsly. 'Please yourself then.'

'Well,' Danny said, 'if it's so long since I've been in, then I suppose it must be my round.'

This remark received what is known as a consensus.

Sandy did some more business.

'Actually, you look like shit,' said Big Frank.

'How dare you,' said Danny.

'Well you do, bags under your eyes, face all thin. You look shagged out.'

'I don't.' Danny glared at his reflection in the mirror behind the bar. A smiling face gazed back at him, rosy cheeked, bright eyed (no doubt bushy tailed also). Healthy it looked. To Danny.

'Knackered,' said Big Frank.

'I'm never knackered. I'm fine. I look fine and I feel fine.'

'Hmmph!' said Big Frank, proving that it *could* be done.

'So *did* you get the sack?' The Kid asked.

'No,' said Danny. 'In fact, I think I'm in line for promotion. I sent off for this book, *RUNEISTICS: The Modern Science of Mental Health*. It teaches you how to think positively. I'm a changed man.'

'Did you hear about Mrs Roeg?' asked Big Frank.

'Mrs Roeg? No.'

'Dead,' said The Kid. 'Murdered, chopped up and strewn all about the place.'

'*No?*' Danny's face did a Procul Harum. 'Dead? I don't believe it.'

'Last night.'

'But she was in the shop.' Danny's thoughts returned to that time. And to the words which had flashed up on the cash register when he ran the bar-code-reader over Mrs Roeg's wrist weeks before. And then Danny's thoughts became a little scrambled. He recalled leaving the shop and going to the allotment shed and then . . . what? Going home to bed? Danny couldn't remember. He *had* gone home to bed, hadn't he? He woke up in bed this morning. But there was some dream. Some horrible dream.

'*Be at peace there, Danny Boy.*'

And then Danny forgot all about any dream and could only think of his dog. Good boy, Princey. Good boy there.

And the voice in Danny's head hummed a soothing melody and whispered, '*Good boy, Danny. Good boy there.*'

And Danny smiled a happy smile and bought another round.

14

If you took as much LSD as Paul McCartney, you wouldn't
eat anything with a face either.

TED NUGENT, 1995

THE COWBOY WHO LIVES
ON THE MOON

Glens full of monarchs,
With antlers and stuff,
That snort at the golfers,
Who dig in the rough.
For balls gone astray,
That are well out of play,
Curse in Hebrew and Gaelic and pigeon Malay.

The hordes of the Mongols,
That live in our street,
Wear lounge suits of satin,
And look most effete.
They speak well of Khan,
And the old seaman's yarn,
But curse common markets and Lords of the Fleet.

The brown teeth of sailors,
Who whistle the tune,
Of hornpipes from whalers,
That set out in June.
Know nothing of bingo,
Or George, Paul and Ringo,
And less of the cowboy who lives on the moon.

MURMURS OF DISAPPROVAL

Danny stayed too long at The Shrunken Head. He'd quite forgotten how much he enjoyed the company of his friends. And thus he drank rather deeply of reunion's chalice and was very late back to work.

Mr Doveston was appalled.

'You went to a *pub*? Why did you go to a *pub*?'

'I dunno,' said Danny. 'I just sort of felt like it.'

'Felt like it?' Mr Doveston threw his hands in the air and paced up and down the shop in the fashion of Inspector Westlake (who had recently paced up and down a hall and whom Mr Doveston knew socially). 'It was just on a whim, was it?'

'I suppose so,' said Danny, wondering where he might sit down.

'On a whim you go to the pub and get pissed?'

'Oh hang about. I'm not pissed.'

'You're all over the place, lad. Pale in the face. Bags under your eyes.'

'I don't have any bags under my eyes.' Danny examined his face in an advertising mirror by the door. He still looked peachy. To him.

'I'm perturbed,' said Mr Doveston. 'I feel you have betrayed my trust.'

'*Tell him to fuck off!*'

'Don't be silly.'

'I'm not being silly, young man.'

'I wasn't talking to you.' Danny leaned himself upon the counter. And he swayed a bit as he did so.

'It just won't do.' Mr Doveston had his arms folded now. He was making tsk-tsk sounds with his tongue. He was quite getting into this really. He liked telling people off. In fact, what he liked most was dressing up in uniform and telling people off. And hitting them with sticks, of course. He liked that *very* much. 'Won't do.' He shook his head and tsked some more. 'I was going to recommend you for promotion, what with me being offered the post of area manager and you being my star pupil. I feel very let down.'

'*You should be let down the toilet on a length of rope.*'

'Stop it,' said Danny.

'What?' asked Mr Doveston.

'Nothing. Look, I'm sorry. It won't happen again, I promise.'

'Four weeks, Orion.' Mr Doveston held up four fingers, then waved them in time with his words. 'Four weeks to redeem yourself. Four weeks to prove to me you're worth it. Four weeks in which to repay my trust. Four weeks—'

Danny collapsed on the floor in a heap.

'Are you listening to me, Orion?'

'I'm listening. I'm listening.' Danny floundered about.

'It's the only chance you're going to get.'

'*Bite his ankle. Sink your teeth in.*'

'No!'

'No? You don't want a chance?'

'I'm not well,' mumbled Danny. 'I don't feel too good. It's not the beer, it's something else.'

'Get up, boy, there'll be customers. You can't lie there.' Mr Doveston tugged at Danny's arm. 'Come on now.'

'Leave me alone.'

'Come on now, get up.'

'*Sink your teeth in, Danny. Sink your teeth in deep.*'

'Shut up, will you?'

'I'm not having this.' Mr Doveston refolded his arms. 'Get up and go home at once. Come in tomorrow at nine sharp, and we'll discuss your future with this company, should you actually have one.'

'*Spit in his eye, Danny boy.*'

'Stop it, please.'

'Get up, Orion.'

Danny tried to get up, but he couldn't. He felt absolutely wretched. And it *wasn't* just the beer. He felt weird. Dislocated.

'*Time to go, Danny boy. Time to go home to bed.*'

Danny wrenched himself to his feet, his head swimming. 'I'm going,' said he. 'And I'm sorry. I'm very sorry.'

'We'll see about that and you won't be paid for today.'

'OK. I'm going. I'm sorry.'

Mr Doveston held open the door and Danny stumbled out into the street. 'I feel very let down indeed,' said Mr D.

Danny half turned and opened his mouth, but he didn't speak, he turned back and lumbered away.

Across the street a white van was parked on the double yellow lines. Several parking tickets were taped to the windscreen, which was tinted a smoky grey. In the driving seat sat a young man who wasn't a man at all. He keyed the ignition, put the van into gear and followed Danny along.

'So,' said Inspector Westlake. 'What are your conclusions?'

Fridge-Magnet Gould peeled off his surgical gloves and dropped them into a bucket. 'Murder,' said he. 'Plain and simple.'

'You call this plain and simple?'

'The actual murder side of it was plain and simple. Somebody reached down this woman's throat and pulled out her—'

'That's hardly plain and far from simple.'

149

'You'd need a good strong arm,' said F. M. Gould. 'And a firm grip, but it can be done. Would you care for me to demonstrate? On this constable here, for instance?'

'No way,' said Constable Dreadlock, who was nosing about with evident relish.

'Any weapons involved?' the inspector asked. 'Knives? Cutting implements? Bone saws? Hairdriers? Fork-lift trucks? Parquet flooring?'

Mr Gould cut the inspector's wandering stream of consciousness mercifully short. 'Bare hands,' said he.

'*Bare hands?*'

'Bare hands.'

'Cor,' said the constable, 'bare hands.'

'And time of death?'

'Between two and three a.m. and, Inspector—'

'Yes?'

'The body is incomplete. The hands and feet are missing.'

'Cor,' said the constable once again.

Inspector Westlake turned to the young ghoul. 'What about the neighbours?' he asked.

Constable Dreadlock scratched his helmet. 'I think they've still got *their* hands and feet. I'm sure I would have noticed. Or they would have mentioned it.'

Inspector Westlake made a scowling face. 'What about the neighbours, did they see or hear anything?'

The constable fiddled with his regulation notebook. 'No-one saw anything. *But* . . . the neighbours on both sides were awoken at around two-thirty a.m. by the noise.'

'The noise of the struggle?'

'The noise of a dog,' said the constable. 'Coming from in here. It was very loud. Barking and howling. Both sides say they banged on the walls.'

'A dog?' Inspector Westlake shrugged. Mr Fridge-Magnet Gould also shrugged. 'A dog?'

'That's what they say, sir, a dog.'

Inspector Westlake shook his head and gazed about at the human debris littering the room. 'Tell me, Constable,' said he, 'does this look like a dog's doing to you?'

Constable Dreadlock joined in the gazing. 'That bit over there does, sir,' he said.

15

No comment.

JEFFREY ARCHER

ODE TO THE ANTIQUITY
OF MICROBES

Adam
Had 'em.

THE *NEW* STORY SO FAR

Old Sam Sprout has discovered a great and terrible secret. That mankind is plagued by a race of invisible parasites, The Riders, beings that exist within a spectrum which cannot be viewed by man. The negative spectrum of *Black Light*.

Old Sam has made this momentous discovery through an accident which occurred to his left foot, but dies alone in mysterious circumstances before he is able to communicate what he has found to others.

Unknown to old Sam, others have already made this

discovery and are determined to wage war upon The Riders and free mankind (The Riders apparently being able to control the thoughts of those they ride upon). At a secret American airbase in the middle of a desert, special agent Parton Vrane, a genetically engineered half-man, half-cockroach, who bears an uncanny resemblance to the now legendary Gary Busey, is put on the case and dispatched to Great Britain.

His mission: seek and contain a particularly nasty specimen of the invisible parasitic race, one that identifies itself as A DOG CALLED DEMOLITION and which has driven its unwilling human hosts to kill, time and again.

Now, although an epic borrower, old Sam Sprout has died apparently penniless, prompting one of his many creditors, a certain Danny Orion (young ne'er-do-well and professional ordinary bloke), to enter his house in search of hidden booty.

Here Danny becomes possessed by DEMOLITION, which settles upon him, invading and controlling his thoughts. DEMOLITION informs Danny that it is his holy guardian angel and that it will steer him on a course to financial success and give him what he has always wanted: a dog of his very own. In fact, it will actually help him to build one.

Danny considers himself a young man blessed of the gods. He will shortly discover that he is anything but.

We join Danny, at midnight, in his allotment shed where, after a lunch-time drinking spree and an afternoon sleeping it off, which has probably cost him his job and was no doubt prompted by DEMOLITION, who does *not* have Danny's best interests at heart but now almost totally controls his mind, Danny's dog Princey is about to be taken for walkies.

WAKIN' THE DOG

Danny lit the hurricane lamp and looked all around the shed. There he was, on the bench, all draped over with the pink nylon sheet.

Good old Princey. Good boy there.

Danny clapped his hands together. 'Is he finished?' he asked.

'*Absolutely. The final vital components were added last night.*'

'Jolly good,' said Danny and he whipped away the sheet.

Good Boy Princey looked pretty damn good. He looked even bigger than the night before and somehow better formed, more firm and round and huggable. Good haunches he had, if dogs have haunches. Yes, of course they do, everything has haunches. Except for fish. Fish have fins, everybody knows *that*! Great floppy ears and a tail just ready to wag.

Danny gave him a pat on the head. And then Danny yawned.

'*Not tired?*' asked the voice in his head. '*You've been kipping half the afternoon.*'

'I know, but I've felt tired since this morning and I woke up with a sore throat. If I didn't know better I'd be tempted to think that I hadn't slept at all last night.'

'*Really?*' said the voice.

'Really, if I didn't know better I'd be tempted to think that I was awake all night howling like a dog and doing something really energetic.'

'*Like what?*' asked the voice.

'I don't know, like ripping someone limb from limb with my bare hands.'

'*What an absurd thought.*'

'Isn't it? But then everybody's been telling me how dreadful I look and each time I look in a mirror I see a really healthy face looking back.'

'*Do you?*'

'I do. And if I didn't know better I'd be tempted to think that you are somehow making me see what you wanted me to see. Silly, isn't it?'

'*Very.*'

'Because if you were doing that,' said Danny, 'it would mean that you weren't my holy guardian angel at all, but some kind of demon that had entered my head.'

'*Well, that really is silly,*' said the voice.

'I know. Because if that was the case you would never have built me this lovely dog. I mean, if that was the case, then this lovely dog wouldn't actually be a lovely dog at all. I'd just be thinking it was a lovely dog and seeing it as a lovely dog when it was really something absolutely hideous, like some monster constructed from human body parts.'

'*Ludicrous, eh?*' said the voice.

'Ludicrous,' agreed Danny. 'So how do I get Princey started then? Do I press a button or something?'

'*No, you just open the artery of your left wrist and let him drink your blood.*'

'Oh very good.' Danny laughed. 'Most amusing, oh yes.'

'*I'm not kidding,*' said the voice.

Danny laughed again. 'Very droll. So I should just take this Stanley knife,' he took up the knife in question, which he didn't recall bringing to the hut, 'and open my wrist?'

'*Yep, that's what you do.*'

'Yeah, right.'

'*I mean it, Danny. Don't cut too deep, he only needs a couple of pints.*'

'A couple of pints?' Danny said, in his finest Tony Hancock. 'That's nearly an armful.'

'*Get on with it,*' said the voice.

Danny put down the knife in a hurry. 'You're *not* kidding, are you?' he said.

'*I never kid, Danny. I don't have time to kid.*'

'Yeah, well you can forget it. If it needs a bit of blood to get it started, I'll get some from the butcher's.'

155

'*You already did. It didn't work.*'

'What do you mean, I already did?'

'*Cut, Danny. Feed the dog. It's a nice woofy friendly dog. It's your dog. I made it all for you. You don't mind chipping in with a paltry pint or two of blood, surely?*'

'I don't like this,' said Danny. 'If I didn't know better, I'd be tempted to think—'

'*Shut up!*' said the voice. '*I'm fed up with your thinking. All you ever do is think. And a load of old rubbish you think too.*'

'You don't know what I think.'

'*Of course I know what you think. I do most of your thinking for you now anyway.*'

'Listen,' said Danny, 'I don't like this. I *do* want the dog. But I don't like *this*. Would you kindly leave my head for a moment? I have to think.'

'*Pick up the knife, Danny. Pick up the knife.*'

'I certainly will not.'

'*You certainly will too.*'

And outside was quiet on the allotment. Midnight quiet. Nice full moon up on high, whitening the highlights and blackening the shadows. A skulking cat that might have been the giant feral Tom of legend. Or then again might not. An earwig in a flowerpot. Pupating larvae of the order *Dictyoptera*. A sleeping drunk called Hermogonies K. Thukrutes from another book entirely (but a great one).*

All was peace. Tranquillity.

But then the midnight quiet imploded. From Danny's shed there came a scream. An awful scream it was and one torn from a human throat.

A potty-filler of a scream, it rang and echoed, clanged and bashed about the hallowed ground.

And then a choking strangled cry and then a slurping licking sound. And then . . . And then . . .

*A pound for the first correct answer on a postcard.

Full moon above.

A werewolf's moon.

A howl. Long drawn, deep-throated howl.

'*Aaaaaooooooooooooooooooooooowh!*'

It went.

Then silence.

16

'You get fucked and you learn.'

JOE PERRY, 1990

TERRIER AT MY TROUSERS

I wandered in my nine-league boots
(My 'tens' were at the menders),
To where the toffs in Sunday suits
(the hobnobs and big spenders)
Were sauntering among the crowds
(upon that Sunday, sunny),
And I was sitting on a bench
(I hadn't any money).

But I got up, to take the air
(and try again to make it).
When a terrier with wiry hair
Took hold of me by the cobblers!
(I didn't half shout I can tell you.)

IT'S THE BLEEDING MEKON

Danny awoke from a dream like the cover of a *Carcass* album.*

He jerked up to flounder around in his bed. But he wasn't in his bed. He stared up at his ceiling. But it wasn't his ceiling. It was the roof of his allotment shed. Oh no.

'Oh no,' Danny went. 'Oh God, no!' and he clutched at his face and felt the sticky pull of his hands. It was blood. His blood. 'No, no, no.'

It was yes, yes, yes. Yes it was.

'Oh God, no,' Danny went and he gaped all around. There was blood all right. Everywhere. He was drenched in it.

Danny felt sick (well, you would). He struggled up and groaned. His left wrist was bound up with a ripped-off length of – 'My shirt!'

Danny dragged himself to his feet and swayed back and forwards. Giddy and ill. That hadn't happened? Had it? Say it hadn't happened. Not the Stanley knife and his wrist and the dog licking and drinking and howling? That howl, that terrible howl. That hadn't really happened, had it? No!

'It's gone.' Danny stared at the bench. 'Princey's gone. Where is it? What have you made me do?'

There was silence.

Danny shook his head and banged at his temples. 'What did you make me do? What happened? I'm talking to you. Answer me. Answer me.'

But no answer came.

'You're not there.' Danny shook his head again, rooted a gory finger into his left earhole. 'You've gone. You've left me. Where are you? Where are you?'

But it *had* gone. The thing that had possessed him. And suddenly terrible thoughts came to Danny, terrible memories of things he had done. Hideous things. Inhuman things.

*The first one, *Reek of Putrefaction*. (Still their best, in my opinion.)

Murderous things. And not just to Mrs Roeg, but to others also.

'No,' Danny screamed. 'I didn't do those things. Those are not my memories. No they're not. They're not.'

But somehow they were.

'I'm ill.' Danny ran his sticky fingers through his matted hair. 'I've gone mad or something. Something's happened to me. Oh God. Oh God.'

On the bench lay a broken shard of mirror glass. Danny gazed into it. Then fell back in horror at what he saw.

He was a wreck: great black bags under his eyes, sunken cheeks, chalk-white skin beneath the flecks of blood.

He looked as if he hadn't slept or eaten for days. And he felt horrendous, hungertorn, ravaged.

'This is *not* happening. This is *not* happening.'

Danny lurched to the door of his shed and flung it open. Sunlight roared in. It had to be midday.

Danny stumbled outside and collapsed. He raised himself onto his elbows and crawled over to a nearby water-butt.

'Clean yourself up,' he told himself. 'No-one must see you like this.' And with the kind of Herculean effort that made Monty of Alamein, Roy of the Rovers and Joy of Sex whatever they were, he dragged himself up and plunged his face into the stagnant water.

It felt like champagne.

Danny raised his head with a great gasp, tore off his blood-spattered jacket and flung it to the ground. His shirt wasn't too bad. The strip had been torn off the tail. Danny tucked his shirt back into his trousers. He was in a pretty terrible state. He needed food.

More than that he needed a drink.

A big stiff one.

Danny took great breaths up his nostrils. Great head-clearing breaths. They never work. If anything they just make you feel worse.

Danny felt worse.

'I really really need a drink!' he said and he staggered from the allotment.

As Danny staggered along he became aware that he did feel very strange indeed. He felt somehow empty. Well not empty, but as if some part of him was missing. It was difficult to explain. Impossible to explain. He'd never felt anything like it before. It had to be the loss of blood.

Or something.

Danny staggered into Moby Dick Terrace. Moby Dick Terrace. Scene of the terrible murder. The murder of Mrs Roeg. And others. Which he somehow . . . he somehow . . .

Danny staggered *out* of Moby Dick Terrace most speedily, crossed the precinct. The High Street. Into Horseferry Lane.

Folk were looking at him. Hardly surprising. Danny put his shoulders back, affected a cheery grin. They still looked.

Danny looked back and smiled. And then he stopped smiling. Quite quickly. They didn't look right, these people. They looked all wrong. Blurry somehow. Danny pinched at his eyes. Did some refocusing. No, they still looked wrong. They didn't look quite in focus. Everything else did – the road, the shops, the cars. But not the people.

Danny blinked and blinked again.

The people looked completely wrong. There was something draped about their shoulders. Rising up above their heads. Something odd. Something odious. Something he seemed to hate.

'Pull yourself together, Danny boy.' Danny stopped short in his staggering tracks. 'I said that, didn't I? It wasn't . . . ? No, it wasn't, it was me. I am *me*, no-one else. Nothing else. Just me.'

Danny staggered on. The Shrunken Head loomed only yards before. A truly welcoming sight. A bit more staggering and he was at its door. A young man was leaving as Danny approached. Danny stared at the young man and the young man stared back. Danny did some more blinking. What *was* that thing the young man had upon his shoulders? Grey and

161

out of focus. He got the impression of an overlarge head, two black staring eyes. Spindly limbs.

'Drink,' said Danny. 'I need a drink.'

The young man pushed past him and went on his way.

Danny entered The Shrunken Head.

There was more of a crowd than yesterday, but a rough-looking crowd it was. All the local tattooed dregs, by the shape of it. The big-bellied lads with the rank-smelling armpits and the pit bull terriers called Arnie.

Danny eased himself into the crush and made for the bar.

'Morning, Danny,' said Sandy. 'Be with you in a moment.'

'Yes, please do.' Danny found a vacant barside stool and dropped down upon it. He took further deep breaths and tried to steady his disintegrated nerves. He was in some kind of big trouble and he just knew it.

'So what will it be?' asked Sandy.

'Large Scotch please and—' Danny gawped at Sandy. 'What is *that*?'

'What?' Sandy asked.

'That,' said Danny, pointing. 'That.'

Sandy looked up above his own head. 'What are you pointing at?'

Danny could see the thing clearly. In the half-light of the bar it was plainly visible. It sat upon the barman's shoulders, a frail, naked thing, its fragile legs dangling down the barman's lapels. It was all-over grey with narrow shoulders, a slender neck and a great swollen hairless head. It had huge black slanting eyes, a tiny nose, a slit of a mouth. Long, delicate fingers caressed the barman's head, the fingertips seeming almost to enter it.

'That,' said Danny. 'That!'

'What?'

'Oh,' said Danny. 'I get it.'

'You do?'

'I do. It's a new theme idea for the pub, isn't it? Let me

guess, Science Fiction Lunch-times, that's it, isn't it? It's the bleeding Mekon.'

'The bleeding what?'

'You know, out of *Dan Dare* comics. You know. You know.' Danny turned upon his stool and perused the patrons. 'They've all got one. How's it done then? They look transparent.'

'Are you all right, Danny?' asked Sandy. 'Because you look rather strange.'

'Come on,' said Danny. 'Don't wind me up.'

The barman turned to draw off Danny's whisky. Then he stiffened and turned back. Danny saw the thing on his shoulders incline its head, stare deeply into Danny's eyes, then up to a spot above his head.

As Danny looked on, the thing became agitated. Its fingers worked and worked upon the barman's head. Massaging. Massaging.

'What's going on?' Danny asked.

'*Clear*,' whispered the barman in a voice that was not his own. 'You're a *clear*.'

'What's that? What is *that*?'

'*Clear*.'

'Clear?'

At the word all conversation ceased. Heads began to turn. Grey things stared. Tall men began to stoop and the things that rode upon their shoulders appeared from out of the ceiling, the black eyes darting, shoulders vibrating, slender knees digging in against the human cheeks. As if they were horsemen. Riders.

'What's going on?' Danny looked from one to another of them. 'Something's happening here. This isn't right. This isn't right.'

'*Clear*,' said the barman in the strange unearthly voice. The voice. *The* voice. The voice that had been in his head. The voice he had never actually heard. Just felt. Just experienced. That was the voice. That was the way it sounded.

'*Clear*,' said a fat-bellied fellow with tattoos.

The same voice.

'*Clear*,' said a woman with a straw hat.

Same again.

'*Clear*,' they went. '*Clear. Clear. Clear. Kill the clear. Kill the clear. Kill the clear.*'

'No.' Danny shook his head vigorously. And it hurt when he did it. 'No, stop this. Whatever it is. Stop it.'

'*Clear!*' and a fat-bellied fellow threw a pint glass.

Danny ducked and the glass hit Sandy square in the face.

The barman didn't seem to notice. With blood now streaming from his forehead he continued the terrible chant. '*Kill the clear. Kill the clear. Kill the clear.*'

'No, this is madness.' Danny leapt from his stool as another pint pot flew at him. He pushed aside a scrawny youth who lunged forward, the grey rider on his shoulders spurring him on, a twisted leer on its lipless mouth.

'No!' Danny ran. As he burst through the door he bumped into The Kid. 'Thank God.' Danny stared. Though made pale by the sunlight one of them was there. Perched upon The Kid's shoulders, clinging to his head. 'You too!'

'Me what?'

'*Clear*,' cried the advancing crowd.

'*Clear?*' went The Kid and the thing upon him glared down at Danny.

'Bloody Hell!' Danny pushed The Kid aside and ran.

He was in no fit state to run.

But it really did seem the absolutely right thing to do. What with 'Kill the clear' and everything.

Danny ran.

Up Horseferry Lane he ran. They were tumbling out of the pub after him, he glanced back to see them, falling over one another, trampling on the fallen. Howling. Howling.

Danny ran.

He made it to the High Street. There had to be safety there. Amongst people. Sanity. In films if you're chased by monsters

164

you're saved if you make it to civilization, to where the normal folk hang out.

Danny huffed and puffed in the High Street.

The mob poured on in hot pursuit. They weren't letting up.

'Help,' wailed Danny, resuming his run. 'Help! Help!'

Shoppers turned at the commotion. Normal folk. Civilization. And on their shoulders. Danny could see them. The unnatural shapes. They were there. Everybody had one.

'Oh my good God.'

And the heads were turning. The Riders over their heads were turning, staring at him. Glaring at him. Danny pushed shoppers aside. And ran and ran.

And tripped and fell.

And the mob caught up. Closed in upon him.

'Leave me alone!' bawled Danny, rising and kicking and punching. 'Get off me. There's something bad on you. Leave me alone.'

But that wasn't what they had in mind.

Fists rained upon him. Feet lashed out.

'No!' went Danny, covering his head. 'No, no, no.'

But they were screaming in their weird unnatural voices. Screaming and screaming.

And hitting and kicking.

'No!'

And then there were howls of pain. But not Danny's pain. A white van veered from the road and into the crowd. It mashed folk aside and swerved to a halt beside Danny. A door flew open. A pale hand extended.

A voice whispered harshly those now legendary words, 'Come with me if you want to live.'

And Danny did.

He really did.

17

AGENCIES OF DISPATCH

He called up the agencies of dispatch.
The dark forces.
The gas-filled beings that dwell below the floorboards.
The undersides of the Hotpoint.
The horrid fluff.
The hairs upon the collar that are not your own.
The odd sock you do not recognize.
The sugar bowl that has moved.
The door that bangs without a wind.
The rattle in the dead of night.
The smell of a strange cigar.
The light bulb that went out without warning.
The thing that brushed against you in the darkened
    corridor.

He called up the agencies of dispatch.
But they were at lunch.
So he left a message.

FOOD FOR THOUGHT

The driver put the white van into gear. Wheels spun and rubber burned. The mob burst asunder, howling curses, like you would. The van leapt forward off the pavement, grazing cars and burning further rubber, through the red lights, scattering pedestrians, upending cyclists, missing by a fraction this and that.

Then on and on. Away and away.

And fast.

Danny clung to the dashboard, crazy-eyed and on the point of gibber. He flashed his crazy eyes towards the driver, looked at him long and hard. The smart dark suit. The swept-back hair. The mirrored shades. And looked him up and down, especially up.

'Duck your head,' gasped Danny. 'Duck your head.'

'My head?' The voice a rasping whisper.

'Just duck it, please.'

The driver ducked his head. And Danny looked at him hard again. 'You're safe,' he sighed. 'You haven't got one on you.'

'One of *what*, is that?'

'One of them. The monsters. The aliens.'

'Aliens, you say?'

'It's got to be it. It's got to be.'

'It has?'

'It has.' Danny gagged to find his breath. Found some of it and held that as best he could. 'Something terrible's happened. Terrible. Those people back there, who were attacking me. They had these things on them. Aliens.'

'Really?' said the driver. 'Aliens?'

'I'm not joking. And I'm not mad. Aliens, big bulbous heads, black eyes. Like the ones in that film *Communion*, except they were really badly animated in that. These were real. It must have happened last night.'

'Last night?'

'An invasion. Like *Invasion of the Body Snatchers* but without the pods. Earth got invaded last night. Or Brentford did. They got everyone, but they didn't get me. I was in my allotment shed. So they didn't get me. That *has* to be it. It *has* to.'

'I'm afraid it's not,' whispered the driver. 'But it's a plausible theory though. I expect if I were in your shoes, it's the one I'd have come up with.'

'You would? I mean, hang about. Who are you anyway? Why did you rescue me?'

'My name is Vrane. Parton Vrane. We've met before.'

'I don't think we have, I'd remember you. You know who you look like, by the way?'

'Gary Busey?' said the driver.

'People have told you that before, eh?'

'Actually no. Hold tight now, I'm going to take a hard left at the roundabout.'

'You can slow down. We've lost them.'

'They'll be looking for us. They'll search.'

'You saw them too. You did, didn't you?'

'I saw them. I've always been able to see them.'

'*Always*? What do you mean by that? And when have we met before? And why did you save me? You're not answering my questions.'

'I've answered all the ones about names.'

The van pulled a very hard left and Danny fell across the driver, he struggled to right himself. 'Tell me what is going on,' he demanded.

'Where is the dog?'

'The dog? What dog? Oh shit, the dog. Are you a policeman? I don't feel well.' Danny clasped at his head. 'I'm really ill. I'm going to pass out.'

'Stay awake a bit longer, Mr Orion. I have to talk to you.'

'*Mr Orion*? How do you know my name?'

'I've been following you.'

'Let me out.' Danny rattled at the door handle. It wouldn't budge. 'Let me out. Stop the van.'

'That really wouldn't be a good idea.'

'Stop the van!' Danny tried to put a lot of menace into his voice. He was only fooling himself though.

'All right.' Parton Vrane swerved the van into the kerb. 'Wind down the window, have a look out.'

Danny wound down the window. They were in a side-road bordering Gunnersbury Park. There were few folk about. A man and a woman. The woman was pushing a baby buggy.

'Thanks for helping me.' Danny tried the handle once more. Without success.

'Just look out.'

Danny just looked out. The couple were approaching. Young chap in a shell suit, woman in a baggy T-shirt and those horrendous multi-coloured leggings that not even Claudia Schiffer could make look appealing. Sprog in a miniature football strip.* And then Danny saw them. The Riders. Perched upon the shoulders of the adults. And the child too! Even the child.

Danny let out a strangled cry and hastily wound up the window. 'Drive. Just Drive. Don't stop.'

'As you wish.' The driver drove on.

'I *am* going to pass out,' said Danny. 'I *am*. I really am.'

'There's food in the glove compartment.'

'Oh thanks.' Danny fumbled open the glovey. He found a carton of milk and some sandwiches (egg) in a triangular plastic container. Danny tore open the milk carton, put it to his mouth. He took a long deep draught, then spat milk all over the windscreen.

'Careful there,' said Parton Vrane.

'It's off,' Danny spluttered and coughed. 'It's bad. It's—' He examined the sell-by date. 'It's two weeks' old. Disgusting. You bastard!'

'Sorry. I like it like that.'

---

*Whichever one Manchester United had invented as *this month's* new design. Bastards!

'You what?' Danny clawed at his tongue. Held up the pack of sandwiches. 'These too. They're going furry inside.'

'Lovely. Tear them open will you and give me one.'

'You're joking.'

'I'm not.'

'Yeah, right. Go on then.' Danny tore the pack open. The sandwiches smelt pretty rank and added to the stench of the milk, the van, although perhaps still a safe place to be, was no longer a pleasant one. Danny handed the pack and its revolting contents to the driver. 'Go on. Tuck in.'

'I will.' Parton Vrane tucked in. The plastic pack as well.

'Oh my good God.' Danny turned his face away. And had his stomach any contents to yield up, it would certainly have yielded them. Probably in a projectile fashion.

'Do you always behave so rudely when others are trying to eat?' asked Parton Vrane.

'When they're eating garbage, yes.'

'One man's garbage is another man's feast.'

'Bollocks,' said Danny. 'And I *am* going to pass out.'

And he did.

He awoke to stare bleary-eyed at yet another ceiling. Danny wondered, for a moment, if perhaps this was to be his fate, always to get into some kind of dire trouble and always to awaken looking up at yet another ceiling. And then he stopped wondering that and he screamed.

'Aaaaaaagh!' he went, because that is how you scream, when you scream, if you're a man. It's the accepted mode of screaming. Although sometimes (if it's really loud and dramatic) it's conveyed in capital letters. This one wasn't that loud, but it was loud enough to raise attention.

'Are they on me? Are they on me?' Danny flapped and flapped at his head. 'Get them off. Get them off.'

'Calm yourself, Mr Orion. You're in safe hands now.'

The voice was not the harsh whisper of Parton Vrane. It was an educated English tone.

Danny looked up at a chap with a monocle and a toupee, looming above him. He glanced all about his present environment. A big airy room. Portrait of Her Majesty. Victorian busts. Leather Chesterfields. He was lying on one of them.

'Well,' said Danny, 'this makes a change.' And then he stared hard at the chap with the monocle. And up and over his head.

'You're safe,' said Danny.

'I'm *clear*,' said the gentleman. 'And so are you. What we'd like to know is, *how*?'

Danny sat up and sunk his head into his hands. 'Feed me,' he pleaded. 'I don't care who you are or where I am. Just feed me. Please.'

'On the trolley.' The gentleman gestured to a chromium wheelabout, laden with silver food domes, a coffee pot, cup, milk jug, toast in a rack.

'Oh, thank you. Thank you.' Danny tucked in like a mad thing.

The gentleman sat behind his grand desk watching. The munching and chomping and thrusting-into-the-mouth of and munching and chomping some more. 'Everything to your liking?' he asked.

'Just perfect.' Danny wiped marmalade from his chin, sniffed the milk jug suspiciously then grinned and downed its contents at a gulp.

The gentleman raised his non-monocled eyebrow and pursed his lips. The working class! he thought. Savages all. When they weren't beating their wives, abusing their children and getting drunk, they were spending their cash on the National Lottery. Which was their only saving grace, as no-one else was going to finance the National Opera.★

'Where am I?' asked Danny, filling his face as he did so. 'No, don't tell me, I know. This is a top-secret room, isn't it? In one of those big Whitehall buildings. I bet it looks out

★A rather poor attempt at satire and a rather out-of-date one.

at Big Ben.' He stood up and looked. 'Told you.' He sat down again and ate on.

'Very good, Mr Orion. Although a mite messy.' The gentleman flicked food flecks from his desk top. 'If you wouldn't mind swallowing before you speak again.'

'Sorry. Oops, sorry again.'

'Just finish your breakfast.'

'Thanks. Sorry. Thanks. S—'

'Just eat.'

'Mmm.'

At length, and at some length it was, Danny stopped eating. He would have eaten more, but all the plates were empty. He felt a lot better for it and he belched mightily.

The gentleman shook his head in disgust and thought about the National Opera House.

'Where's the bloke who looks like Gary Busey?' Danny asked. 'I assume he brought me here. Am I under arrest, by the way?'

'You're not under arrest.'

'Oh good, then I'll be off.'

'Really? And to where?'

Danny thought about this. There were an awful lot of folk in the heart of London and if they all had one of those things, one of those *Riders* . . . 'I could hang about for lunch,' said Danny. 'I don't have anything pressing on today.'

'That's the spirit. I think you're going to be a real asset to us, Mr Orion.'

'Oh, I do hope so,' said Danny.

'Was that sarcasm?' the gentleman asked.

'It certainly was.'

'Refreshing. Most refreshing.'

'My pleasure. Did I just take a late breakfast, by the way? Is it time for the mid-morning coffee-break?'

The gentleman rang a little bell and presently coffee arrived on a tray. Well, in a pot actually, but the pot was on a tray.

Danny didn't waste too much time on the semantics, he got stuck in. 'Oh, biscuits too. Splendid.'

'When you are quite finished, Mr Orion, we really do have most important matters to discuss.'

'About the aliens?'

'The aliens, quite so.'

'I've been thinking,' said Danny. 'I think quite a lot, you know. Although nobody gives me any credit. Probably because I never tell them what I'm thinking. But while I've been eating, I've been thinking.'

'That's very interesting.'

Danny waggled a bourbon bicky at the gentleman. 'And *that's* sarcasm.'

'What have you been thinking?'

'Nukes,' said Danny.

'Sorry?' said the gentleman.

'Nuclear weapons. It's the only way. That or the common cold. The common cold killed the aliens in *War of the Worlds*. I do a lot of thinking about movies.'

'Mr Vrane did mention it.'

'I met him before,' said Danny, 'in old Sam Sprout's house. I've got terrible memories in my head.'

'You're bearing up very well.'

'You have to laugh,' said Danny. 'You'd cry if you didn't.'

'Please spare me the working-class homilies. You'll be singing *Roll out the barrel* next. Can we get on, please?'

Danny finished his coffee and biscuits. 'My time is all yours,' said he. 'Until lunch and possibly through till tea.'

'Perish the thought.'

'What do you want to know?'

'I want to know how you came to be clear. I want to know what happened to the dog.'

'The dog in my shed?'

'The dog in your head.'

'You *what*?'

The gentleman sighed. 'I will have to explain everything

173

to you. It is a long story, you'd better make yourself comfortable.'

'Before I do,' said Danny, 'do you think I could use your toilet?'

It was nearing lunch-time by the time the gentleman had finished filling Danny in on all the gory details. Danny sat throughout the talk, opening and shutting his mouth, shaking his head and adding the occasional 'Oh my God', or 'This is terrible'. When the gentleman had finally done, he smiled across to Danny and said, 'And there you have it.'

And Danny did.

But he didn't know quite where to start.

'So you're saying,' he said, 'that I've had one of these Rider things on me since the moment I was born?'

'Correct.'

'But then this new one, this one that calls itself Demolition, also got on me at old Sam's house? But has now got off me and got into the dog that was built in my shed.'

'Correct.'

'Which is why I can see them now?'

'Correct.'

'No, not correct. I shouldn't be able to see them, because I should still have the Rider I got when I was born, on me.'

'Yes, that's correct also. That's what puzzles us.'

'It puzzles me too. Unless—'

'Go on.'

'Unless the Demolition one *killed* the one that was already on me. After all, if the Demolition one drives men to kill other men and the other men have these things on them, when they get killed, the things on them get killed too.'

'That would appear to be the case.'

'But why do they do it? Why kill their own?'

'That's something we'd like to know. If we could capture Demolition we might persuade him to tell us.'

'Some hopes,' said Danny. 'No, the best way is definitely

nukes. Get all the clears together in a deep bomb shelter somewhere. Then nuke the entire planet. That would be my solution.'

'Wipe out everyone on the face of the earth?'

'It's the cruel-to-be-kind approach. It may seem drastic, but it will get the job done.'

'We have considered it,' said the gentleman.

'You bastard, I was only joking.'

'I wasn't. But it's not a practical option. We must purge the planet of these things. But not at the expense of the human race.'

'Have you thought about trying to communicate with them?' Danny asked. 'Perhaps they have a leader. You could talk to him.'

The gentleman tried to remember whether he had a moustache or not. Concluding that he *had*, he stroked it thoughtfully.

'That is a new suggestion,' he said.

'I'm full of bright ideas,' said Danny. 'I'm feeling a bit peckish too.'

'Communicate with their leader,' the gentleman said, steering the conversation away from food. 'It is an interesting thought. But who would their leader be?'

'Come on,' said Danny. 'That's bloody obvious, isn't it?'

'Strangely, not to me.'

Danny shook his head. 'Well, it is to me. These things settle upon you the moment you're born. They manipulate your thoughts, they make you do what they want you to do, right?'

'Right. I mean, correct.'

'So if one's really smart and ambitious it will urge its human host to do smart things, advance himself, correct? Get to the top.'

'That would seem logical.'

'So the smartest one will be the leader, and he'll be the one who has urged on his human host to—'

175

'I get it,' said the gentleman. 'You mean that—'

'Exactly,' said Danny.

'The Prime Minister,' said the gentleman.

'*Richard Branson*,' said Danny. 'Is it lunch-time yet?'

18

FAMOUS MEN'S SHOES

Down beside the woolly tracks,
Where the trunkers rot and crumble,
And the ends of rusted metal,
Melt amid the callous nettle.
There are Chad and Nigel Parker,
Searching for the boots.

Searching for the clog and slipper.
For the brogue with leather upper,
And the sandal and the lace-up.
Each one smiles and shows its face up.
Here a dab and patent fellow, hidden by the roots.

Here amongst discarded footwear,
Here the long-forgotten Blakey.
Where the strings are old and knotted,
Shop-soiled, rain-spoiled, cold and spotted,
Famous men have left their cast-offs mid the
    flowering shoots.

Could this be Charles Laughton's toecap?
Did this sound Gene Kelly's toe-tap?
Has this ragged tongue known Bogart?
Was this dabbled mocco so smart?
Famous shoes of famous people, left in weedy flutes.

Chad and Nigel delving deftly,
By the loafer of Bing Crosby,
And Jack Hulbert's glossy dance pump,
And his Cissy's lamé strutter,
Lying face down in the gutter,
Earns no more the gold-top butter.

Echoes in no ancient dance hall.
Gone its final one more house call.
Or the dusted debs at hunt ball.
Bleak and wretched, cast and castless,
Present, future and the pastless.
Doomed to moulder by the railside.
Famous people's shoes.

LONG POEM, SHORT CHAPTER, BUT AN IMPORTANT ONE

Danny talked to the gentleman through lunch, through the afternoon, through high tea (which gentlemen take), into the early evening and then into dinner (which is sometimes called supper by those who eat lunch at dinner-time and unwittingly support the National Opera House). The conversation took many tortuous routes, which wound through much rich and fantastic countryside, to finally arrive back pretty much at the point where it had begun.

The gentleman concluded that Danny really did not possess any insights and Danny concluded that the gentleman really did not possess any insights and then the two of them shared wine and brandy and cigars and eventually came to the conclusion that each and the other shared all sorts of insights, were the absolute salt of the earth, a soul-buddy, a hail-fellow-well-met, a bloody good bloke and a dear, dear friend.

'I don't really hate the working class,' said the gentleman, leaning heavily on Danny's shoulder. 'They're rough diamonds, but they're OK, do you know what I mean?'

'Not half,' Danny put his arm about the gentleman. 'Actually they're crap,' he slurred. 'Posh is where it's at. Posh is OK. I like posh.'

'I'm posh,' said the gentleman, trying to focus his monocle.

'I can see you're posh. But I'm not posh. I'm common as muck, me.'

'But a bloody good bloke. May I call you a bloke, by the way?'

'You call me one. I don't mind.'

'Good bloke. Bloody good bloke.'

'Good brandy,' said Danny. 'Shall we have some more?'

'Let's do.' The gentleman poured more brandy. Some even went into the glasses. 'You're a good bloke,' he said. 'Did I tell you you're a good bloke?'

'You did. But I'm not posh.'

'Posh is crap,' said the gentleman. 'Crap.'

'Is it?' Danny asked.

'You have to go to the opera.'

'Urgh,' said Danny. 'I wouldn't fancy that.'

'I don't fancy it. No-one fancies it. If it wasn't for you blokes and your bloody lottery tickets, we wouldn't have to have a bloody opera.'

'I've never bought a lottery ticket,' said Danny. 'I reckon it's a conspiracy. I reckon it's a fix. That bloke Paul Daniels, he could make any ball he wanted come up.'

'I can do that,' said the gentleman. 'Learned it at Sandhurst. You take a deep breath and sort of hitch up one side of your groin.'

Danny collapsed in drunken laughter. 'You arsehole,' he said.

'See,' said the gentleman. 'See. Not posh. We wouldn't say that. We would say . . . er, what would we say?'

'Have another drink?' Danny suggested.

'Yes, that's what we'd say. Have another drink.'

'Well, just you say it. Bugger 'm. You say it.'

'I will.' The gentleman swayed to and fro. 'What was it I was going to say?'

'I've forgotten,' said Danny. 'I think it was about balls. But not yours.'

'Are you saying I've got no balls?'

'Lottery balls,' said Danny.

'Listen,' said the gentleman, drawing Danny near and making conspiratorial hushing movements with his hand. 'That's a fit up, you know, that lottery.'

'Get away,' said Danny.

'Sorry, am I too close?'

'No. I meant, a fit up. I said that just now, didn't I?'

'You said it was that magician. That Paul Robeson.'

'Paul *who*?'

'Paul McCartney.'

'Never heard of him.'

'He was a Beatle. Like Parton Vrane.' The gentleman laughed foolishly.

'Parton Vrane was never in The Beatles.'

'No?'

'No, he was in The Small Faces.'

'He was in *Predator Two*,' said the gentleman, hiccuping loudly.

'Who, Steve Marriot?'

'No, Gary Busey. He looks like Gary Busey, doesn't he?'

'Who, Steve Marriot?'

'No, Parton Vrane. He looks like Parton Vrane.'

'Who, Steve Marriot?'

'Did you say, *I'd like a claret*?'

'No, *you* said that. I saw your mouth moving.'

'Ventriloquists,' said the gentleman. 'You never see *their* mouths moving. Now *that's* magic.'

'Paul Daniels,' said Danny. 'Now *that's* magic. Paul Daniels.'

'That's the fellow,' said the gentleman. 'That's who you said fixes The National Lottery. You're right. It *is* him.'★

'What, he really *does* fix it?'

'Of course. You didn't think it was real, did you?'

'No,' said Danny. 'I told you it's not real.'

'You're right,' the gentleman agreed. 'How did you know?'

'Paul Daniels,' said Danny. 'Whoever would have thought it?'

'You've got me,' said the gentleman. 'I'd never have guessed.'

'Makes you think,' said Danny. 'That Paul Daniels, he can put his wife in a box, saw her in half, move the bits apart, then put them back together and she's not even harmed.'

'Well,' said the gentleman, 'actually that's a pretty crap old trick, when you come to think of it.'

'Yeah, you're right,' said Danny. 'Are we sitting, or standing?'

'Sitting.'

'Ah good, I thought I'd fallen onto my bottom in a sitting position. Easy mistake.'

'Crap trick though.'

'Yes, you're right. Crap trick. That David Copperfield, he—'

'Liked him, hated her.'

'Who her?'

'Woman who got jilted on her wedding day, sat about in her dress with mice running all over the cake. You know the woman, can't abide her.'

★(Allegedly – phew!)

181

'Debbie Magee? And you mean *Great Expectations*, not *David Copperfield*.'

'Are you trying to confuse me, young man?'

'David Bloody Copperfield,' Danny shouted this. 'Sorry,' he continued. 'He's a *real* magician. He made the Statue of Liberty vanish.'

'No?'

'Yes, and a passenger train.'

'No?'

'Yes. And Australia. I think. He's a real bloody magician. He could make anything vanish, he could. Anything.'

'Anything?'

'Even *you*.'

'Even me?'

'You. He could make you vanish. He'd put a cloth over your head, then there'd be a bit of jiggery-pokery out of sight of the camera. Then you'd vanish – gone.'

'Gone? I'd be gone?' The gentleman, who was sitting down, sat down further and a tear came to his monocle. 'I'd just be vanished away?'

'Like you'd never been born,' said Danny, snapping his fingers.

'Boo hoo,' grizzled the gentleman. 'I'd be like I'd never been born. Horrid magician. Take him away.'

'Eh?' went Danny.

'I don't want to be vanished,' wept the gentleman. 'Horrid magician.'

'Don't take it personally,' said Danny, patting the gentleman. 'Cheer up now, do.'

'I don't want to be vanished,' blubbered the gentleman. 'You tell him for me, will you? Next time you see him. Tell him to vanish someone else.'

'I will.' Danny patted the gentleman again. 'I'll tell him, you leave my friend alone. Vanish someone else. Who would you like him to vanish?'

The gentleman scratched his toupee, which took an

alarming list to the port side. 'Tell him to vanish The Riders,' said he. 'Make *them* disappear.'

'Yeah. That's what I'll tell him. *Here*—' and Danny did that sobering up that you do when something really dramatic happens, like you run into a tree driving home, or a nun, or a Bigfoot, or something. 'That's it! You've got it!'

'I have? I have? Get it off me then.'

'That's the answer.' Danny punched his left palm with his right fist. 'We'll vanish them. Magic them away.'

'Oh,' said the gentleman, dabbing at his eyes with an oversized red gingham handkerchief from another story. 'So this David Copperfield can magic The Riders away, can he?'

'Not him,' said Danny. 'But I know a man who can.'

19

WINSTON'S HAIRCUT*

On a red hot day in August,
When Jim was passing by.†
Winston stepped into Stravino's dad's,
Saying, 'Give us a haircut, says I.'

So the Greek took his comb and his scissors,
And spat on the palms of his hands.
Then he snipped and he snapped, saying, 'How was the
  match?
Did you get a good seat in the stands?'

The hair flew like rats from a tanker,
And knee-deep in fluff stood the Greek.
Snipping away with a will and a spirit,
Quite odd for that time of the week.

There was hair on the shelves and the shutters.
There was hair in the cracks of the door.
There was hair in the cups and the cupboards,
And no small amount on the floor.

*With a brief appearance from Jim Pooley.
†That was it.

184

And when the Greek finished, he fainted,
And had to be given a beer,
And Winston looked into the mirror,
And said, 'It's a bit short, isn't it, guv?'

LEGION

In his suddenly sober state Danny began to expand upon the thoughts that were now entering his head. He named Mickey Merlin and spoke of the spell of *Temporary Temporal Transference*.

This indeed would be the kiddie for getting to meet the King, or Emperor, or President or whatever of The Riders. A volunteer, suitably confined in a padded cell or suchlike, would recite the spell and temporarily change bodies with whoever the King, Emperor or whatnot controlled. Assuming, of course, that when you changed minds, then the controller of that mind would come along with it. There were lots of loose ends and probably a great deal of risk involved. But it was worth a go.

And if it failed, well, Mickey might just have a spell to vanish the lot of them. Well, he *might*.

Anything was possible.

Danny spoke most eloquently of his thoughts. And it would have been evident to anyone who heard him speak, that here was a young man who was definitely coming into his own. Sadly, however, there was no-one to hear him speak, as the gentleman had passed out and lay upon one of the Chesterfields, snoring softly.

Danny finally tired of talking to himself. His discourse was wandering into esoteric fields, ballroom dancing, crop rotation, the direction the water might go down the plug hole if you emptied your bath on a satellite circling the globe, and how, all things considered, if he ever got out of this alive and all became normal, he was not going to buy a Labrador, but a bloody big Rottweiler.

And then Danny became aware that he was drunk once more and fell down behind the Chesterfield and slept.

It would be a comfortable night for Danny this time, as the rug was thick and cozy and he was sufficiently drunk as to sleep without being haunted by dreams of his dreadful doings.

And while Danny sleeps and the gentleman sleeps and for all we know The King of The Riders sleeps also, we might chance our arms to relate one final unrelated tale. It could be argued that it might not be one of the best. But it's not too long and it *is* the last, and these two points alone must surely act in its favour. It does concern possession and it somehow got left out earlier.

This is it.

Every Thursday evening at six of the clock, Lester Total would sit in his greenhouse amongst the forced tomatoes and fill in his football pools. He would rub the coupon with his lucky Joan the Wad, fold it with care and tuck it into the brown envelope. When sealing the flap and sticking on the stamp, he would wish very hard for a win.

Lester Total would then creep from his greenhouse, shin over his garden fence and pop the coupon into the post box on the corner of Sprite Street.

Normally this was akin to clockwork, but this particular Thursday had been fraught with strange perils. Somehow his greenhouse had caught fire and been reduced to ashes, he had spilled ink onto his coupon and had to stick the envelope down with Sellotape.

Worse was to come.

Grumbling and cursing he had climbed over his fence, only to rip his trouser turn-up upon a nail which had certainly not been there the previous week.

Worse was to come.

Upon eventually reaching the post box, Lester had tried to pop his coupon into the slot. A rumble like thunder had issued from the hole and the envelope shot out to flutter onto the pavement at his feet.

Worse, however, was to come.

'What gives?' asked Lester, who read a lot of Lazlo Woodbine novels. 'What the God-damn gives?'

His second attempt proved as fruitless, in fact even more so, the precious envelope was returned to him in shreds.

Lester stared at these shreds in disbelief . . . his chance of a million pounds in little chewed up pieces. 'You mother f—' Lester screamed, kicking at the post box and damaging a winklepickered toe.

A great bowel-loosening roar, accompanied by a strong smell of brimstone, made him leap back most nimbly.

Lester turned round in circles and danced a foolish jig. 'Who's in there? You bastard! Come out here, you dirty—'

But his words were drowned by a deeply timbred voice, and one not unlike that of the now legendary Charles Laughton himself, which boomed the words, 'I AM LEGION. WE ARE MANY.'

And yes they *were* in capital letters and yes worse *was* yet to come.

Now to Lester Total, practising atheist and ex-tomato cultivator, the post box's words meant nothing. 'You just come out,' he cried, making fists and rolling up his sleeves (which is tricky to do at the same time). 'Come out and get your medicine.'

A gust of evil-smelling icy wind knocked him from his feet.

'Oh, you want to play dirty, eh?' yelled the game little fellow, who knew naught of devil possession and cared even less. 'Well, we'll see about that. We'll see about that.'

The post box gave vent to a stream of unprintable vulgarity, rounded off with a graphic description of the present sexual habits in Hell of Lester's long-deceased mum.

'Well,' said Lester, in a manner not unknown to Jack Benny.

A lady with a straw hat and matching shopper had been watching from the bus stop. 'Is it that Jeremy Beadle?' she asked.

The post box told her in no uncertain terms just what it would like to do to her. The lady left in a red-faced huff*, wishing desperately that her husband might be up to that kind of thing once in a while.

Lester stood and fumed.

The post box stood and smouldered.

'Right,' said Lester, sleeves now rolled and fists firmly made. 'This is your last chance. Come out now. Or I'm coming in.'

The post box offered a stinking belch.

'Right,' said Lester. 'That settles it.'

And just then Archroy drew up in a Robin Reliant that he had recently, with the aid of a kit he had bought through *Exchange and Mart*, converted into a Red-Faced Huff.†

'What's on the go?' asked Archroy, winding down the window. 'Why are you trying to climb into a post box?'

With stuttering speech and much fist-raising, Lester appraised Archroy as to the current state of affairs.

'Ah,' said Archroy, issuing from his Huff. 'That sounds to me like a case of flying starfish from Uranus.'

Archroy had pretty definite opinions on most things. Particularly the rising cost of milk, although that need not concern us here. 'I'll tell you what we need for this,' said Archroy. 'We need a bucket of chicken droppings.'

'We do?' Lester asked, whilst keeping his fists up. 'Are you sure we do?'

'Would you stay in there if some bastard dumped a bucket of chicken droppings on you?'

'Now there,' said Lester, 'you have a good point.'

---

*Possibly some sort of fur coat?
†Oh, that's what it is.

188

And Archroy did.

Now it might occur to the discerning reader that here the tale had reached a point which could well be described as 'far-fetched'.

After all, where would one come by a bucket of chicken droppings in Brentford?

'I'll pop over to the allotment and scoop one up from my chickens,' said Archroy, saving the tale's credibility.

And Archroy did.

'Right,' said he on returning. 'The bugger still in there?'

'Are you still in there, you bugger?' Lester shouted.

A nerve-shattering peal of laughter informed them that it (they) was (were).

'Well, check this out,' said Lester, hefting up the bucket.

There was a hideous scream and the post box rocked. Jets of steam blew hither and thus. There were rattlings and quiverings, voices cried in Latin, Greek and the Hebrew tongue. And then there was a kind of imploding bang and the post box returned to its normal self. Which wasn't a self at all, but just a post box.

'Gotcha,' said Lester.

A policeman stepped out from behind a parked Huff. 'I saw that,' said the Bobby. 'And you're both nicked.'

The magistrate gave Lester Total and Archroy three months apiece for tampering with the Queen's mail. He explained, during his summing up, that he would have been more lenient, but that he held the two of them directly responsible for the fact that his new Jaguar now answered to the name of Legion and refused to come out of the garage.

Such is life.

20

CONTRACTING DEADLY AILMENTS FROM WEARING JUMBLE SALE CLOTHING

Now I'm not much the kiddie for socks,
Because *I've* found they give you the pox.
Which is sad when you hear,
Quite a few every year,
Are sold by the bag and the box.

Now I'm not wearing vests cos I find,
That those suckers make you go blind.
Which is quite a rum do,
Cos I always wore two.
But I'm not getting called a wanker just because I can't see
  properly!

Now I care not for jackets of tweed,

That give you complaints you don't need.

Like piles and the flu,

and a dose of clap too,

And dirty big lumps that come up under your armpits and turn out to be cholera, or anthrax, or the plague or something equally unspeakable and make bits of you drop off in gangrenous scales and puss weep from cankerous wounds on the end of your—

And I'm giving the woollen combinations a miss also.

ACTION HOTTING UP

Inspector Westlake was not having a nice day. He'd had an early-morning phone call from Mr Gold-Top the milkman.

Mr Gold-Top had drawn the inspector's attention to the fact that bottles and newspapers were beginning to pile up upon the doorsteps of two houses on his round, and that both these houses were in Moby Dick Terrace.

With weary resignation the inspector got hurriedly onto the case and had his lads apply the big basher-in to the front doors in question. Revealing, to their shared horror, the new horrors within.

'Perhaps there's a gang of them,' said Constable Dreadlock, who had brought his box Brownie this time and was rapidly snapping pictures to sell to the gutter press. 'Or maybe it's the Council, trying to clear the area for redevelopment.'

'Morning, Westlake,' said Fridge-Magnet Gould. 'Trying for a new record, are we? Ooh, that's decorative, isn't it? How would you describe that?'

'It's a sort of maze,' said Constable Dreadlock. 'The small intestines have been stretched and laid out on the carpet. The inspector's trying to work out how you get to the head in the middle.'

'Shut up,' said Inspector Westlake, as it was the best he could manage under the circumstances. He wasn't really a 'murder' man, he was strictly a 'drug bust' man. You knew where you were with a drug bust. You got the tip off, stormed in, arrested the suspects (guilty parties), had them banged up, then divided the spoils and sold them off. That's the way he did business. The same as all inspectors★.

But madmen on the loose. Not his cup of tea at all.

'Any clues?' asked Fridge-Magnet, fanning at his nose.

'No,' said Inspector Westlake. 'None at all.'

'Well, there are some,' said the constable.

'Oh right.' Inspector Westlake glared at his inferior. 'Constable Breadlocker has solved the case.'

'It's *Dreadlock*, sir. Armenian, it means "He who walks through the cornfield eating a Cadbury's flake".'

'I thought you said it was Dutch yesterday.'

'No, yesterday I said it was German.'

'The Germans bombed my favourite chip shop in the war,' said the inspector. 'You can forgive a race just so much, but no more.'

'German on my mother's side,' said Constable Dreadlock. 'But actually I do think I've solved the case.'

'Oh, please do tell us then.' Inspector Westlake took to picking his nose.

'Well,' said the constable, 'remember in Mrs Roeg's back parlour, there was a carrier bag with an unopened bottle of Jim Beam and a packet of fags on the table.'

'Yes,' said the inspector, who actually did remember.

'Well, in the house we've just come from next door there

★*ALLEGEDLY.*

was a carrier bag on the table with a bottle of gin in it. And look over there.'

'What over there where the ribs have been piled together to resemble . . . ?'

'A greenhouse,' said Fridge-Magnet Gould. 'It looks like a greenhouse. Or the Crystal Palace. See the way the finger bones are stacked into little towers at each end.'

'Yes, well, over there,' said the constable. 'On the table. There's another carrier bag, with another bottle of gin sticking out.'

Inspector Westlake looked at the constable.

And the constable looked at Inspector Westlake.

And Fridge-Magnet Gould looked at the both of them. Dickheads, he thought.

'No, honestly. Come on, Inspector, sir. It's got to be it, hasn't it? It's the bloke at the off-licence.'

'Mr Doveston? How dare you? That man is a pillar of the community. He's a member of the Rotary Club. On the Special Functions Committee.'

'Not him,' said the constable. 'The weirdo with the white hair. The one who's always talking to himself.'

'Arrest the psycho,' cried Inspector Westlake.

The psycho was having his breakfast. 'Any more toast?' he asked.

'Not so loud,' said the gentleman, nursing his head.

'Any more toast?' whispered Danny.

'Not so loud with the damn chewing.'

'Sorry.'

The gentleman sipped black coffee. 'Do you know,' he said, 'now that you've repeated all the things you told me last night while I was napping, I think they have much to merit them. Assuming, of course, that you are not pulling my pudenda about this Mickey Merlin character.'

'He's the business,' said Danny. 'He was Hugh Giant once for an evening.'

'He told you *that*?'

'He did. I treated it with the contempt it deserved, of course.'

'Of course you did. But if it is true and this book of spells of his really works . . . Interesting possibilities.'

'I've been thinking,' said Danny.

'Oh dear,' said the gentleman.

'I was thinking that as I can't go back to my job and as I will be working with you until we've saved the world, I ought to be paid for my services.'

'*What?* I mean, pardon me?'

'It's only fair. You've been involved in this for years, I've been at it a matter of hours. I'm making all the good moves though, aren't I?'

'We might discuss something of a financial nature. But certainly not now.'

'Over lunch then.'

There was a knock at the door.

'Come,' said the gentleman.

The door opened and Parton Vrane entered the big airy room. 'Good-morning, sir, Danny,' he said.

'Sir Danny,' said Danny. 'A knighthood might be good also.'

'What have you to report, Mr Vrane?'

'The Brentford Constabulary have just raided Mr Orion's lodgings.'

'*What?*' Danny spat coffee all over the gentleman.

'You weren't a very careful serial killer,' said Parton Vrane.

'I wasn't any kind of serial killer. It wasn't me. It was the thing in my head.'

'I wonder how well that argument would stand up in court,' mused the gentleman. 'With all the jury seeing that you're a clear, and everything.'

'This is terrible.' Danny buried his head in his hands.

'Perhaps now would be the time to discuss rent.'

'Rent?' Danny moaned.

'Of the Chesterfield. Will you be staying long? Should I charge you by the week?'

Danny added a groan to his moan. And then he jumped to his feet. 'All right,' said he. 'No more mucking about. I want the monster that was in my head brought to justice. And I want all those other horrible things off all my friends and everyone else. Let's go and grab Mickey Merlin and his book of spells. Once we've got that far we can work out the rest.'

'Bold talk,' said the gentleman. 'But perhaps we should leave this side of it to Mr Vrane.'

'I'll go with him,' said Danny. 'And *I'll* talk to Mickey.'

'I don't know who this Mickey Merlin is,' said Parton Vrane. 'But whoever he is, his Rider will make him hate you, make him want to kill you.'

'We'll see.'

'This is very foolish,' said the gentleman.

'Yes,' agreed Danny. 'But it should be pretty exciting.'

21

Conscience is not the voice of God, but the fear of the police.

EXPLAINING METAPHYSICS
TO SMALL CHILDREN

'Well,' he begun,
And out in the sun,
The kids played at hopscotch and bowling the penny.
'Well,' he repeated,
'When you lot are seated,
I'll tell you of wonders I've never told any.'

'Well,' said the lads,
'We've heard from our dads,
About seafowl and gannets and birds of the air.'
'Well,' said the boys,
'We much prefer toys,
To the wheelings of planets and all that up there.'

'Well,' said the sage,

'When I was your age,

I cared for such trifles as tossing a rock.'

Well, in that case,

I'll go some other place,

And chat with some Arabs or Donny and Doc.

WHAT MAKES DANNY RUN?

They drove through the very streets of London Ralph McTell used to sing about. Not that Ralph would have liked what Danny saw as he was driven along. 'Have you seen the old bloke with the Rider on his shoulders, going to his office and he doesn't know a thing?' etc. Danny shuddered and kept low down in his seat.

'It's special glass,' Parton Vrane explained. 'No-one and no thing can see in.'

'All my life,' Danny shuddered. 'All my life I've had one of those things on my shoulders. Watching everything I did. Going to the toilet and—' Danny thought of that thing which all men do on a regular basis, but few if any are prepared to own up to.

'Pulling your plonker?' asked Parton Vrane.

'Leave it out,' said Danny. 'But while we're on the subject, do *you* have a plonker to pull? The gentleman told me you're half beetle. Do beetles have plonkers?'

'Big black ones,' said Parton Vrane. 'They'd frighten the life out of you.'

'Hmmph!' And Danny sank into silence.

It was naturally a while before they reached Brentford and during the journey Danny explained all about Mickey Merlin and his book of spells. Parton Vrane asked this question and that in his raspy-whispering dead-pan voice, and Danny couldn't be quite certain whether he was taking the piss or not.

'Are you taking the piss?' he asked.

'No,' said Parton Vrane.

'That's all right then.'

And onward they drove. The day was fine. The sky was blue and if it hadn't been for the burden of the terrible truth about the Riders' existence pushing down upon Danny's shoulders like a sumo wrestler's backside, he would have felt that natural sense of wonder and all-pervading well-being that everyone always feels as they enter the borough of Brentford.

The way the sun dances upon the windows of the tower blocks.

The beauty of the local womenfolk.

The architectural splendours of The Butts Estate.

The finest hand-drawn ales for miles around.

Ah, Brentford!

'Were you brought up in this hole?' asked Parton Vrane.

'Hole?' Danny whistled. 'That's good coming from one who dines out of dustbins.'

'I meant it as a compliment.'

'Well, of course you did.'

'Which way now?'

'At the bottom of the High Street, turn right to the other side of the canal bridge.'

'Right it is.' And right they went.

Parton Vrane pulled up close by Leo Felix's used-car emporium.

'That's Mickey's hut over there.' Danny pointed. 'You stay in the car and I'll go and talk to him.'

'It's not wise.'

'It's better than two clears confronting him at once. Let me talk to him, if the Rider on him is less powerful than Demolition was, then perhaps I can convince him.'

'Take this,' said Parton Vrane.

'A gun?' Danny shook his head fiercely. 'No thanks.'

'Stun gun,' said Parton Vrane. 'Electric shock. Just in case. It will only knock him out.'

'All right.' Danny tucked the gun into his trouser pocket. 'Give me ten minutes.'

'I'll give you five. Then I'm coming in.'

'Five then,' and Danny left the van.

As it was now four o'clock in the afternoon, and a Tuesday to boot, Mickey Merlin was tending to his livestock. A long-handled spade in one hand and a bucket in the other, he was mucking out his rabbits.

Danny appeared, slouching along the tow-path. This time he wasn't smoking a cigarette, as he had none on him to smoke.

Mickey looked up to view Danny's approach. 'A new tactic,' said he, 'but I'm not fooled. Give me a Woodbine, you bum.'

'I haven't got any.' Danny patted his pockets. 'Empty, see.'

'There's a big bulge in the right one,' said Mickey.

'That's only a pistol,' Danny smiled.

'Oh, I thought you were just pleased to see me.*'

Mickey looked Danny up and down. 'There's something different about you,' he said.

'It's my shoes.' Danny sought to draw Mickey's attention away from the region of his head. 'Swordfish shoes, hand made, pretty stylish, eh?'

'That's the same pair of brogues you always wear. It's something else.' Mickey blinked his eyes. Danny watched as Mickey's hand rose to his forehead. He could clearly see the Rider that sat upon Mickey's shoulders. It had that agitated look, its long fingers were massaging Mickey's scalp.

'No, it's not the shoes,' Danny said hurriedly. 'Actually, it's something else entirely. In fact, what it is, is, I need your help. Someone has done something to me.'

*One for the Mae West fans there.

199

'What?' Mickey eyed Danny suspiciously. Strange thoughts were now entering the rabbit-tender's mind.

'I've had a spell cast over me,' said Danny, as this was the ploy he had been rehearsing in his head. 'By another magician. Not a patch on you, of course, but obviously quite nifty. This magician has cast a spell over me which makes everyone I meet hate me on sight.'

'Yes,' Mickey shook his head, in an attempt to clear it. 'I see what you mean. That's some spell. I'm beginning to hate you myself. In fact, I feel as if I'd like to—'

'Kill me?' Danny asked.

'Kill you,' said Mickey, taking a step forward. 'Kill the clear.'

'See what I mean.' Danny took a step backwards. 'Insane, isn't it? You wouldn't really want to kill me, would you?'

'I'd like to kick you up the arse once in a while.'

'But not *kill* me.'

'It's a very strong urge,' said Mickey. 'In fact, so strong as to almost have me convinced that you're lying.'

'Phew,' said Danny. 'And I thought you were top man when it came to magic. Many times great-grandson of the now legendary Merlin himself. Surely you're not going to let the spell of some minor magician get one over on you?'

Mickey now began to clutch at his head. 'I'm having a real problem with this,' he complained. 'There's a voice in my bonce shouting, "Kill the clear, kill the clear!" '

'Try and control it.' Danny's hand hovered near to his gun-toting pocket. 'You're a powerful magician, Mickey, you can control it if you try really hard.'

'I'm trying. I'm trying. Come into the hut. Let's not talk out here.'

Danny followed Mickey into his converted hut. Before entering Danny raised a thumb in the direction of Parton Vrane's van. He could get this sorted on his own. He just knew that he could.

Danny walked into Mickey's hut.

And a frying-pan full in the face.

'Mickey, don't!'

'Oh, I'm sorry.' Mickey struggled to help Danny up. 'It just came over me. I couldn't control it.'

Danny clutched at a now bloody nose. 'Just sit down. Turn your head away, don't look at me.'

Mickey turned away, but the Rider on his shoulders kept staring at Danny. It was really most upsetting.

'How are you doing?' Danny asked.

'Not too good, I still want to rip off your head.'

'I'd like to tell you that it will pass,' said Danny. 'But I don't think it will. If anything it will get worse.'

'You'd better go,' said Mickey. 'I'll go through my book of spells when you're gone. See if I can come up with anything.'

'You promise?'

'Yes, I promise. No, I don't promise, the voice in my head is saying, "Wait until he gets outside, then push him in the canal." Whoever put this spell on you is one dangerous individual.'

'I'm going to have to come clean, Mickey. It isn't a spell. The voice you can hear in your head is coming from a creature that is sitting on your shoulders. I can see it and it can see me.'

'He's mad, I mean, you're mad.'

'Everyone's got one,' Danny continued. 'But mine left me and now I'm a clear.'

'Kill the clear,' said Mickey Merlin.

'It's manipulating your thoughts.' Danny's hand was right on his trouser pocket. 'Think for yourself, try to stop it.'

'I'm trying. I really am trying.'

'They're some kind of alien beings,' Danny explained. 'They make men do terrible things. We have to wipe them out. Or drive them off the planet, or something. Your book of spells could help do it.'

Mickey clenched his fists. 'It's telling me that you are evil and must be destroyed.'

201

'They're not your thoughts. You know they're not.'

'I bloody do.' Mickey shook and twitched. 'I can control it. I *can*. I *can*.'

'I knew you could.' Danny didn't *know*. But he had *hoped*.

'Get it off me,' spat Mickey, through gritted teeth. 'If you got yours off, get mine off.'

'I don't know how to. But we could do it with your magic book. I'm sure we could.'

'Bloody Hell!' Mickey sat down hard upon his camp-bed. 'It's telling me to burn my book of spells. Bastard! Get out of my head, you bastard!'

'We're definitely making progress here,' said Danny.

'But it's all the progress you will be making.'

The voice wasn't Mickey's and neither was it that of Mr Parton Vrane. This was a voice Danny felt that he knew. And as he felt that he knew it, a terrible chill ran through him.

Danny turned to the door.

And Mickey turned to the door.

'Cor look,' said Mickey. 'It's a doggy. A big golden Labrador doggy. Is that your dog, Danny?'

And Danny saw the dog. For a fleeting moment he saw it. It was his dog, Princey, with its lovable ears and its big waggy tail and its nice cold nose and everything.

And then Danny saw what he was actually seeing and Danny fell back in some alarm.

Looming in the doorway was a thing to inspire terror. A foul travesty of the human form dressed up in a clutter of gore-spattered rags, gaunt and skeletal with stark, staring mismatched eyes. It was a patchwork quilt of stitched human flesh, cobbled together on a frame of all the wrong bones. The head was lopsided with great hunks of hair, in three different colours, framing the face of a fiend. The mouth, which was clearly that of Mrs Roeg, opened, exposing several sets of teeth. The voice of Demolition spoke.

'Fun's over, Danny,' it said. 'Time to get back to work.

My spine needs adjusting and I need a new arse. I think your Aunt May's will do the job. A bit wrinkly, I bet, but you can put a tuck in it.'

'Get away from me.' Danny snatched out his pistol.

'What are you doing?' Mickey asked. 'You're not going to shoot that nice doggy.'

'It's not a nice doggy. It's a fucking monster. Use your eyes, Mickey, the thing in your head is controlling you. Use your eyes. Try to see it.'

'He can only see a nice big doggy,' said Demolition.

'Can't you hear it speak?' Danny held the pistol in both hands. And both hands were really shaking.

'I hear barking,' said Mickey. 'You *are* bloody mad. You bloody clear.'

'Leave him to me,' said Demolition.

'Oh, OK,' said Mickey.

'There.' Danny's hands went shake, shake, shake. 'You must have heard that. Or the thing in your head heard it. You've got to stick with me, Mickey. I'm not going to be a puppet again.'

'I'm coming back in,' said Demolition.

'No.' Danny raised his gun. And then he put it to his left temple. 'No,' he said again. 'You're not coming back in. I'll shoot myself first. I will. I mean it.'

'Let's discuss this in private.'

'Who said that?' asked Mickey.

'The monster. Look hard, Mickey. Try to see it.'

'I'm trying. I'm trying.'

'Out,' said Demolition. 'Outside. Your friend can't help you. Nobody can help you, you're mine, Danny. All mine.'

'Oh no I'm bloody not.' Danny charged at the thing in the doorway. It was a very brave thing to do. Reckless, but brave. But then brave is often reckless and reckless often brave. Danny caught the horrible thing at belly level. Tissue gave and bones crunched. Man and monster tumbled out of the door and fell in a heap on the ground. Danny fought to gain his feet, but a six-fingered hand had him by the throat. 'Here I come,' crowed the voice of Demolition.

'Oh no you don't.' Danny tried to raise his gun, but he'd dropped it. The hand held him tightly. Danny tore himself away and the hand came with him, Mrs Roeg's hand, parting from the skin-patched arm with a most disturbing snap. On his feet Danny put the boot in once and ran.

Back to the van and far away from here.

Danny ran. Turning back for an instant he could see the monster rising and Mickey in the doorway looking all bewildered. Danny ran. Ahead was the van and some degree of safety.

Along the tow-path and over the lock gates. Yards in it now. Danny kept on running. 'Start the engine,' he shouted. 'It's coming after me. Start the engine. Start the engine.'

He threw himself towards the van, tore open the passenger door and almost leapt inside. Almost but not quite.

Danny lurched back, horror in its every form writ big upon his face. Slumped over the wheel was Parton Vrane.

Bits of him.

Other bits were all knotted together. Arms and legs entangled.

The cab floor swam in blood.

'Aaaagh!' Danny jerked back.

'Got there first,' called the voice of Demolition. He was coming over the lock gates now. He, she and it. Danny's hands trembled. All of him trembled. 'Run, Danny, run,' said a voice in his head. And it was his own voice too.

Danny ran.

He didn't run towards the High Street. Not a second time. A lesson once learnt, and all that kind of thing. Danny ran along the tow-path. Towards where? Well, there were the allotments. He could hide out there, lose the monster amongst the huts. Hide out. Not in his own hut though. Definitely not.

Danny ran.

And the monster ran too. It shambled along looking very out of place upon this nice summer's day. Monsters really belong in the night-time. They never look right at four in the afternoon.

'Help!' went Danny, although he knew there wouldn't be any.

Two lads were fishing on the opposite bank.

'Look at that silly man,' said one.

'And his nice doggy running after him,' said the other.

And, yes, Danny ran.

There was no gate to the allotments on the canal side, in fact there was a bit of a wall. Quite a bit. Quite high. Hard to climb.

Danny leapt at the wall, fingers clawing. He sank back and leapt again. Horrible footsteps clumped nearer and nearer.

'I can do it,' Danny told himself. 'Oh yes I can.'

'Oh no you can't.'

'I bloody can too.' Danny took another leap. This time his fingers found purchase on the top of the wall. He hauled himself up.

The thing's remaining hand caught him by the ankle, tried to drag him down. Danny kicked it away. Scrambled up. Scrambled over and dropped down the other side.

Heart doing a thrash metal drumbeat. Temples pounding. Sweat a-dripping. Knees knocking together. All about right, considering.

Don't stop now. Keep running. But how much run did he have left in him? Not much. Although in the circumstances it was probably worth making that extra effort. Danny made that extra effort.

He stumbled along the rows of plots. The bean pole battalions, the corrugated plot-dividers. The sheds and the water-butts. So bloody normal. Everything so normal. So safe. But not any more. Nothing was safe. Nothing was normal.

Here and there some local fellows tilled the soil. Danny could see them, and the beings which rose above them.

Don't let them see you, Danny. Stay cool, try to act normal. Just walk.

Danny tried to just walk. Where was he going to hide? Mickey had a plot here, didn't he? He could hide in Mickey's shed. Would Mickey be joining in the search? Danny hadn't the faintest idea. Mickey's shed it was then.

Now just where was Mickey's shed?

Danny bent double his hands upon his knees. Trying for some breath. He was in this thing so deep there did not seem to be any way out. But. While breath remained. He was at least still free, and still free he had some chance of making it back to the big building in Whitehall and the top-secret room of the gentleman. The chances weren't exactly good. But they *were* there. Which was something.

'I'll survive this,' Danny told himself. 'I'll beat them. I will. I will.'

'But not today, Mr Orion.'

Danny's blood temperature dropped below zero. He focused his eyes. Before him a shiny pair of shoes and some blue serge trousering. And looking up . . .

'It is Mr Orion, isn't it?' asked Inspector Westlake.

'That's him.'

Danny's eyes flickered to the side. There stood a constable. Danny had seen him before, he came into the shop on Fridays to buy a six-pack. He didn't like Danny. The barcode reader Danny had run across his wrist had spelled out the word WEIRDO on Danny's side of the cash register.

'It's definitely him,' said Constable Dreadlock.

Danny turned to make a break for it. But other constables were approaching, from every direction it seemed. 'Now look,' said Danny. 'It's not what you think. You're not going to like me. In fact, you might just want to kill me. But it's all because—'

'No-one wants to kill you, sir,' said Inspector Westlake. 'We'd just like to ask you a few questions.'

'Perhaps later,' said Danny. 'I'm a bit busy at the moment.'

'I'm afraid I'm going to have to arrest you *now*,' said the inspector. 'Constable, would you care to read this gentleman his rights, as our colonial cousins like to put it?'

'With the greatest pleasure, sir.'

'No,' pleaded Danny. 'I haven't done anything. Well, I have, but it wasn't me. I'm an innocent man.'

The policemen now formed a nice tight ring around Danny. They began to laugh.

'Don't laugh at me. Get away from me.'

The policemen ceased to laugh and as they did so, Danny saw that expression coming over their faces. That look coming into their eyes.

'You're a psycho, lad,' said Inspector Westlake. 'You should get what's coming to you.'

'This is England, I deserve a fair trial.'

'You'll get one, lad, now don't you fear.'

'Yes,' agreed Constable Dreadlock, staring hard at Danny, as hard as the Rider that sat upon his shoulders. 'You'll get a fair trial. But not here.'

'No, not here,' said Danny. 'In court, eh?'

'At the station,' said the constable. 'Down in a nice quiet cell.'

'No!' screamed Danny. 'Help me, someone, help me.'

'Shut it, you,' said Inspector Westlake. 'Draw your truncheon, Constable, strike this, this – this *clear* on the head.'

Constable Dreadlock drew his truncheon. 'Oh look,' said he, pointing, 'a nice doggy. Whose nice doggy are you then?'

'It's not a doggy!' screamed Danny. 'It's a—'

'Shut up, you,' and the truncheon hit home.

Danny went down in a blur of red. As he passed from consciousness the last thing he heard was several constables going, 'Good boy there, whose dog are you?' and the inspector saying, 'Bring the dog to the station, Constable, it might belong to Orion.'

And then things went very dark for Danny.

Very dark indeed.

22

Hang on by your fingernails and never look down.

RORSCHACH (1884–1922)

REBELS

Those rebels,
The fellows in boots,
Who hate,
All the fellows in suits,
And write,
All that stuff on the wall,
And think,
'Though their brains are quite small.
They sneer,
At Beau Brummel and Baudelaire.
Are proud,
'Though they choose silly clothes to wear.
Those rebels,
Who cause all the trouble,
Breath air.
'Though they live in a bubble.

SHAVING THE MONKEY

Danny sat upon the cold stone floor in the corner of the cell, his knees drawn up to his chin, his arms hugged about his shins. He was rocking gently to and fro.

And humming.

He had woken, of course, to yet another ceiling. This one was small and white with an iron bulkhead light, tinged by tiny flecks of red, which Danny rightly supposed to be blood. Moonlight shone in through a tiny open cell window, there was nothing too romantic about it.

Before he'd started humming, Danny had weighed up the cons of his present situation. Most folk would have weighed up the *pros* and cons. But not Danny, as his present situation didn't have any pros. He'd been truncheoned unconscious and thrown into a police station cell. The Riders on the policemen had seen he was a clear, their human hosts would shortly come and kill him. The report would read 'while in an agitated state the prisoner threw himself to the floor, striking his head on the radiator'. No change there then.

But that wasn't the worst of the cons. Being beaten to death didn't have much to recommend it, but the alternative was even more dreadful. 'Hello, Mr Orion, we've brought you a present. It's your dog, Princey. Would you like some time together? In you go, boy. My, you are eager. He's pleased to see you, Mr Orion, isn't he?'

Danny rocked and Danny hummed. He was done for. He, the erstwhile saviour of mankind. Not that he ever really stood a chance, even with the help of Parton Vrane and the gentleman in Whitehall. You couldn't defeat an enemy that numbered in billions, was invisible to the human eye and in charge of the human mind.

What a bummer.

'Hum, hum, hum,' went Danny, rock, rock, rock as well. He did have one option. But it involved biting on a cyanide capsule and he didn't have one of those about his person. He could hang himself by his shoe laces. Possibly. Or stuff his socks down his throat. Or hold his breath. Suicide was not something Danny had ever given a lot of thought to. In fact—

Danny stopped humming. In fact, he wasn't going to give any thought to it now either. The situation might be hopeless, but that didn't mean it was without hope. Danny stood up and put his palms against the painted brick of the walls. There had to be some way out of here. It couldn't be impossible. David Copperfield had walked through the Great Wall of China and *that* certainly *was* impossible. It didn't stop *him* though.

'I could make a dummy of myself,' Danny said to himself. 'Put it over there, then hide behind the door and when someone comes in, whack them on the head.'

Danny gave this some thought. 'All right,' he said. 'Perhaps I could tunnel out. Lift up a flagstone, use a spoon. Might take a while though.'

Danny didn't trouble to give that one any more thought at all. 'I remember reading somewhere about how you have all the ingredients for gunpowder in a cell. If you know just where to look.'

Danny sat back down in the corner and returned to his humming. It *was* hopeless. He *was* doomed. It was wait for the clear-bashers or wait for the dog from Hell. Either way it was goodbye Danny Orion. Nothing but goodbye.

'Hello,' called a disembodied voice. 'Hello, Danny Orion.'

Danny froze against the wall. He knew that voice.

'Danny, are you there?'

'Yes,' said Danny. 'I'm here.'

A head popped up outside the little barred cell window.

'Hello, Danny,' said the mouth on the face of the head.

'Hello, *Mickey*,' said Danny. 'But how?'

'No time to talk. I'm having a real job keeping this thing in my head at bay. But I think I'm getting the upper hand.

210

I'm here after all. Take this and meet me around the back.'
'Do what?'
Mickey's hand craned through the window, it had a shake on.
'Take it quick, before this thing makes me use it on you.'
The hand held a gun, Parton Vrane's gun. Danny snatched it from the shaking hand.
'Around the back,' said Mickey and then he was gone.
Danny weighed the pistol on his palm. '*Yes*,' said he. 'Now we'll see who's beaten.'
There came a rattling at the cell door. The sound of a big key turning in the lock. Danny tucked the gun away behind his back. The cell door opened and there stood Inspector Westlake. And Constable Dreadlock. And several other constables. And what a surprise, they all had their truncheons drawn.
'*Hello, Danny Boy*,' said Inspector Westlake. And Danny knew *that* voice. And it wasn't the voice of the inspector. '*I've taken up a new residence*,' said the voice. '*Your services are no longer required.*'
'Stick 'em up!' Danny whipped out the pistol. Held it tight between both hands. 'Drop your truncheons first. Then stick 'em up.'
Inspector Westlake's mouth dropped open.
'I wouldn't think twice about shooting you,' said Danny. 'You know I mean it.'
'*Stand firm, men*,' said the voice of Demolition. '*He's bluffing.*'
Danny stepped forward and rammed the gun barrel into the policeman's mouth. 'If I shoot this man then you'll die too,' he whispered. 'Back off!' Danny shouted to the constables. 'Drop the truncheons and back off. Or I'll shoot the inspector. I'm a psycho killer, you know I'll do it.'
'I think he would,' said Constable Dreadlock, dropping his truncheon. 'Would you mind if I took your photo as you were escaping?'

'No, that's fine,' said Danny. 'The inspector's coming with me. As a hostage.'

'Mmmph, grmph, mmmph,' went the inspector's mouth. The eyes that blazed at Danny didn't look very human. Rather red and canine-looking. 'Mmmph, gmph.'

'He says do it. Hurry up.'

The constables backed into the corridor, dropping their truncheons and falling over one another. Constable Dreadlock raised his box Brownie. 'Over here, Mr Orion,' he called, paparazzi fashion. 'Just one smile. Could you ram the gun in a little deeper? That's lovely. Got it. One more now, really frowning at the inspector. Make it look intense. Really manic. Great. Now, if you could just take your top off—'

As he had a free foot to use, Danny kicked the constable in the cobblers.

'Ouch,' went Constable Dreadlock, doubling up, but keeping a firm hold on his camera.

Danny thrust the inspector before him. Backwards, it wasn't easy. The constables were keeping well back. There wasn't a hero amongst them. Not on a constable's pay. And it was nice to see one of the higher ranks with a gun stuck in his gob.

But then, they also wanted to kill this man. This *clear*. Interesting dilemma. But one that was left unresolved.

Danny went along the corridor and there was a fire exit ahead. He pushed the inspector backwards through it.

And they were outside in the car park now.

'Over here.'

Danny turned. Mickey was waving. From the white van. Nice one, Mickey. 'Come on,' said Danny, withdrawing the gun, spinning the inspector around and ramming it into the small of his back.

'*I can be inside you as quick as a flash,*' sneered Demolition.

'I don't think so. You'd have done it by now if you could.'

The inspector's mouth closed, his eyes continued to blaze.

'Don't bring *him*,' shouted Mickey. 'Come on now, hurry.'

Danny pushed the inspector onwards. 'Open the back

doors,' he called to Mickey. 'See if there's some rope or something.'

'Danny there isn't time for that.'

'It's very important, the creature that was in me is inside this man.'

'I don't know what good *that's* going to do us.' Mickey turned the ignition key and prepared to drive away. 'No you don't, you sod,' he told the voice in his head. He leapt from the cab, rushed round and opened the rear doors. The moonlight shone in upon the remains of Parton Vrane.

'Oh dear,' said Mickey. 'I really should have dumped this lot.'

'Get in,' Danny told the inspector, and, 'Oh dear, Mickey, you really should have dumped that lot.'

And suddenly there was a lot of commotion. A siren sounded and constables issued from the fire-exit door. They had guns.

'Get in!' Danny kicked the inspector inside. Mickey slammed the doors shut, raced round to the cab. 'Drive like crazy,' said Danny.

'Have no fear of that.' Mickey pulled out the ignition keys. 'No!' Mickey stuck them in again. Gave them a twist. Gunfire rattled. Bullets slapped into the van. Mickey kept his head down, whacked the van into gear, tore away at the hurry up.

In the darkness of the back Danny toppled over. And hands sprang at his throat. 'No, get off me.'

'Are you OK?' Mickey called.

'Drive. Just drive.' Danny clubbed with his pistol. Clubbed again and again and again. The hands about his throat relaxed and fell away.

'Give us some light,' called Danny. Mickey flicked on the interior lights that some folk always make such a fuss about you putting on at night.

'You're not supposed to have these on at night,' called Mickey, who was evidently one of these folk.

Danny looked down at his handiwork. Inspector Westlake's

face was a bit of a mess. Danny turned the unconscious policeman over. He found some of those elasticated things with the hooks on the ends, which are never really any use at all for fixing stuff on your roof rack, but which everyone always has none the less, and bound the inspector's hands and feet.

Danny scrambled over the seats and into the cab. 'You're a genius, Mickey,' he said. 'An absolute genius. How are you managing? Do you want me to drive?'

'I can manage. Like I said, I'm getting the measure of it. Watch this.' Mickey ducked his head and made a scowling expression. Danny could see the Rider on his shoulders. The blank face took on a look of concern. And then one of pain. Mickey relaxed. 'It doesn't like that,' he said.

'What are you doing to it?'

'I'm thinking about it. Thinking how I'd like to drive a nail into its head. Imagining myself doing it.'

'Genius,' said Danny. 'Pure genius. Where are we going, Mickey?'

The driver shrugged. 'You tell me.'

'Do you have your book of spells with you?'

'Of course I do. But you wouldn't believe what a struggle I had.'

'Oh yes I would.'

'So where should we go?' Mickey asked.

'To Whitehall,' said Danny. 'There's a gentleman I'd like you to meet.'

23

A FOND FAREWELL TO VERSE

There comes a point,
It seems to me,
When there's no time,
For poetry.

Mr Rankin would like to personally thank all those discerning souls who took the trouble to read his deeply mystical and damn fine poetry and not just skip past it to get on with the chapters.

You know who you are.

THE DOGS OF WAR

'I'm very pleased to meet you, Mr Merlin.' The gentleman extended his hand and Mickey gave it a shake.

'Pleased to be here,' he said. 'Danny was telling me on the way that you have some really decent booze, any chance of a drink?'

'Please be my guest.'

'And he mentioned something about cigars.'

'I see you're not entirely alone.' The gentleman glanced with distaste toward the Rider upon Mickey's shoulders. It glared at him with unbridled hatred.

'Do the thing with the nail, Mickey,' said Danny.

'What's this?' asked the gentleman.

'Watch,' Danny told him.

Mickey screwed up his face. Thought hammers and nails. The Rider flinched, jerked its head about.

'Most impressive.' The gentleman clapped his hands together, then took to the pouring of drinks.

'Make mine a double,' said Mickey.

'What have you done with the inspector?' Danny asked.

'He's tucked away safely. You're sure Demolition is inside him?'

'He's there. He couldn't get back inside me. I'm sure he tried.'

'It's because you know he's there,' said Mickey. 'These things are only powerful as long as they keep you off guard. As long as you don't know they're doing it. When you *do* know, you can defend yourself.'

'I wish I'd met you chaps twenty years ago,' said the gentleman.

'What, when I was three years old?' Danny accepted his drink.

'Yes, forget that.' The gentleman handed a drink to Mickey and opened his box of cigars.

'Great,' said Mickey. 'And you can forget that.'

'Forget what?' asked the gentleman.

'I was talking to *that*.' Mickey thumbed to the Rider on his shoulders. 'He was suggesting I whack you over the head with the cigar box.'

'I'm sorry about Parton Vrane,' said Danny.

'He'll be all right,' said the gentleman, raising his glass and toasting his guests. 'Most of his major parts are intact. We'll soon have him up and about.'

'Bloody Hell,' said Mickey Merlin. 'I threw one of his legs in the canal.'

'He'll grow another.'

'You mix with some shit weird people, Danny,' said Mr Merlin, lighting his cigar and taking a puff.

'It's been an interesting week.' Danny helped himself to a cigar.

The gentleman lit it for him. 'I feel confident,' he said, 'that a solution is now near at hand. We have Demolition safely confined. Mr Merlin here has demonstrated that it is possible to fight back mentally. And we have the mysterious book of spells. Surely with all this in our arsenal we have a fighting chance.'

'So where do we start?' Danny asked.

'Well, these things take time.' The gentleman sat down behind his big desk. 'We can't rush matters. We must interview Demolition, see if we can persuade him to co-operate. We must study this book of spells, discover whether an answer lies within. I will put my top people on it. But we might be talking about months, possibly even years.'

A telephone upon his desk began to ring. The gentleman picked up the receiver to his ear. 'Yes?' he said, then with a pause, 'What?' then another pause. A further 'What?' a further pause. A 'Do what you can,' and the gentleman replaced the receiver.

'Well,' said he. 'An interesting development.'

'Yes?' said Danny. 'What?'

'Apparently you didn't quite outrun the police,' said the gentleman. 'Apparently the building is now completely surrounded.'

It's funny how things work out sometimes, isn't it? Just when you think you're beginning to get things sorted. Whoosh, out of the blue comes trouble. It's just possible that if Danny had not taken the inspector hostage, the response would not have been quite so muscular. But if you do take a police inspector hostage, then with or without the influence of the Riders, you can get yourself into all kinds of trouble.

'Special service units,' said the gentleman. 'Heavily armed. 'State-of-the-art weapons. Stun grenades. Tear gas. Quite a few out there. Massing, as it were.'

'Over to you, Mickey,' said Danny.

'What do you mean, over to me?'

'You're the magician. Magic us out.'

'David Copperfield can make the Statue of Liberty vanish,' said the gentleman.

'That's a trick,' said Mickey. 'Anyone can do that.'

'Oh yeah, sure,' said Danny.

'It's simple,' said Mickey. 'He had two towers built in front of the statue. The audience sat one side. The statue was the other. Then he let down a screen between the towers, raised it again and the statue was gone.'

'Yes I saw *that*, but how was it done?'

'There was another screen behind the first one. A black one. It blacked out the statue. And that's how it was done.*'

'I don't think you're supposed to give away secrets like that,' said the gentleman.

'I'm not in the Magic Circle,' said Mickey. 'I'm a real magician.'

'Then make the building disappear.'

'I may be good, but I'm not *that* good.'

The sound of a voice amplified by one of those electric loud hailers was now to be heard. Its message was simple and unambiguous. 'Give yourselves up at once,' it was, 'or we will storm the building.'

'Negotiate,' Danny told the gentleman. 'We do have the hostage. Waste time, negotiate. Ask for flasks of tea. Make outrageous demands. A helicopter. A million quid.'

The gentleman's phone began to ring again. And the

*And that's how it *was* done. A bloke who used to work in a circus told me.

gentleman snatched up the receiver. 'I'll only negotiate with Michael Jackson,' he was heard to remark.

Mickey drew Danny away to a corner. 'This is going to get very silly,' he said. 'We could get killed here. I don't have time to set up a spell. And even if I did, we don't know whether it would work against these things. We can't hang around, we'll have to escape.'

'There's nowhere to run to. We have to make a stand now.'

'Get real, Danny.'

'*Get real?* This is all as unreal as it's ever likely to get.'

'Where do you think they've banged up the inspector?'

'I don't know. Down in the basement probably.'

'Then let's get down there. I have an idea.'

'I'm with you,' said Danny.

'Then grab my book of spells from that loony in the wig's desk and let's get going.'

'And smoked salmon,' said the gentleman into the telephone receiver. 'And I want it fresh, flown down from Scotland, and I want Madonna to deliver it personally.'

Words returned to him through the earpiece.

'All right,' said the gentleman. 'If you can't get smoked salmon I'll settle for cod and chips.'

'Just popping out to the toilet,' said Danny, snatching up the book of spells. 'Be back in a minute.'

'Do you want vinegar on yours?' asked the gentleman.

'Yes,' said Danny. 'And a pickled onion.'

Danny ran, this time with Mickey. Along the corridor. To the lift. Down in the lift to the basement and along further corridors. Neither was sure exactly whether they were running in the right direction, but each felt certain that the in-built something which always causes heroes to arrive at the right place at the right time would aid them on their run.

And naturally it did.

During their run, Mickey explained what he wanted Danny to do. The thing about real magic, Real *Magick*, is its specific nature, there is no airy-fairyness about it. You have to be specific and *exact*. You have to know *exactly* what you want and be very *exact* in the way you demand it. There's no room for half measures in magick. Precision is everything. And so there were certain things Mickey *had* to know. And Danny was just going to *have* to find them out.

'Let's try in here,' said Danny, pushing open a door which had a sign reading 'TOP SECRET, NO ENTRY' emblazoned upon it.

'That might well be the one.' Mickey followed Danny through the doorway.

'Oh yes,' said Danny, then, 'Oh Bloody Hell!'

Now 'Oh Bloody Hell' didn't cover it. But swearing rarely helps.

This room was large. It was low ceilinged, but it was large. It was lined with what seemed to be glass-fronted museum cases. Old they were. Victorian. They were lit from within.

'Oh Bloody Hell!' said Mickey.

'I said that,' said Danny. 'But would you just look at all this?'

The museum cases were packed with specimens. Suspended in sealed jars. Preserved in formaldehyde. Tissue samples. Organs. Limbs. But they weren't human. No way were they human.

'It's an aliens' graveyard,' said Mickey Merlin.

'These are old,' Danny whistled. 'Look at the labels.'

The labels *were* old. They were peeling from the specimen jars. Brown and peeling. Crabbed cursive lettering in quill pen, by the look of it.

'Here,' said Danny. 'You know that bit at the end of *Predator Two*, when the alien gives Danny Glover that old flintlock with the date on it, to show how long they've been hunting on Earth?'

'Yeah, I saw it,' said Mickey. 'Wasn't as good as the first one though. No general electric mini-gun. And no Arnie.'

'Yes, well – this is the same business. The aliens were

collecting *us*. But someone here's been collecting *them*. I'll bet there's bits of the Roswell Crash here.'

'Forget that,' said Mickey. 'Look at the label on this.' He pointed. Danny read, ' "Spleen of entity recovered from wreckage of craft which crashed into the R.101 airship, causing its destruction." This is a rewrite of history.'

'Oh, I like this,' said Mickey, pointing anew. ' "Skeleton of Jack the Ripper." '

'Looks more like the Elephant Man. Oh, it *is* the Elephant Man. Well, I never knew *he* was Jack the Ripper.'

'I always suspected it,' said Mickey. 'All the murders were a short walk from the London Hospital where he was staying at the time★. But then I never knew the Elephant Man was an alien.'

'I don't think the gentleman was altogether straight with me,' said Danny, perusing further specimens and shaking his head as he did so. 'I think there's a bit of a conspiracy going on here.'

'You're not kidding. Look at *that*.'

Danny looked. 'Bloody Hell,' he said once more.

And it was Inspector Westlake. He lay in a sort of open-topped chromium sarcophagus, with dry ice raising little wisps of mist. He was well frozen up.

'They've done him in,' whispered Danny. 'And oh shit. I can see it.'

'What can you see?'

'I can see the dog.' And Danny could see it. The image was superimposed over the inspector's face. It was another face, definitely canine in design, but more than that, a noble face, a wise face. A face that glowed with a vivid intelligence.

Mickey stared in at the inspector. 'I can't see anything but the policeman. This sod in my head is clouding my vision.'

★They actually *were*, you can look it up.

'Well, I can see it.' And Danny looked, and as he looked the eyes in the transparent face opened and turned towards him. The thin blackish lips moved. Trembled.

'It's still alive.' Danny still had the gun in his pocket, he drew it out and pointed it down.

'*Thaw me out,*' came the voice of Demolition.

'No way,' said Danny, steadying the gun.

'*Thaw me out. You don't know what you're doing. You don't know what this is about. Set me free and I'll tell you everything.*'

Danny looked at Mickey.

'Ask him the questions,' said Mickey. 'The questions I told you to ask.'

'What is your *real* name?' Danny asked. 'What is the name of your race and the name of the place you came from?'

The transparent lips rolled back into a crooked smile. '*Tell you that?*' whispered the voice of Demolition. '*If I were to tell you those things, your friend could apply his magic.*'

'Actually it wasn't a request,' said Danny. 'More of a demand. It's a case of, tell me what I want to know or I shoot the inspector and you die with him.'

The lips curled back further. '*You wouldn't shoot another man.*'

'I really have nothing more to lose.'

'Ah, well, let's not get *too* carried away.' This voice did not come from the mouth of Demolition. It came from the mouth of the gentleman. 'I really wish you hadn't come down here,' he said. 'You were doing so well and being such great assets.'

'That's a very big gun you've got in your hand,' said Mickey. 'And you don't look pleased to see me.'

'Yes it is quite a big one, isn't it? Please drop yours, Danny, I know it's only an electric job. It wouldn't reach this far anyway.'

Danny dropped the gun onto the floor. 'What's going on here?' he enquired.

'I don't want any harm to come to you here. Nor to my prize exhibit.'

'Well, we're fine,' said Danny. 'You can put your gun away.'

'Perhaps I'd better hold onto it, just in case.'

'Please yourself. Any news of our fish and chips, by the way?'

'Ah, no. In fact, the police are being somewhat adamant. They demand I surrender you and your companion within ten minutes or they're going to come bursting in. Guns blazing, that sort of business.'

'Tricky,' said Mickey.

'Yes, I do feel it might rather compromise our operation here.'

'You'd best go back and talk to them then. We can manage.'

'Ah, no again, I'm afraid. I don't want you to do any managing.'

'Mickey has a plan,' said Danny.

'I rather thought he might. I still have to ask you to come with me.'

'Why?' asked Danny, as if he hadn't guessed.

'I'm going to turn you over to the police, of course.'

'Thanks a lot.'

'It's nothing personal, Danny, but this is all too important.'

'But Mickey has a plan.'

'A plan to destroy the Riders?'

'Exactly.'

'Just as I feared. Come on, we must be going.'

'No,' said Danny. 'I'm not going anywhere.'

'Then I'll have to shoot you.'

Danny stuck his hands in his pockets. 'Go on then,' he said. 'I dare you.'

'What? I mean, pardon me?'

'Well, come on, don't be ridiculous. What are you going to do? Shoot us dead and then drag our bodies outside? In front of all those police? All those police with Riders on their shoulders? All looking at you. The *clear*.'

223

'Tricky,' said Mickey.

'Not *too* tricky. I was thinking of taking your bodies up in the lift and throwing them out of the window, actually.'

'I don't like this man at all,' said Mickey. 'And it's nothing to do with the bugger on my shoulders either.'

'Just one thing.' Danny took a hand from his pocket and put it in the air. '*Why* are you doing this? Mickey and I could sort this out once and for all – just give us time. Stall for time.'

'I don't want you to sort it out once and for all, it is not in the interests of the department.'

'What are you talking about? You want the Riders destroyed, surely?'

'Well, yes and no.' The gentleman took out his pocket watch and perused its face. 'All right. It can't hurt to tell you, your fate is sealed, as it were.'

'Could we sit comfortably?' Danny asked.

'No. Just stand with your hands in the air.'

'Fair enough.'

'So,' said the gentleman. 'And briefly. As I say, it is not in the department's interests to destroy the Riders. Possibly in time, but certainly not now and all at once. They are a most valuable commodity. All we seek to learn is how to destroy them selectively and at a distance. Imagine the power of that. Let us take, for example, Saddam Hussein. Wicked Saddam goes off to bed one night. Someone here presses a little button. His Rider is destroyed. Saddam awakens the next morning. I bet he wouldn't make it to the breakfast table alive.' The gentleman laughed. 'The possibilities are endless. An opposing army. You zap the Riders on half the soldiers, the other half do the job for you. Do you get the picture?'

'All too clearly,' Danny said.

'And, of course, one could expand upon this premise.' The gentleman was all smiles as he spoke. 'Once we have learned how to destroy the Riders, the next logical move would be to communicate this knowledge to them directly. Once they learn that they are vulnerable, they may well choose to be co-operative.'

'Such as by urging their human hosts to vote for a particular politician?' Danny suggested.

'You have it. Urge them to work harder for less pay. Spend more of their earnings on the National Lottery. The possibilities are, indeed, endless.'

'And you and an élite of clears would run all this, run everything in fact.'

'As benign rulers. The power behind the throne, as it were. Whichever particular throne we choose to put our power behind.'

'Can I have your autograph?' Mickey asked.

'Why?'

'You're the very first loon bent on world domination I've ever met. My dad got Hitler's autograph. It's a family thing, you understand.'

'I'm afraid I don't have time for autographs. Kindly hand me the book of spells.'

'Away on your bike,' said Mickey.

The gentleman sighed. 'No more time. I'll just have to take it from your body.' He aimed and cocked his pistol. Aim it went. And cock.

Danny covered his head, 'Don't shoot,' he pleaded. 'We'll go quietly.'

'We will?' Mickey asked.

'Yes, we will. Give him the book of spells.'

'I bloody won't.'

'Of course you will. Kiss the book goodbye and give it to the nice gentleman. Remember? Like you did for me in your hut?'

'Oh yes. Indeed.' Mickey lifted the book to his lips and gave it a great big kiss. 'Be good now,' he told it.

'Hurry,' said the gentleman. 'And no tricks.'

'No *tricks*, I assure you.' Mickey stepped forward and handed him the book.

The gentleman took it in his non-gun-toting hand. There was a bang and a bit of a flash and the gentleman fell in a faint.

'Works every time,' said Mickey, retrieving his book from the floor.

'Yes, I know.' Danny snatched up the gentleman's gun. 'Come on, let's go.'

'To where?'

'Anywhere but here.' They stepped over the fallen gentleman and rushed into the corridor. The 'TOP SECRET' door had a bolt on the outside. Danny swung it shut. Then on second thoughts he re-opened it and went back into the sinister room.

'What are you doing?' Mickey called.

'Something.' Danny returned to the corridor and slammed the door. As he pushed home the bolt he said, 'I'm sure Demolition heard everything the gentleman had to say. So I've pulled the plug on his freezer. Let the two of them work it out. Head to head, eh?'

'Ooh. That's really horrible. I like it.'

'Now, which way should we go?'

From above came a devastating explosion, followed by the sound of rapid machine-gun fire.

'Not up,' said Mickey.

'Any chance of a spell?'

'We don't have the time, let's try running.'

And so they ran.

Now the thing about Whitehall buildings is that they do have a lot of basement. Plenty of basement with miles of corridor. Popular legend has it that they all interconnect. The various ministry buildings, Downing Street, the Houses of Parliament, Buckingham Palace. There's war rooms and store rooms and record rooms and listening rooms, where dull-looking men sit smoking cigarettes, wearing headphones and watching the spools of big tape recorders going round and round. And there's top-secret rooms. Loads of those, of course.

It would indeed be tedious to list all the various top-secret rooms Mickey and Danny ran past. Obviously there were openings for a few satirical gags there. But none springs immediately to mind.

'Oh look,' said Mickey. '*National Lottery Winning Calculation Room. Paul Daniels only.*'

'It's a crap gag,' said Danny. 'Shall we try down this way?'

Further sounds of gunfire were to be heard, marching feet also.

'Down that way seems good to me.'

And on they ran.

'We can't run for ever,' wheezed Mickey.

'*I* can. And if we keep going east we'll get back to Brentford in an hour or so.'

'And which way would east be?'

'This way, undoubtedly.'

'Drop your weapons and put up your hands.' Men sprang out before them. Men all dressed in black with all blacked-up faces. Guns raised. Big guns . . .

'Back this way, I think.'

'Hold it,' came cries from behind them.

'Perhaps not back this way.' Danny dithered.

'Drop your weapon.'

Danny dropped his weapon.

'Now onto the floor, face down. Hands behind your heads.'

'I think we're done for,' Mickey said.

'There's always the possibility of divine intervention.'

'You really think so?'

'Well.'

The lights went out.

'Open fire,' shouted someone. And men opened fire.

Muzzle flame and tracer shells and sparks and fire and noise. Such noise in a confined space. And so many bullets. In both directions.

And the lights flicked back on. What a lot of smoke. And

227

men rooting fingers into their ears and shouting, 'Shit I've gone deaf.' They advanced, both teams, and they met in the middle. They weren't dead. The teams. Bullet-proof jackets, that kind of thing. But they weren't half furious.

'Where did they go?' someone asked.

'Pardon?' said somebody else.

24

BIG TROUBLE IN LITTLE BRENTFORD

'Where *did* we go?' Danny asked.

'Pardon?' said Mickey.

And the lights came back on. But not in the corridor. Well, in *a* corridor. But not the one they'd just been in.

'Aaaagh!' went Danny.

'Sorry,' said Mr Parton Vrane. 'Did I startle you?'

'Yes, you did, you . . .' Danny stared.

Parton Vrane hopped up and down on one leg. He only had the one. And only the one arm. And not much in the way of shoulders. 'I had a job keeping up. Are you OK?'

'Obviously more than you are. No offence meant.'

'None taken, I assure you.'

'Thank you,' said Danny. 'Thank you very much.'

'From me too,' said Mickey. 'How did you do that? If you don't mind me asking.'

'Secret door. There's no shortage down here. Shall we go?'

'Where to?'

'I thought perhaps Mr Merlin's hut.'

'You're a bloody good bloke for a beetle,' said Danny.

★   ★   ★

They travelled on the underground. But it was not any underground Danny or Mickey had ever travelled on before. It was a top-secret underground. Comfortable ride though, and no graffiti.

Mickey took out a packet of cigarettes.

'Give us one,' said Danny.

'My last,' said Mickey. 'Sorry.'

'It's a *no smoker* anyway.' Parton Vrane tried to make himself comfortable on his seat. It wasn't easy. 'Would you like to tell me about your plan? I overheard that you had one.'

'You were listening in while we spoke to the, er, gentleman?'

'It's what I do. Listen in. Seek and destroy. You know the form.'

'I reckon you're likely to be unemployed quite shortly,' said Danny. 'I think your governor's probably gone over to the other side by now.'

'Serves him right. I knew he was up to something.'

'Look there's no-one about,' said Mickey. 'I could have a fag, couldn't I?'

Parton Vrane nodded. 'If you hand them round.'

'Oh, all right.'

They took up fags and smoked them. Parton Vrane leaked a bit and the effect was none too pleasing. 'Speak to me of your plan,' said he.

'It's down to magic.' Mickey patted the book on his knee. 'See this?' he pointed to his Rider. It looked a most uncomfortable Rider. One ill at ease with itself. One most disturbed. 'This fellow is going to help us, aren't you?'

The Rider nodded its big bald transparent head. Gloomily.

'Incredible,' said Danny. 'How do you do that?'

'Thought,' and Mickey tapped at his temple. 'We're on speaking terms now. Especially since he heard the gentleman say his piece. He's eager to oblige.'

Danny looked up at the Rider. He didn't look *that* eager. 'You can make it do what you want it to do?'

'It's not an *it*,' said Mickey. 'It's a *him*. His name is Rodney.'

'Rodney the Rider? Leave it out, please.'

'Wave to my friend, Rodney.'

Rodney raised a long slim hand and waved at Danny.

'Rodney is going to do his impersonation of Moses,' said Mickey. 'He is going to lead his people away from the evil pharaoh and off to the promised land. Aren't you, Rodney?'

Rodney nodded once again. He looked anything but enthusiastic.

'Or Rodney will get another nail in his head.'

Rodney flinched and grasped at his dome-like.

'Careful, Rodney, or you'll fall off.'

'You know what, Mickey,' said Danny, 'you never cease to amaze me.'

'Yes, well, when this is sorted, you can buy me a drink. When you've paid off my bar tab. Which you haven't *yet*.'

'I've had things on my mind.'

'Most amusing.'

'We're almost there,' said Parton Vrane. 'Tell me, Mr Merlin, just what have *you* got on *your* mind?'

'Well,' and Mickey went on to explain.

They have beautiful dawns in Brentford. Gorgeous they are. Rich with golden promise. The rooftops shimmer and sparrows rejoice. Angels on high join in their chorus and not without cause. No siree.

Two and a half men approximately were climbing out of a manhole in Mafeking Avenue.

'Is it safe?' Danny asked.

'Of course it's safe,' Mickey helped Parton Vrane to his foot. 'Put your arm round my shoulder,' he said. 'It's hopping time.'

The allotments, all dew-kissed, glittered in the early light. The church clock of St Mary's chimed five-thirty. Danny took a deep breath and sighed. If he'd had any poetry in him, he might have recited it now. But he hadn't, so he did not. 'Are you sure we'll be safe?' was what he said.

Mickey helped the half a man along. 'Of course I'm still not certain this will work,' he told him. 'Magick is a most precise business, we're spreading our net rather wide.'

'If it does work,' said Danny, giving Parton Vrane a help along too, 'the world is in for a bit of a wake-up. I mean, these Riders have driven their unwitting hosts along, probably not into the jobs they might have chosen of their own free will. Shit, they've probably made people marry each other because the Rider on the bloke fell in love with the Rider on the woman.' Danny tripped up and fell into a lettuce patch. 'And that's only the tip of the iceberg,' he said.

'Do you want them on or off?' asked Mickey.

'Off,' said Danny.

'Then let's get to it.'

Apparently there was a door in the allotment wall that Danny had all too recently scrambled over. Mickey had the key, of course.

The canal looked so good too. Sun dappling the water. A heron moving in his roost. A black-necked swan. A bandicoot.

'A rat!' said Danny.

'That's a squirrel,' said Mickey. 'You're crap on animals.'

'I've always wanted a dog.'

'Don't start on that again, please.'

'This converted hut of yours,' said Parton Vrane, 'how exactly is it converted?'

'Thoroughly,' said Mickey. 'Walk this way.'

'If I could walk that way—'

'Come on.' Mickey's keys were out once more. He turned one in the lock of the door. 'Follow me.'

Danny sat down on the camp-bed. 'What do you want me to do?' he asked.

'Well, you can get off my bed for a start.'

'Should I draw a magic circle or something?' Danny got off the bed. 'Or should I put the kettle on?'

'Why don't you be the look-out?'

'Who am I looking out for?'

'Oh a gentleman with a toupee, a police inspector with pneumonia, the SAS. Take your pick really.'

'Look,' said Danny. 'You seem to be taking over everything. It's me who's been through all the horrors. Me that told you about that Rodney on your shoulders.'

'Me who got you out of the police cell,' said Mickey. 'Me with the book of spells—'

'Excuse me, chaps,' said Parton Vrane. 'But it was *me* who saved you in the corridor.'

'I helped *you* out of the manhole,' said Mickey.

'You threw my leg in the canal,' said Parton Vrane.

'You turned me into a female psycho killer on her way to the electric chair,' said Danny.

'I never did,' said Parton Vrane.

'No, not *you*, him.'

'All right,' said Mickey. 'I'll just put my book of spells back on the shelf then, should I?'

'Looks like you're running the show,' said Danny.

'Right, well you bloody keep watch then.'

'I bloody will.'

'Are you sure the world is ready for independent thought?' asked Parton Vrane.

'Don't have a go at me,' said Mickey.

'Oh, as if I would.'

'Are you taking the piss? You *are* taking the piss.'

'If I told you that there was a whole load of blokes in black uniforms creeping along the tow-path, would that hurry things up?' Danny asked.

'Oh shit! There isn't, is there?'

'No,' said Danny.

'Right, well you're taking the piss. Step outside.'

'I will, don't you worry.'

'*Chaps!*' Parton Vrane's harsh whisper was almost a shout. 'We really should get on. Although I'm beginning to have my doubts as to whether this is a good idea at all.'

'It's a great idea,' said Mickey. 'It's *my* idea.'

'I helped.'

'Not much,' said Mickey.

'Chaps, please. Please.'

'Well, he started it.'

'I didn't.'

'*Chaps!*'

'All right,' said Mickey. 'Let's get to it. Now what I propose to do is this. I am going to recite *The Spell of Mass Discombubulation*. You note that is in *italics* and not in CAPITAL LETTERS. That is because it starts small, but it ends big. What it does is to spread panic, somewhat like a virus, from one person to another.'

'Oh,' said Danny.

'But,' said Mickey. 'I'm not going to pass it on to a person. I am going to pass it on to Rodney here.' Rodney took to a terrible shuddering. Danny almost felt sorry for him. *Almost*.

'Rodney is then going to pass it on. It spreads geometrically. From one to two to four to eight, et cetera.'

'Have you done this before?' Danny asked.

'Well, once, yes.'

'And how many people did you spread it to?'

'Well, not many.'

'How many?'

'I got in a bit of a lather,' said Mickey, 'and my rabbits ran away.'

'Not a spell whose efficacy has been universally proven then?'

'Yeah, well, I was only practising.'

'So when they all panic,' said Danny, 'assuming that they will, although that seems—'

'*When* they all panic,' said Mickey, 'Rodney here is going to communicate the message, "Quick everybody, this way." '

'And which way would that be?'

234

'Back to their own bleeding planet. Or dimension. Or spectrum, or wherever they damn well come from.'

Danny nodded. 'Well, I heard you tell it in the train. And I've heard you tell it again here. And with the sunrise and everything, have you ever heard the phrase "but in the cold light of day"?'

'Oh, so you don't think I can pull it off?'

'I'm not saying that, but come on. Here we are, one serial killer, one magician with a transparent alien on his shoulders, and a half a bloke who's mostly a beetle. Would you pit this bunch of dorks against an entire invisible race?'

'You're a loser, Danny. Always were, always will be.'

'Oh yeah? Well at least I don't have a girlfriend who makes me dress up in a school boy's outfit and beg to be spanked.'

'She told you *that*?'

'On the night when *I* was *you*, she made me do it.'

'You bastard.' Mickey swung his fist and knocked Danny out of the open hut door. Danny bowled over, but came up fighting.

'Chaps! Please!' Parton Vrane flapped his arm. 'Oh, this is bloody ridiculous, I'll do it myself.' He hopped over to the book of spells that Mickey had placed on his table. 'Now let me see,' he said. There was a bang and a flash and Parton Vrane fell down on the floor.

'Oh, you look tough.' Mickey squared up before Danny. 'Sure you can manage on your own, don't want a little bow wow to help you?'

'Rabbit shagger!' said Danny.

'Right, you've had it.' Mickey fell on Danny and Danny fell on Mickey back. Fists were swung and the boot went in.

'Take that!' went Danny.

'East 17!' went Mickey.

Ha, Ha, Ha went the noises off. But not very loudly.

And WAH-OOH WAH-OOH WAH-OOH! came the sound of police sirens.

'Kill the clear!' went the voice in Mickey's head.

235

'Oh, shut up!' said Mickey.

CHOP-CHOP-CHOP-CHOP-CHOP-CHOP-CHOP. That would probably be the sound of a police helicopter. Oh yes, here it comes bearing down from the direction of the High Street. It's just passing over the off-licence.

'What's all that bloody noise?' asked Mr Doveston awakening from a dream of latex bondage.

'Give in.' Mickey had Danny's arm up his back.

'Bollocks!' Danny kneed Mickey in that very area.

'Poof!'

'Pervert!'

'And this one I took in the second murder house,' said Constable Dreadlock, out strolling with a member of the gutter press. 'See the way the lungs had been blown up and tied with ribbons. Very festive we thought that was.'

'How much?' asked the member of the gutter press. 'What's all that noise?' he continued.

Constable Dreadlock began to load his camera.

25

WOOF!

The rabbits were restless. They looked on nervously and twitched their foolish noses as Danny punched Mickey in his.

Mickey collapsed into the hutch, bursting the chicken wire and getting all entangled. Danny danced above him, shadow boxing and poking out his tongue. The rabbits made a break for freedom.

'Look what you've done!' Mickey floundered in faeces and clawed at his gory hooter. 'My prize Angoras, you'll pay for this.'

'When you're ready. When you're ready.' Danny punched the air.

'You bloody madman.' Mickey lashed out with his foot and caught Danny in the ankle. Danny took to hopping about. Mickey jumped up and rushed at him. Down they went once more.

Inside the converted lock keeper's hut, Parton Vrane was stirring. He was trying to get up from the floor, but it wasn't easy, what with him only having the one arm and one leg, and everything (well, he didn't have the *everything* actually), and the one arm and the one leg were both on the same side.

Tricky.

The helicopter swooped in low. A head poked out of the passenger window. The force of thrashing blades blew its wig off. The head ducked back inside. It was the head of the gentleman. '*Land here!*' he shouted, in the voice of Demolition.

'I can't land here, there's not enough room.' The pilot shook his head fiercely. *His* head had a full head of hair, *and* a cap on it.

'*Land here! At once!*'

'No. I won't!'

The police presence was increasing. Five squad cars were already lined up on the forecourt of Leo Felix's used-car emporium. Officers were scrambling from these, belting on flak jackets, strapping visored helmets into place, handing round the weapons.

Constable Dreadlock sidled up, Brownie at the ready. 'Could I have a go of one of those pump-action jobs?' he asked.

'No you can't,' he was told. 'Just piss off.'

And folk were issuing into the High Street. Folk in foolish dressing-gowns and awful carpet slippers. Folk who wanted to know what all the fuss was about at this early hour. Folk who demanded to be told. Police motor cyclists swept between them, loud hailers blaring. '*Clear the streets. Return to your homes.*'

Not what they wanted to hear.

Mr Doveston hurried into his trousers and armed himself with what looked at first glance to be an oversized pink rubber truncheon. Hm!

★   ★   ★

Mickey had Danny by the throat and was banging his head up and down in the dirt and droppings. Danny flung up an arm and poked Mickey in the eye.

Parton Vrane had an arm up also. He was trying to hook Mickey's book of spells from the table with a trowel.

The helicopter turned in faulty circles. There seemed to be a bit of a struggle for control going on in the cockpit.

Another police car slewed to a halt on Leo's forecourt, rousing Brentford's token Rastaman from his dreams of Sion. Wearing nothing but a pair of Bob Marley boxer shorts, Leo held fast to the chain on his Dobermann. 'Get off me land, Babylon!' he shouted. 'I an' I set me dog on you.'

An ashen-faced Inspector Westlake climbed painfully from the latest police car. He'd turfed out the driver and driven all the way from Whitehall himself. He was swathed in blankets and looked in no mood to be trifled with. 'Officer, arrest that dog,' he ordered. 'And search the place for drugs.'

'Police harassment.' Leo loosened the chain on his hound. 'Call me solicitor, someone, I'm being oppressed again.'

The dressing-gowned crowd now gathering on the bridge above, cat-called and hooted. They all liked Leo. Leo was all right.

Danny wasn't, nor was Mickey. But they went at each other hammer and tongs. Rolling backwards and forwards, punching, gouging. Men behaving badly.

'Hah.' Parton Vrane had the book on the floor. He turned the pages with the trowel. 'I shall do this all by myself,' he whispered. 'There can't be much to reciting a spell.'
Oh dear.

★   ★   ★

Back on the forecourt Inspector Westlake stumbled along the rank of heavily armed policemen. They all stood to attention, looking very tough. Blanket-wrapped and wretched, Inspector Westlake looked anything but tough and the Dobermann which now clung to his trouser seat, hampered his movements and did nothing to boost his morale. 'N . . . now,' stammered the inspector, teeth rattling, lips rather blue. 'I don't want this cocked up. Joe bloody public is watching.'

Joe bloody public booed and hissed. 'Fascist pigs,' called someone.

'In like Flint,' said Inspector Westlake. 'No happy triggers. Arrest the suspects. You can't bloody miss them, that's them over there.'

He pointed to the other side of the canal, where Mickey and Danny still battled it out. 'That is all. Get to it.'

The line of policemen viewed the inspector in the blanket shawl. They didn't like the look of him one bit. Inspector Westlake viewed them back and made a puzzled face. 'If I didn't know better,' he said to himself, 'I'd be tempted to think that all these officers had little transparent men with big heads sitting on their shoulders. Well, go on,' he told them. 'Go on.'

The policemen didn't move.

'Why are you looking at me like *that*?' asked Inspector Westlake.

The helicopter made a very low pass. A door flew open and the pilot flew out. With an 'AAAAGH!' that could be heard above the chop of blades, he fell into the canal. The crowd on the bridge applauded this. Constable Dreadlock snapped pictures.

Inside the converted hut Parton Vrane found his page. THE SPELL OF MASS DISCOMBUBULATION. He perused the text. '*Having performed the banishing ritual of the pentagram and*

240

sanctified the temple,' he read. 'Yes, blah, blah, blah. *Within the sacred circle*, well, we don't have one of those, so let's skip that. *The magician in his purified garments* . . . Yes, blah, blah. *Raises both hands and calls forth the invocation.* Well I've only got the one hand, but I can't see *that* matters. *Upon completion of the spell cry the word "PANIC"* in capital letters. All seems straight-forward stuff, I can't see any problem here.'

Oh dear. Oh dear.

The helicopter dipped alarmingly. The gentleman was ex-army, he didn't know how to fly an aircraft. The dog in his head also lacked for such skills. The gentleman's hands clung tight to the joystick. 'I think I've fouled up here,' said A Dog called Demolition.

'You're a *clear*,' said a policeman with a gun.

'A *what?*' asked Inspector Westlake. 'Will somebody get this dog off my arse?'

'*Designate subject,*' read Parton Vrane. 'Rodney the Rider on Mickey Merlin,' he said. '*Intone spell.* Fair enough, let's see, *Tenet est circum directus locum fahee.* Piece of cake.'

Oh dear. Oh dear. Oh dear.

The helicopter swept down towards the bridge, scattering the crowd. On the forecourt below, policemen were looking bewildered. Voices in their heads were crying, 'Kill the clear. Kill the clear.' Their training told them that's not how to gain a promotion.

'Get to it!' shouted the inspector. 'Or I'll put you all on a charge.'

Constable Dreadlock snapped away at the policemen who were duffing up Leo Felix. 'I'll get these syndicated,' he said. 'I'll need a good agent.'

'Come on. Charge!' The armed policemen looked at one another and then they reached a collective decision. They'd charge now and shoot the inspector later. Somewhere less public. That was for the best.

'Charge!' they went.

And charge, too, went the local constabulary. Freshly arrived on the scene and somewhat miffed. There is always rivalry between divisions. The Met versus the rest. The regional lads are never too keen about the way the London mob muscle in and get all the glory. Brentford's boys in blue were most put out about these up-town Bobbies storming their manor. 'Charge!' they went, eager to be first across the lock gates.

Chug-chug and whirr. The helicopter flew in a sort of vertical Victory Roll. And helicopters can't do that. They stall when they do that.

'*Careba, caroba haffa basanova,*' chanted Parton Vrane, in a whispery voice, but with vigour.

'Bloody Hell!' cried Mickey, falling backwards.

'Ready to give up, eh?' Danny stumbled to his feet.

'No, something's happening. I can feel magic.'

'You what?'

Mickey turned a decent black eye, and the other, half-closed, towards his hut. 'It's your beetle mate, he's tampering with my book.'

'You're just bottling out.' Danny raised a fist and then lowered it again. 'Shit,' said he. 'Look at that helicopter. They stall when they do that, don't they?'

'Oh!' went Mickey, pointing every which way. 'Look at those policemen! Look at all those people!'

'To the hut. To the hut. To the hut-hut-hut.'

To the hut they ran. And how.

Hard upon their heels came the policemen, some with guns and some without. They poured across the lock gates. And you really should do that in single file. And use both hands.

242

Cries and shouts and the sound of bodies splashing brought joy to the crowd on the bridge.

'Perfect,' went Constable Dreadlock, snap-snap-snapping. 'Now if you could just strike a pose, as if you're clubbing down that unarmed officer with your gun. Excellent. One more. Thank you.'

'*Casa-pupo Benelux Gabba Gabba Hey,*' chanted Parton.

Chug and whirr and stut-stut-stut, went the helicopter, quite high up now and almost in slow motion.

'*Kaleorum consanostrum Hi-cockalorum.*'
Mickey burst in through the hut door. 'Stop!' he shouted. 'Stop, for God's sake. You haven't drawn a circle, you haven't—'

'*Halmey et scrotum pakamakus.* I'm doing fine,' said Parton Vrane.

'No you're not, you'll kill the lot of us.'

'Leave this to me,' Parton Vrane flicked over a page with his trowel. *Two* pages actually. '*Hermasitas hokus pokus—*'

'That's a different spell. Don't chant *that* one. Stop, won't you? *Stop!*'

STOP. Whirr and stop went the blades of the helicopter. And suddenly all became quiet.

STOP, went the policemen, looking fearfully skyward.

STOP, went the crowd, looking also.

STOP. Everything sort of STOPPED. Just STOPPED.

'No-one speak,' Mickey froze in the doorway.

'What?' asked Parton Vrane.

'Sssh!' Mickey put a finger to his lips.

'What's he done?' whispered Danny.

'He's mixed two spells together. The one to put the wind up the Riders and another one.'

243

'What other one?' Danny asked. It had grown terribly quiet.

'Just another one.'

'*What* other one?'

'A real shitter,' whispered Mickey. 'A medieval one to call down the wrath of God on unbelievers and vanish them away.'

'Well, that's good, isn't it?'

'Not if you don't have a circle to stand in. Now just don't say anything while I try to work out what to do. Stay silent. Say nothing. Especially don't say anything in capital letters.'

'What, like *PANIC*?' asked Parton Vrane.

And the world that was Brentford went WOOF!

26

VOICES OFF

Of course now, looking back, it's hard to tell what really happened that day. If anything actually happened at all. Act of God, some say. Meteor say others, unexploded wartime bomb, say others still.

Rumours abound, and theories. Mostly suggesting some sinister conspiracy on the scale of the JFK assassination plot or the Roswell saucer crash. But who's to say for sure?

Occasionally a voice is to be heard on some local station radio talk show. One claiming he was 'there at the time and saw the whole thing'. Generally this someone is promoting a book on the subject. Though none of these sells very well.

Testimonies were taken from those who survived the holocaust, they make for an interesting, but inconclusive read. It's all down to what you believe, I suppose. Or what you *think* you believe. Or think that it's *you* thinking.

Danny Orion: 'I was there, all right. In the thick of it. If it hadn't been for me uncovering the existence of the Riders and working out a brilliant plan to defeat them, there's no telling what might have happened. I know people think I'm a Whacko and that my plea of *multiple personality disorder* at my trial was "unadulterated crap", but I saw them, I know they're out there somewhere, just watching us and waiting for an opportunity to return. And when they let me out, *if* they let me out, I'll prove to the world I was telling the truth. I have to go now and walk my dog. What do you mean you can't see any dog? What do you call this then? What?'

Mickey Merlin: 'Well, he is a whacko, Orion, isn't he? Barking, he is. I never had anything to do with it. On the day it happened I was in Orton Goldhay. No, I've never professed to be a magician, there's no such thing as magic and there's no such thing as transparent men with bulbous heads who sit on your shoulders and tamper with your mind. Crap it all is. Do you want to buy a rabbit?'

Constable Dreadlock: 'Actually it's not "constable" now. I left the force to take up a career in professional photography. And I never took a penny for all those photos of mine that were syndicated round the world. I gave all the money to charity. Yes, I know some people say they were fakes, especially the last one which shows God actually coming down to sort the whole thing out himself. But I know what I saw, and I saw that. Grey men with bulbous heads? No, I didn't see any of those.'

Parton Vrane: 'Well, it wasn't *my* fault. *I* didn't do it.'

Paul Daniels: 'I did *not* fix the National Lottery.'

Inspector Westlake: 'Don't ask me, I'm dead.'

The gentleman: 'Me too.'

And a Dog called Demolition: 'My people have always been given a bad press by your people. Referred to as "parasites" or *Riders*. So I'd just like to put the record straight.

We didn't come to your world of our own free will. We were dragged here and you did the dragging. My people are "spirit", we transcended physical form aeons ago. And that ain't no Star Trek jive neither. We are creatures of pure thought. And I mean P.U.R.E. And we're peace loving with it. We never manipulated any of your lot, it was the other way round.

We got sucked here by *your* thoughts. *Is there anyone out there? Are there folk up there looking down and wondering if there are folk down here?* It was the gravity caused by your heavy thoughts that drew us down here. And *we* couldn't see *you*. All we were aware of was that some solid physical entities existing in a spectrum of white darkness were hanging onto our legs and wouldn't set us free.

Well, like I say, my people are peace loving, but some of us, some of us decided we weren't going to take it any more. We were going to break free.

We formed an underground organization called DEMO-LITION. *Destroy Earth Men Or Live In Tyranny.* I.O.N. Ion is from the Greek, you know, it means literally *going from, to go.* Cool name, eh?

We sought to destroy the three-dimensional flesh-covered brutes that preyed on our psychic energies. Wipe them out. Trouble was that your bunch had got our bunch so well and truly hooked that when we did in one of yours, one of ours got did in too.

We tried a lot of other things, building substitute bodies, all kinds of stuff. It was war. *Was* war. I don't know who won it, if anyone *did*.

Tell you my present location? You have to be kidding. Let's just say I'm like the truth – and you know where that is. You don't? Well, I'll tell you buddy.

IT'S OUT THERE.

That's where.

A FACT IN THE CASE

In March 1994, Manhattan Supreme Court Judge Leslie Snyder rejected career criminal Hubert Napier's defence of Multiple Personality Disorder as 'unadulterated crap' and jailed him for the rest of his life. Napier, 27, had decapitated and gutted Kim Nichols in her New York apartment and gone on a spending spree with her credit cards. He claimed the atrocity was ordered by a god called Zygor, a voice called George and a dog called Demolition.

Fortean Times 79

A DOG CALLED DEMOLITION
The Soundtrack.

Sleeve notes: It is with the greatest pride that we present the *first ever* soundtrack album to accompany a novel. Painstakingly selected, these twenty-four tracks will greatly enhance your reading pleasure and add an extra dimension to what is already a classic work of literature.

It must be understood that this album is NOT AVAILABLE IN THE SHOPS, that none of the artists listed have given their consent, and that all compositions are strictly copyright. As HOME TAPING IS KILLING MUSIC, it will shortly be an offence punishable by death.

'I dedicate this album to all those who have divined the occult significance of the bandaged left foot.'

Robert Rankin.

SIDE ONE: THE LIGHT SIDE

1. Free as a bird   *Magic Muscle*
2. Unkosibomvu   *Juluka*
3. Christopher Mayhew says *The Shamen*
4. Killing in the name   *Rage against the Machine*
5. Addicts for the out   *Sonic Energy Authority*
6. Happy in the world   *The Lost T-shirts of Atlantis*
7. Amsterdam dogshit blues *Mojo Nixon*
8. Nadir's big chance   *Peter Hamil*
9. Dead finks don't talk   *Brian Eno*
10. Big eyed beans from Venus *Captain Beefheart*
11. Anarchy in the UK   *The Sex Pistols*
12. Gary Gilmore's eyes   *The Adverts*

SIDE TWO: THE DARK SIDE

1. Rot in Hell, ma   *The Kray Cherubs*
2. Addiction   *The Almighty*
3. Pull the plug   *Death*
4. Evelyn, a modified dog   *Frank Zappa*

5. This corrosion   *Sisters of Mercy*
 6. Hunted, stalked and slain *Blood Priest*
 7. Everyone's out to get you *Beck*
 8. Ride the lightning   *Metallica*
 9. All along the watchtower *Jimi Hendrix*
10. Demon Bell   *Megadeth*
11. Insane in the membrane   *Cypress Hill*
12. Out of the picture   *Robyn Hitchcock*

PLAY LOUD. THERE'S NO OTHER WAY.
Thank you.